THE LISTS

T.O. REYNOLDS

THE LISTS
Copyright © 2024   T.O. Reynolds

All rights reserved. No part of this book may be used or reproduced by any means, graphic, electronic, or mechanical, including photocopying, recording, taping or by any information storage retrieval system without the written permission of the author except in the case of brief quotations embodied in critical articles and reviews.

Because of the dynamic nature of the Internet, any web addresses or links contained in this book may have changed since publication and may no longer be valid. The views expressed in this work are solely those of the author and do not necessarily reflect the views of the publisher, and the publisher hereby disclaims any responsibility for them.

Library of Congress Control Number: 2024943893
　　　　　　　　　　　　Paperback: 979-8-89306-071-3
　　　　　　　　　　　　　　eBook: 979-8-89306-072-0

Printed in the United States of America

CONTENTS

2020 .... *xvii*
Prologue .... *xix*
Someplace near Washington DC, 2020 .... *xix*
The Beginning Or The End? .... *xxiii*
(Sometimes The Best Place To Begin Is At The End) .... *xxiii*

2002 to 2008 .... *xxxiii*

Chapter 1	How It Started	1
Chapter 2	Trip Preparations	9
Chapter 3	The New England States	15
Chapter 4	Traveling In Northeastern United States And Canada	19
Chapter 5	A Change In Plans?	25
Chapter 6	The Junkyard	31
Chapter 7	The Veteran's Administration	43
Chapter 8	Job Hunting	57
Chapter 9	The Windy City	65
Chapter 10	Cause And Effect	71
Chapter 11	Explaining The Lists	83
Chapter 12	Motivation, Aka Termination	87
Chapter 13	The Lists	97
Chapter 14	The Lists: A Domestic Summary	107
Chapter 15	The Lists: A Foreign Summary	119

Chapter 16	(Logistics—Mobilization)	131
Chapter 17	Looking Back: 2012 Domestic Issues	135
Chapter 18	Looking Back: 2012 Foreign Issues	155

2013 ... 165

Chapter 19	Looking Back: 2013, Domestic	167
Chapter 20	Looking Back: 2013, Foreign	179

2014 ... 187

Chapter 21	Looking Back: 2014, Domestic	189
Chapter 22	Looking Back: 2014, Foreign	205

2015 ... 215

Chapter 23	Looking Back: 2015, Domestic	217
Chapter 24	Looking Back: 2015, Foreign	227

2016 ... 235

Chapter 25	(Looking Back-2016-Domestic)	237
Chapter 26	Looking Back: 2016, Foreign	243
Chapter 27	2016 (Late)	249

2017 ... 259

Chapter 28	Looking Back: 2017, Domestic	261
Chapter 29	(Looking Back-2017-Foreign)	275

2018 and 2019 ... 283

Chapter 30	Looking Back: Domestic And Foreign 2018/2019	285
Chapter 31	(The Final Chapter-Or Is It?)	289

Epilogue ... 311
Postscript ... 315
About The Author ... 317

For Barbara
My best friend, confidant, lover, proofreader and motivator—who just happens to be my wife.

This is a message for my grandchildren.

LEARN FROM YESTERDAY,
ENJOY TODAY,
PLAN FOR TOMORROW,
THE FUTURE IS YOURS.

Michael
Jeremy and Kristen
Christa
Amanda
Amber
Taylor
Christopher
Brittany
Joshua
William
John

And the kings of the earth, and the great men, and the rich men, and the captains, and the mighty men, and every bondman, and every freeman, hid themselves in the den and in the rocks of the mountains.

—Revelations 6:15

Dear Reader:

You are obviously reading *The Lists*, so this letter applies to you. You are now considered an involved participant and can no longer claim ignorance of the negative forces working to destroy our fragile planet. Nor will you be able to avoid adhering to the requirements set forth in *The Lists*. Hopefully, you will no longer consider yourself a member of the silent majority. The details for your assignment are as follows:

First, you have two weeks to finish reading *The Lists* in its entirety.

Second, you will be allowed three weeks to begin demonstra-ting your support for the goals and objectives as explained. This support includes communicating with friends, neighbors, relatives, politicians, business leaders, clergy, and others. You will attempt to enlighten and motivate them into becoming active participants in eliminating pollution, practicing energy and natural resource conservation, population control, and demanding your elected or appointed representatives begin to serve the people, not themselves, and you will hold them accountable if this does not happen.

Please remember that your future, my future, everyone's future depends on pro-activities of people like you and me. We must not fail!

Thank you in advance for your efforts,

T. O. (Tom) Reynolds

This is a copy of the cover letter sent to individuals respon-sible for implementation of an assignment from The Lists. All letters were sent personal and confidential in expensive and official-looking envelopes displaying the seal of the CAG (the Citizen's Advisory Group is a figment of my imagination and included only to add credence to assignments).

> To: (appropriate name) Date: (appropriate date)
> From: "The Lists" and The Citizen's Advisory Group
> Subject: An Assignment for you.
> I ask that you take the time to read this letter and the attached assignment very carefully. This is not a prank, and we are not nutcases. How you react after reviewing the content will determine what happens to you. Your continued well-being and, possibly, the well-being of others close to you depends on your actions. It doesn't matter whether you agree with what you've been asked to do. You are in a position permitting you to accomplish the task, and you are now responsible for doing so. You must believe failure to complete the assignment will have dire consequences.
> You may read the attached assignment and then toss it in the trash. We sincerely advise against this. If you elect to ignore this communication, you will still be held accountable. As stated above, without timely completion, there will be serious consequences.
> You may think of contacting law enforcement or security personnel. We strongly advise against this simply because they will create a wall of interference impeding your ability to complete this assignment. The authorities will not be able to find us. Whether you involve the authorities or not, you remain accountable for timely completion of your assignment.

We ask that you to take this communiqué at face value, begin to form a plan of action, and complete your task. The assignment you've received is nothing like the old TV program *Mission Impossible;* there is no clause stating, "Should you accept this assignment —." THIS IS YOUR ASSIGNMENT! The clock has started ticking. There may be others assigned to assist, but you'll never know who they are or what role they play in its completion. You are being monitored independently. Your performance will be measured on what you accomplish, so you need not worry about others failing to carry out their part of an assignment and dragging you down.

A detailed description of your assignment follows. It is in English and is very well written. Obviously, there will be no Q&A. Foreign assignments may require translation. We recommend you select translators from trusted staff personnel.

Take the moral high ground! Complete your assignment. Civilization is depending on you! Live a long and prosperous life.

The Lists & CAG

This is an EXAMPLE of an assignment given to a domestic participant:

Mr./Ms./Mrs. _____ Date: __/__/__

I ask you to carefully read this letter. Think about its content and the consequences involved before you disregard it.

For more than two years, you have led a group of well-financed and highly placed individuals in an effort to prevent making it illegal for individuals to own or sell fully automatic assault weapons or extended ammunition clips for various weapons.

You and your compatriots, some of whom are members in good standing in the NRA, have maintained this position in spite of being witness to at least nine episodes over the last two years involving multiple deaths caused by these weapons being in the hands of criminals or deranged individuals. Eight of those who died were in law enforcement. You continue to publicly claim the following: "If the laws that currently exist were properly enforced, these deaths may not have happened." You know full well there are either weak or no existing federal laws to prevent this from happening. The absence of regulations is largely due to your misguided efforts.

Your assignment is to immediately cease involve-ment or support for individuals or groups actively engaged in preventing new laws from being introduced to regulate these weapons. We are not asking you to assist in drafting or passaging of new regulations. Others are tasked with that assignment.

Your cooperation is appreciated. You must believe that noncompliance will be dealt with accordingly. It's your choice. Make the right one!

TL/TCAG

2020

PROLOGUE

Someplace near Washington DC, 2020

I can't believe it's been eighteen years. It seems like only yesterday we decided to retire. Twelve years ago, my life's purpose began to change, and ten years ago, I became a wanted fugitive. Without reservation, I can say what I made happen over the years has made the world a better place for all of us. I never intended to write a book about my involvement or how The Lists came to be. I knew any facts presented in the narrative would undoubtedly provide clues for law-enforcement agencies that had been searching for me since assignments and terminations began. However, my circumstances have changed. I've been arrested! So I've made up my mind to tell the story about the birth of The Lists since fear of detection is no longer a deterrent. I want to inform my family and the public about what really happened. I know where to begin the story, and even though it's not over, I have a pretty good idea how it will end.

Society needs to know why leaders all over the world suddenly began to act responsibly to save our planet. I don't want this publication to come across as the work of a lunatic but to serve as a warning to individuals or organizations trying to undermine the basic principles of human rights or those polluting our planet. As you begin to understand The Lists and, hopefully, take time to reflect on what's happened over the last decade, I think you'll agree something, perhaps The Lists, motivated many leaders, not just politicians, to change. Today, the powers that be need to remember what happened and ensure their future actions do not necessitate a sequel to The Lists, with their names on it this time. I'm incarcerated, and I'm approaching supersenior status. My replacement had already taken over management of The Lists before I was removed. He is well aware of the rules, who the key players are, and most importantly, which corrective tactics to use if needed.

The Lists were entirely my doing. It took more than three years to develop the initial plan, including the *why*, the *who*, and the *how*. The Lists are designed to ensure in spite of greed, entitlement mentality, and lack of positive actions from a variety of world leaders; the earth would survive and our lives would be improved. The plan was based on the KISS (simple is best) principle and maintained a sense of urgency to "git er done" without creating chaos. Chaos could have forced us to return to the dark ages.

Civilization was rapidly running out of time in many survival areas. The problems of global warming, pollution, overpopulation, disease, renewable energy, greed, corruption, drugs, immigration, terrorism, education, entitlements, crime, unemployment, disease, and insufficient supply of potable water and food, etc., had been known for years. In most instances, solutions (or at least some positive actions) were readily available. However, there was a distinct lack of worldwide participation in correcting these problems. Because of an extremely biased media and an apathetic public (you and me, bro), very little pressure was being exerted on politicians or leaders in any capacity. There was an obvious disconnect with reality. The public had been brainwashed into complacency, and world leaders suffered from delusions of competency. Something had to change! The basic question was, who would lead us to change or what would drive us to change? Existing world leadership seemed unwilling or incapable of dealing with the situation. This cast of characters found it easier to bicker and moan about the inabilities of the other guy rather than buckle down and get some work done. Should we remove existing leadership and risk anarchy or try some way to motivate them to correct the situation? How could we get them to act responsibly and quickly? What does history tell us about motivating leaders? How about a pat on the back for a job well done? Yeah! Right! What about fear of exposure in the media? LOL! It was obvious there was a disconnect between the leadership and the public. The leaders knew what was best for us without listening to us and without consulting with us.

This is why The Lists were born. It took almost two years to compile a list of the most irresponsible leaders. Survival became the motivational tool. The objective was to force those in positions of power to recognize the need for immediate, proactive changes for society as a whole. Within the framework of The Lists, survival wasn't defined as getting elected, re-elected, appointed to another term, receiving an exorbitant bonus or adding a million dollars to an off shore account. Survival, as spelled out in The Lists had a much more potent meaning. Those who received an assignment had to answer a simple question; "Did you or those close to you want to keep on living?"

When I attended services at the Hope Lutheran Church I had a simple prayer. "Please give me the wisdom to know what should be changed and the courage to make it happen." I felt that if I were able to reach the right person it could have a positive effect on hundreds or even thousands.

Once you begin reading The Lists, I'd advise you to finish the entire book before jumping to any conclusions. Also, if I make some glaring mistakes, please forgive me. I'm writing from memory. My situation allows no access to personal records, T.V., on line services or any type of news media. I hope that where my recollections are in error, my editor or publisher will provide the necessary corrections prior to publication.

THE BEGINNING OR THE END?

(Sometimes The Best Place To Begin Is At The End)

The authorities are not legally permitted to use the same techniques to obtain the truth from prisoners as once was the case and not long ago. What happened at Abu Ghraib and Gitmo changed all that. Waterboarding, electrodes, freezing, altering extremities, sleep deprivation, starvation, thirst, drugs, sexual intimidation, etc., are no longer used to motivate prisoners or, in my case, persons of interest. Over the past twenty-two months, I have been legally tortured, but my torture *de jour* has been isolation. There have been times when I truly believed the mental anguish caused by isolating a human being is worse than any type of physical torture that can be administered. I've been told to get used to it. They classify me as a terrorist. I think of myself as a results-oriented human rights activist. I won't give them the information they want, and they have no intention of improving my quality of life until I do. This could take awhile!

How did I wind up in this situation? I still haven't figured out how I screwed up, how they found me. For almost eight years, I avoided detection by the most sophisticated law-enforcement agencies on the planet. It could have happened because of a termination package that wasn't mailed as scheduled. A forwarder, with whom I had an arrangement for five years, died unexpectedly in early 2017. The package he was to have mailed lay around his office for a few months until one of his family members, a twenty-two-year-old international soccer star, got curious. Instead of mailing it, he opened it, found an expensive bottle of wine (thankfully threw the card away), removed the cork, took a drink, and died seven hours later, creating an international incident reported over and over again on TV. This could have provided the authorities with a clue, allowing them to backtrack to me! Or I could have mumbled something incriminating about The Lists when put to sleep while undergoing surgery for a broken ankle in late 2017. If this happened and it was reported at the time, I'm sure I would have been apprehended before leaving the hospital. I doubt they found me by good detective work. That only happens on TV. In any event, I've been captured!

This is what I do know. Two years ago, I finished having dinner at my favorite Italian restaurant, Red Sauce, in The Villages in Central Florida. I paid the check, walked out to the parking lot to my replica '29 Ford Street Rod golf cart, and then everything went blank. That's right! I vanished. Family, friends, even my protégé Mike, have no idea what happened to me or even if I'm still alive. I guess my house, golf cart, Tesla, everything are still there, but I'm gone. I don't remember how I was abducted, but I have flashbacks of dozing in a van and a helicopter. I woke up sometime later (a day or a week?) in a twelve-by-twelve concrete room (cell?), no cell mate, no windows, an explosion-proof light fixture in the center of a sixteen-foot-high ceiling. There was a solid metal door, a bed with a welded frame bolted to the wall, a reasonably comfortable mattress (no sheets, blankets, or pillows), a stainless steel sink built like an anvil, and a matching commode. A roll of paper towels was next to the sink and a roll of TP next to the commode. The room was pleasantly warm. I was dressed in a light-blue two-piece paper pajama set and slippers (no underwear or socks). I needed a shave (looked like a two-day growth, which provided a hint regarding time passing?). I was starving and very thirsty! It was totally silent.

This has been my home for almost two years. It's impossible to be comfortable here. Except for the isolation, I'm treated well. I miss my leather recliner, my HDTV, and a cold beer. I'm permitted to select reading material from a censored list provided by my captors. I choose meals from a weekly menu. The coffee is terrible, but milk shakes at lunch are great! No glass and no metal utensils are provided. I'm allowed to shower once a day, and I exercise in a secluded workout room up to two hours a day. I have no visitors. The only people I've seen are guards (in military-style uniforms I don't recognize), medical doctors, and shrinks a.k.a. interrogators. When I ask why I'm here, they frequently mention the Patriot Act or National Security. I do know I'm being held by a branch (Homeland Security?) of the federal government in a maximum-security compound. Based on the changing seasons (I get a glimpse of the trees in the distance when I'm taken to the interview room), I'd guess I'm somewhere in the mountains near Quantico, Virginia. My crime? I don't think the authorities know what I'm really guilty of! I haven't been charged. I've not had a trial. When I ask to make my legally permitted phone call, they just laugh at me. During repeated interrogations, I've been able to get hints as to what they suspect. They think they know what I did but can't prove anything. They'd love to know if I did it, why I did it, and verify how I did it, but I'm not sharing. They won't put me on trial for fear that public disclosure would result in mayhem in the Washington political community, and demands for retribution and restitution from foreign governments would be enormous. It's kind of a modern version of what used to be called a Mexican standoff.

I'm a political prisoner with little hope of getting out of here. A few years ago, before my incarceration, I contemplated writing my memoirs, but I was always too busy. Now, I'm not so busy, but I decided to tell the story of The Lists instead. I have lots to gain, including potential financial rewards, when (not *if*) my story is published. My family deserves to know what happened to me, and I hope they'll realize why I did what I did. Under the circumstances, deciding to go public wasn't difficult. Being able to go public was. Remember, I'm being held in isolation at a maximum-security facility. I didn't think my captors would have a problem allowing me to write my memoirs; it could be used as a confession, and it would never be made public, so it would not become a cause célèbre. There were several problems to contend with. First, I would have to use my memory to report over ten years' history: events, names, places, and statistics. Was I up to the task? Next I'd need to find a way to secretly document the story, find an insider willing to assist me (and maybe get paid for it), and locate an editor or a publisher interested in (and willing to pay for) the story. Oh well! Nothing ventured, nothing gained. I made up my mind to give it a try.

So here's how I handled it. I informed my interrogators I wanted to write my memoirs. I'm sure they had quite a laugh but, for selfish reasons, approved my request. Days passed, and then one morning a guard handed me a laptop computer and simply said, "Get busy!" I'm sure they were anticipating receipt of some incriminating information.

The computer didn't fit my plan, so I refused, feigning ignorance of computers and a lack of typing skills. The next morning, a tablet, two short pencils (weapons?), and a miniature eyebrow pencil sharpener was delivered. I wasted no time and began writing. I planned to keep two sets of notes. Set no. 1 would be my memoirs, starting about age twelve. This was the copy for them to read and, hopefully, to keep them occupied. It provided just enough information for them to allow me to keep writing but never supplied enough details for them to fully comprehend what The Lists had been responsible for, no information about my successor, or what was planned to happen.

Set no. 2 became the tell-all version of The Lists, the book you're now reading. I had no doubts I'd be able to get it to a publisher. My security guard, I'll call him Pete (probably hired as a contractor just like in Iraq) delivered and picked up my lunch tray on what I thought was Monday through Friday since a different guard served my meals the other two days (Saturday and Sunday?). One day, I slipped him a note scribbled on a used napkin. I used mustard to write it and asked if he'd be interested in making some easy money. The next day the napkin on my tray had a yes written on it. That's how Pete became my contact with the outside world.

Now I had to figure out a way to get the handwritten pages to him without detection. I found that I could tightly roll up one or two pages and slide them into a used milk shake straw. (Try this sometime.) Of course, the first thing I did was make him pass a test. The first page I had him process instructed him to mail it to an address I'd listed but not to include a return address. The address I'd given him was for a vacant lot near where I used to live in Ohio. The page had information about a fictitious termination scheduled the next week.

I'm sure Pete read the page, and I was certain, if he were an informant, my interrogators would be interviewing me PDQ. I'd get no more milk shakes. Nothing changed. My daily routine continued, and so did the milk shakes. Hopefully, the test letter is lying in a dead letter bin in a post office basement somewhere in Ohio.

A month later, Pete provided confirmation that communi-cations were established with an editor I'd found from a couple of articles in the prison library. He'd already received a Pulitzer for breaking a scandal at the UN, and I was certain he would like to have another hot story. My first contact with the editor, via Pete and the straw, contained a request for him to edit my work and to find a publisher for it. The second contact was verification from him that he'd received the first sixteen pages (it had taken me almost two months to write and smuggle them out) and had located a publisher who was interested. The third communiqué was his agreement to try and decipher my newly invented shorthand and rewrite the pages when received. If it took me two months to get the first sixteen pages out, I figured I'd be about ninety when the book was finished and everyone would have lost any interest in publishing it, let alone ever reading it. My newly invented shorthand was simply using a lot of abbreviations and skipping obviously needed words like *the, and, that, were,* etc. The fourth contact was after receipt of fifty pages. It informed me what the publisher was willing to pay and an agreement they'd hold publication until the end. Contact no. 5, after receipt of chapter 16, stated they agreed to my terms regarding payment for the book, the sale or transfer of my property in Florida, and for 65 percent of book sales to go to my family. The sixth note from the editor informed me the publisher had received everything through chapter 26 and advised me they were getting very anxious to go to press. It had taken most of the last twenty-two months to write and smuggle the pages out, two at a time (even with my shorthand). Now, they were telling me to hurry it up!

The editor or publishing company undoubtedly made revi-sions to the grammar and the format. I'm sure they corrected some factual errors I made for the 2018 and 2019 time frame. It was extremely difficult to keep a flowing story line. Hopefully, they were able to sort it out. I'll probably never have an opportunity to read the book. I hope it turns out to be a good read.

I assumed I'd know when the book was published. There undoubtedly would be repercussions with increased pressure at interrogations and revocation of privileges. I hadn't thought about what would happen to Pete. I'm sure he was astute enough to realize what would happen when the book was published, and his superiors started looking for the leak. I anticipated certain government sources would take a lot of heat (maybe a few would lose their jobs, probably be promoted). They would adamantly deny an individual or group had anything to do with causing so many deaths over the last decade. "There was no conspiracy! There was no serial killer on the loose!" They'd claim the book was a work of fiction, and politicians, national or international leaders need not worry. The world would be told the government had no knowledge of me. I could really disappear! At least my family will know what happened to me; they won't know where I am or if they'll ever see me again. Months ago, I had thought about sending a message to my successor Mike and my oldest son, Tim, via Pete, informing of my situation but felt it would be much safer if family members knew nothing about The Lists and my successor remained unknown.

When I began The Lists, I had every intention of trying to change the world.

After a short while, reality set in, and I realized it would be an impossible task. I decided it would be more prudent to take on a couple of problem areas negatively impacting civilization and our planet. However, as time went on, my knowledge of the problems became clearer, and the method I could use to motivate the responsible parties seemed fairly simple. My motto became "in for a penny, in for a pound." I resolved in my own mind, unlike Don Quixote and his impossible dream, that limited success would be acceptable. I had no idea what to expect.

Did you happen to notice over the last eight years that so many political, financial, industrial, military, educational, entertainment, or media personnel began to die unexpectedly from natural causes, and their successors began to exhibit humane tendencies? Or that the constant bipartisan bickering in Washington all but disappeared? Or why foreign powers, excluding most Muslim-controlled countries, introduced beneficial changes internally and began to talk openly (sometimes honestly) with their neighbors?

As you read on, you'll find that hundreds of deaths (terminations) were initiated because irresponsible entities failed to meet the needs of society and the mandates of The Lists. One hundred sixty-one totally corrupted individuals were identified and marked for termination in the first eighteen months. Over a period of eight years, about five hundred deaths would occur. This included eighty-four deaths counted as collateral damage. These sacrifices were made to ensure that civilization and our planet survived and our quality of life improved over the years. Many greedy, power-hungry individuals or governments, modern-day robber barons, have been eliminated, but history tells us there is always someone willing to try again. As I warned earlier, politicians, oil magnates, industrialists, terrorist organizations, financial managers, media or entertainment personalities, lobbyists, and those in the legal system need to be aware that my replacement is already monitoring their activities.

Would I do it again? Absolutely! But I'd begin sooner, and I'd try harder to avoid being caught. Since my successor is in place, there will be no lull in initiating corrective actions required by The Lists. Planning activities a year in advance provided adequate time to prepare for completion of the final segments of the original plan and determine what future actions need to be initiated. Will it be necessary for The Lists no. 2? That depends on you and on world leadership. The alarm clock has gone off and provided a wake-up call for a civilization that had been asleep for too long. As you'll see from my example, one motivated person can and has made a difference. Now, it's your turn! Here's the story of The Lists.

2002 TO 2008

CHAPTER 1

HOW IT STARTED

After thirty-six years of forced labor, I managed to convince myself (and my wife, Barbara) that it was time to take early retirement. We had been living in Huntington Beach, California, for almost eight years but decided to leave the "left coast" and return to the "right coast": that's where the in-laws, "out-laws," kids, and grandkids all lived. Years before retirement, we had selected Smith Mountain Lake, in the Blue Ridge Mountains of Virginia, as the place we would escape to. We purchased a beautiful waterfront home fifteen years ago. The plan was to sell as much stuff as possible before moving across the country to the lake house. While my wife was packing boxes, she learned how to sell unneeded items on eBay. I managed to find a suitable replacement to take over management of the manufacturing operation I had run for almost ten years. We closed out or transferred bank accounts, insurance coverage, and utilities. It only took five weeks to sell our condo on the harbor. Four months after deciding to retire, we said good-bye to Al and Johnita, John and Vicki, Elliot and

Susan, Kay and Michael, and all our friends in the Corvette Club of Southern California, promising to keep in touch. It was the twenty-sixth of September when we pulled out of the underground garage for the last time and headed east. The moving van would not arrive in Virginia for eight days, so we were able to take time to stop and smell the roses on the way to our new home.

We arrived at the lake house October 4. The weather was beautiful, and there were wine and cheese festivals everywhere. We put the top down on the Vette and enjoyed trips on the Blue Ridge Parkway. The kids and grandkids visited over the Thanksgiving holiday. I began enjoying a life of leisure and often wondered why we hadn't made this move earlier. Retirement was lots of fun. We had stashed away a small fortune, acquired legally. I received a traditional early-retirement pension (reduced by 35 percent) along with interest from investments and royalties from several patents I'd filed over the years. Social Security would come later (if any money remained in the fund, not just federal IOUs).

While making preparations for our move back east, Barbara had sold some of our extra things on eBay, and her interest in making this a business had grown. She intended to wait until after the moving dust had settled before beginning. It was a good thing she waited. We only lasted six months at the lake. After spending eight years in Southern California, it was more than a little shock to our systems when late December and January's weather hit us in Virginia. We put her business and our travel plans on hold and began a search for a warmer retirement location.

The house and the Vette were winterized. We waved good-bye to Carl and Cindy and BH and Saundra as we pulled out of the driveway and headed south. It was the last week of February and it was 24 degrees. We'd found out about a great retirement community we planned to check out on the way to visit our son Tim, his wife, Cheryl, granddaughter Christa, and grandson Will in Orlando. We weren't enthused about retirement communities but thought we'd look around the area. It took three days to get to a place called The Villages. When we drove into the Spanish Springs Town Square, it was a little after 5:00 p.m., and it was happy hour. There were people dancing to a live band on the center stage gazebo. We found a place to park and joined the party. Three days later, we bought a home on one of the forty-six golf courses. Two days after that, we bought a golf cart. We sold the lake house in Virginia two months later and never looked back.

We were completely relocated again by early May, and by October, we joined several clubs, including the Red Hats and The Village Corvettes, and were rapidly making new friends. I began golfing two or three days a week, and Barb finally began her eBay business. Together, we found flea markets, auction houses, and looked through the classified ads for garage sales. We agreed the distance we would drive to a flea market or an auction would be no more than 150 miles, although when she found some special goodies advertised, the limit was stretched a few times. It didn't take very long before the oversized garage began to fill up with the treasures she accumulated. Between golfing, clubbing, and eBaying, it wasn't long before we had to make an appointment to see each other. She was actually making money with her business and enjoying every minute.

Our plans to travel extensively wouldn't be influenced by her business venture. As a matter of fact, searching for new sources of supply only added to the need for travel throughout Florida and Southern Georgia.

Barbara loved a movie called *50 First Dates*, so the day I retired I promised her we'd have ten thousand first dates. She liked the idea. Right from the start of our retirement, we traveled: locally the first two years while moving and setting up Barb's new business venture and to foreign locations after that. Our philosophy was "If you can dream it, you can do it!"

Places we'd always wanted to visit were now just a travel agent away. We'd already traveled to Alaska, Australia, New Zealand, Fiji, Tahiti, Bangkok, Hawaii, Vietnam, China, and Mexico while living on the West Coast. Now Spain, Portugal, England, France, Germany, Russia, Italy, Costa Rica, and other destinations became memories refreshed by piles of digitized photographs.

When necessary, we helped the kids do their thing, and the grandkids received the proper "grandparental" guidance (and frequently, money). Life was good. We took courses for wine tasting, gourmet cooking, computer literacy (special emphasis on how to use the Net), and ballroom dancing. We golfed, swam, and joined about twenty clubs. We knew about the constant and escalating turmoil in much of our country and the rest of the world, but we didn't pay much attention except for escalating gasoline prices and, of course, the vivid memory of 9/11 and some of the restrictions we ran into during our travels. We weren't directly affected by terrorist activities or the multiple wars going on (the draft had been eliminated, and none of our kids was in the military. Listening to the politicians and the media, we believed these conflicts would probably be resolved before the grandkids were old enough to become involved). Fortunately, the Wall Street/banking rip-offs hadn't impacted our finances. We were healthy and not overly concerned about health care insurance. We'd deal with Medicare when it became necessary.

We were retired, living in a great community, and our children were working at good jobs, so the unemployment situation was of little concern to us. Don't get the wrong idea; we didn't live in a vacuum. We felt good about doing our part to help the less fortunate. We donated food to the local homeless shelter and contributed financially to a number of charities. We thought, "What the hell? Our leaders will get around to correcting the world's problems, eventually. Let's go play another round of golf and then have drinks on the lanai." Without actually realizing it, we became the epitome of the silent majority, proof that ignorance really is bliss.

Then one bright and sunny morning, my life took an imme-diate and totally unexpected turn. We had developed an enjoyable morning ritual. I would quietly leave our bed about seven each morning (after years of getting up at this time to go to work, it was difficult to break the habit), make coffee, open the blinds, fetch the morning paper, shower, shave, and throw on my robe. Then at 8:00 a.m., the love of my life would usually pull off the covers and follow her nose to the freshly brewed coffee pot. After a kiss and a *good morning* to each other, we'd sit in the breakfast nook, sip our coffee, read the paper, point out items of interest to each other, and compare schedules for the day. We'd share friends and family updates, the latest neighborhood gossip, various upcoming club events, and a review of wish list plans for travel. Afterward, we'd get dressed and then officially begin our day, usually with a light breakfast. Then it was e-mail catch-up time before venturing out to shop, golf, or visit the Market of Marion, our local flea market, to replenish Barb's supplies.

On this particular morning, following my routine tasks, I poured my coffee and began browsing through the newspaper. At eight thirty, my wife hadn't made her usual appearance. I tiptoed to the bedroom door and, as quietly as possible, peeked in. She was still under the covers and not stirring. While this was highly unusual, it was no cause for alarm. I assumed that she just wanted to sleep in a bit longer. By 9:00 a.m., I was more than a little worried and entered the bedroom with the intention of waking my sleeping beauty so we could begin our day.

Several hours later, after she had been transported to the hospital by ambulance, the attending physician informed me that she had peacefully passed away as a result of a heart attack. Our happy retirement together had come to an abrupt end. We'd only made it to 598 first dates. We'd shared so much together. We met in high school. I went on to college. She went to work. We married just before I began a tour of duty in the Marines. Then I started working, and she became Mom. Our six children were our lives. We attended their weddings and were blessed with eleven grandchildren. Infrequently, we visited her brother and sister-in-law, an uncle, and a couple of long-distance cousins—our only relatives. Now, the future was forever changed. My wife had once confided to me that when it was time for her to go, she wanted it to be quick. Her motto was "Happy. Healthy. Happy. Healthy. Dead!" She hated hospitals, and a DNR order was on record. Thankfully, she got her wish.

The following weeks were a blur of activity, most of which are difficult for me to remember. After the funeral and for the next several months, I guess I was on cruise control. The children, our friends, and neighbors helped me adjust. I was told by several people, including our minister, we'd had a meaningful life together, but I needed to reevaluate future plans for my life. Barb's eBay business was forgotten for the time being. It would be rejuvenated later, but for completely different reasons.

I opted for a time-out. I'd take a trip, maybe three or four months, and focus on other things. I'm certain my support group breathed a sigh of relief when they heard my plan. The kids even suggested I give serious consideration to writing my memoirs. The next decision: where to go? I didn't have a bucket list prepared (this would come later), so I spent several weeks at the library, online, and discussing options with travel agents. Apparently, my list included a few destinations considered politically volatile and not recommended for tourism by the State Department. Places my wife and I had planned to visit were now on an advisory list.

I took the safe and easy way out, selecting destinations within the United States and in Canada (Mexico was on the don't-go-there list because of some drug violence). A neighbor suggested I look into purchasing a motor home (an RV) and drive from one place to the next. This would allow me to see the sights without the hassle of making hotel reservations, flying, or rental cars. It sounded like a great idea. The economy made it a buyer's market for either a used or a new motor home. After a couple of weeks of searching, I located a midsized thirty-two-foot-long unit less than two years old and equipped with every creature comfort known to man! It had the necessary household amenities, including a fully equipped kitchen, a desk, a small gasoline generator, a powerful diesel engine, a GPS, a slide-out room extension, a fair-sized bathroom with a shower, a built-in TV, a stereo system, a nice bedroom with a queen bed (guests could bunk on the pull-out sofa bed in the living room), and there were lots of places to store stuff. I fell in love with the swivel-style captain's chairs in the cockpit. When I first saw all the instruments and switches, it felt like I was piloting a 747! I visited my AAA office, got a stack of maps and some helpful hints. During the preparations, I found myself looking forward to hitting the road.

CHAPTER 2

TRIP PREPARATIONS

I arranged to have the rig thoroughly checked out by a professional RV dealership. I bought recommended provisions and practiced driving through the neighborhood, especially backing up (thank goodness for the rearview TV camera) and parking. I found setting up camp in a practice field (my yard wasn't big enough, and I don't think my neighbors would have appreciated my parking in the driveway) wasn't as easy as just turning off the motor and pulling the parking brake lever. Denny, a friend of mine from The Village Vettes Club, came over to give me assistance and help me consume some cold cans of Budweiser. Linda, Denny's wife, was still working, so he was available. After several failed attempts at leveling the motor home and connecting the utilities, we pulled out the instruction manuals and read them cover to cover. Everything worked the way it was supposed to, and after a few more trial runs, I considered myself competent. Denny even gave me a thumbs-up.

By nature, I'm not overly optimistic or pessimistic, but I am always realistic. That's why I used Velcro straps to hide my 9 pistol and a spare clip under the dashboard. It was well hidden but still accessible. Who knows? I could run into a mean bear in one of the campgrounds I planned to visit. I'd mastered using my new digital camera and used more Velcro strips to hold it securely to the top of the center console in the cab. Maybe I'd get a photo of me shooting the bear! The plan was to spend the first four or five weeks touring the New England states and then travel in a counterclockwise direction across the continent. I was working my way through the mapping process when it became obvious that three months wasn't going to allow enough time for the trip I'd outlined. It looked more like it would take eight months. Time was not an issue, so a longer trip presented no problems. After New England, I'd head west and swing back and forth over the US/Canadian border, hitting the high spots, starting with Montreal, Ottawa, Toronto, Kingston, Niagara Falls, Buffalo, Cleveland, Detroit, Chicago, etc. If I timed it right, I'd be able to reach Calgary in time for the Stampede Rodeo in August.

Weather permitting, I'd proceed north, stopping in the Banff and Lake Louise en route to Alaska, via the ALCAN highway, where I'd visit the Denali National Park and pan for gold in "them thar hills" near Eagle! My parents had made this trip years ago. Next, I'd drop down south to Vancouver for a few days, visit Whistler Resort, and take the ferry to Victoria and Butchart Gardens. I'd reenter the United States and point my rig south, just in time to avoid cold weather. My itinerary would be updated weekly to get the most out of my trip and ensure I had a place to park the motor home when I arrived at each destination. The plan included extending invitations to two of the older grandkids to join me (one at a time) for a week during their summer vacation.

It took about two months to complete the preparations (I was still playing golf and bowling), but the motor home was now equipped (I followed recommendations found in an RV magazine), the fuel tanks filled to the brim, the GPS all checked out, traveler's checks and some cash were in my fanny pack. I was anxious to hit the road. Arrangements were made for the house and yard to be looked after in my absence. A neighbor agreed to hold my mail, and we'd find a way to forward anything important. Warren and Linda, good friends and neighbors, held a bon voyage party the night before I left. Going-away gifts included a six-pack of Diet Coke in a foam cooler, twenty-four chocolate chip cookies in a Tupperware container, a Willie Nelson CD titled *On the Road Again*, and Lucy, a blow-up traveling companion. It was a great send-off, one I'd remember for many years after my trip was completed. Lucy is still in a closet somewhere. I finally hit the road in April 2008.

Like anything reasonably complex done for the first few times, there's a learning curve involved. Getting familiar with a large and somewhat complicated vehicle was an adventure, but I persevered. The first stop at a campground proved to be more difficult than the practice setups. With the assistance of a couple of veteran RV enthusiasts, I got the rig properly positioned and connected to the lifelines. I'm sure my helpers had some humorous stories to tell around the campfire that night. Feeling reasonably proud of my success at setting up camp without hitting anything, I went inside and began cleaning up the mess of spilled food and broken containers all over the kitchen floor. I'll never again forget to lock the refrigerator door before hitting the road.

After a few days on the highway, I mastered the gauges and switches on the dashboard and the center console. I'd even figured out how to use the CD player, and Willie Nelson entertained me frequently. I bought a few more CDs of ABBA, the Beach Boys and the Momas and the Popas. When driving a motor home around the country, a GPS, CB radio, and truck stops are necessities. An RV guide becomes your bible. Without these items and the support of fellow RVers, I wouldn't have survived the first week on the road. When needed, Walmart parking lots are a great place to park overnight and replenish supplies.

On the fourth day of the trip, I stopped at a service plaza to fill up and clean the windshield. This is a time-consuming process. The tanks hold forty gallons of diesel fuel, and the windshield is as big as the side of a small building. While I was working on this task, a young couple stopped at the pump next to me in a dilapidated extended-cab pickup truck. The truck was loaded with household goods covered with the traditional blue tarp. A U-Haul trailer was attached to the back bumper. Two little girls were in the back seat of the truck, eating Ritz crackers out of the box. After a minute trying to get the pump to accept his credit card, the young man's shoulders slumped, and he walked around to his wife's side of the truck. She began to cry and so did the kids. It didn't take an Einstein to figure out they were having some money problems. The young man approached me with a watch in his hand, excused himself, and asked if I would be interested in buying a good watch for $20. Before I could answer him, he told me why he needed to sell the timepiece.

He'd lost his job about seven months ago. He'd been working for five years as a mechanic at a small manufacturing plant in New Jersey when all of a sudden it went bankrupt. He was unsuccessful in finding another job in the area. Apparently, local unemployment was very high, with numerous businesses going broke. His unemployment checks had stopped. Then, out of the blue, his brother had called him two days ago and told him that he'd found him a job as a maintenance man for an apartment complex. The pay wasn't great, but a two-bedroom apartment was part of the compensation. He was supposed to start on Monday morning. They had celebrated the good news by packing everything the truck could carry and spent most of the money they had left renting the trailer. It was Saturday! They were broke, the girls were hungry, and they still had more than two hundred miles to go. All he needed was enough to fill up the tank, so he could get to his new job. That's why he was trying to sell his watch.

I knew this couldn't be a con job. Who'd go to all this trouble for $20? So here's what I did. I filled up his gas tank and treated the family to a gourmet lunch at the service plaza restaurant. The young man and I finished our coffee just as the ladies returned from the restroom. We stood in the parking lot and said our good-byes. I got hugs from the little girls, was blessed by Mom, and got a hearty handshake from a very appreciative dad. While the gals were in the restroom, I had convinced him he would need a few bucks for toll, gas, and some food until he reached his brother's place. I gave him five $20s, and I really meant it when I wished them good luck. It was a short visit with a tearful good-bye. It was the reason I stopped at a Walmart the next day. I bought a bound journal so I could begin recording the stories I'd decided to collect on my trip.

It was taking me an average of fifty minutes to set up my RV at night. I also noted every couple of days I'd just finish getting camp ready and then remember I'd forgotten to buy some necessity (like beer or chips).

Rather than decamp, drive to the local market, and then recamp, I did without. There were quite a few RVs towing small cars, but that wasn't for me. Others traveled with bicycles or small motorcycles loaded on racks attached to the back bumper. Here was an obvious solution to my grocery store runs. I really didn't want a bicycle, so I started looking for a new toy—a motorcycle.

I found it informative to talk to the other RVers before rushing off to buy something, so I asked some advice about my planned acquisition. Everyone was more than willing to share experiences and give advice. Several recommended smaller Harleys while others said that a Vespa scooter was what I needed (and a lot easier to load/unload than a Harley). I really couldn't picture myself on a Vespa, and a hog seemed a bit much since it would probably mean hauling a trailer behind the RV. I already had enough fun backing up without adding to the problem. So I settled on a midsized Honda 250cc. It looks like something that would be born if a Harley and a Vespa had an offspring. It's small, it handles easily, is nice looking, is powerful, and is light enough so that it's not a lot of work to load/unload from a rear-mounted platform (no trailer needed). After practicing for a couple of days, I managed to pass my driver's test. Yes, I bought a Bell helmet. No, I didn't buy leathers or get a tat. I enjoyed riding it, so I frequently forgot necessities and got to use the bike for grocery runs. It also accompanied me on quite a few sightseeing trips. My kids thought I was going through my second childhood (I'd already gone through my midlife crisis when I bought my Corvette), but the grandkids couldn't wait to get a ride on Grandpa's motorcycle!

"Onward and upward!"

CHAPTER 3

THE NEW ENGLAND STATES

The early stages of the trip took me into Connecticut, Rhode Island, Vermont, New Hampshire, Massachusetts, and Maine. The weather was warm and beautiful. After the initial screwups in setting up camp and transitioning from inept to expert with my GPS, I was enjoying the open road. I looked forward to my daily adventures while refueling at truck stops or the RV parks where I spent the night. I really met some interesting characters. After camp was ready, folks would gather around a campfire most evenings and willingly share a treat (or a beer). It seemed that everybody had stories to tell and couldn't wait to do so. As the days and weeks passed, it became evident this wasn't the same world we saw on the nightly news on ABC, CBS, NBC, or CNN. Fox News was the closest the media came to actually reporting reality, but that was still a stretch. I was seeing the real stories, firsthand. At times they were humorous and uplifting, but most times they were just the opposite. Each night I entered the stories and experiences in the journal. Who knows? I might write a travelogue for future RVers to enjoy or an article for *Reader's Digest*. The kids would probably have to wait awhile for my memoirs.

The longer I was on the road, the more I became aware of what was happening in our country. I began to notice things I completely overlooked only weeks before. These were not isolated incidents. People were out of work. There were a growing number of "will work for food" or "I need a job—not a promise" signs held by dejected-looking individuals at intersections. Foreclosure signs appeared on many front lawns. Stores and factories had windows boarded up, their gates and doors locked. State and national parks were a mess. Roads and bridges were falling apart. When I left the interstate, I had to drive carefully, or I could have torn the front end off the RV in some of the potholes I saw. There was lot of evidence of air and water pollution. Trash barrels were overflowing at the roadside rests, and the restrooms were totally unsanitary. I heard stories of gang violence taking control of many metropolitan areas, and even law enforcement stayed out of these places. Some of my new trucker friends said this was a by-product of unemployment and uncontrolled immigration! Others said it was because of the growing drug problem. I don't believe that was the case in the New England states, but later, I began to think that uncontrolled immigration, illegal drugs, and unemployment were a very big problem in many areas of the country. I had known for years that the no. 1 state with an immigration problem was California (probably drugs too). I was surprised to see similar troubled areas existed in parts of Canada.

Thank goodness Betsy (this was the name I'd given to my GPS since she had a pleasant female voice) helped me avoid most of these trouble spots, and I liked the mental security my under-the-dash 9 mm provided. Even though I managed to avoid these areas, there were many occasions when I felt like a foreigner in my own country. I also noticed the days were getting much warmer than normal.

It was about this time I took a break for a pleasant visit with my fifteen-year-old grandson, Jeremy. His joining me had been planned several months before my trip began. Originally he was to be with me for ten days. He was to fly into Boston where I'd meet him at the Logan Airport, and after touring the Cape and canoeing in Acadia National Park, he would fly home out of Bangor. However, his priorities had changed (I think her name was Kristen), and his visit was shortened to five days. We managed to alter his flights so that he would fly in and out of Bangor. This gave me the opportunity to visit a crowded international airport in a large RV. It wasn't a pleasant experience. Imagine arriving at a busy terminal only to find your unit wasn't welcome at the normal parking areas and wouldn't even fit into the concrete parking structures. With the help of a local police officer, I finally found a $10 parking spot in a field about three miles from the airport and a $6 shuttle (one way) ready to transport me to/from the terminal. I'd find out later it was much more convenient to stay overnight at one of the hotels surrounding most airports and use their free shuttle service to/from the terminal.

Jeremy's change in plans prevented our visit to the Cape, but we still had plenty of time to tour Acadia, do lots of sightseeing, and sample some great seafood.

Watching Jeremy consume his first lobster proved to be interesting, and of course, his learning how to ride my Honda was a thrill. Although a short visit, it was very enjoyable and memorable. I hope Jeremy will remember it; I know I will.

It was time to resume my vacation trip. I decided to include some political information to go along with my social journal entries. I'd continue to chronicle my observations and conversations in the journal (now converted to a laptop computer with a huge memory thanks to a visit to Best Buy). When completed, I'd probably publish my findings online and maybe in hard copy. I guess my objective would be to increase the public's awareness of these social problems by sharing my experiences with them. Then I imagined that maybe, collectively, we could try to influence our government leaders to initiate some needed changes.

CHAPTER 4

TRAVELING IN NORTHEASTERN UNITED STATES AND CANADA

I continued my travels through New England. I loved traveling through the mountains of Vermont and New Hampshire. I crossed into Canada near a quaint city named Sherbrooke in Quebec. It reminded me of places I'd visited in France years ago while on a business trip. Getting through customs was a breeze. Of course I lied about having any firearms with me—no need to complicate things. Next, I crossed the St. Lawrence River and visited Montreal, then the beautiful Canadian capital, Ottawa. I can't say the French Canadians in Quebec welcomed me with open arms, and they weren't a bit bashful when it came to discussions about the shortcomings of the United States. The Province of Ontario has a very picturesque city, Kingston, on the banks of Lake Ontario at the beginning of the St. Lawrence River. Next came Toronto where I visited the Blue Jays's baseball stadium. When I reached Niagara Falls, I spent two nights on the Canadian side and two nights in the United States. The Canadian side had a much-nicer campground and the falls were more photogenic than from the US side. With Betsy's help, I skirted around Buffalo, New York, trying to miss the congestion, pollution, and potholes and headed west, passing through the Lake Erie wine country. I visited several wineries and stocked up with gifts I planned to distribute to the neighbors after returning home. My next destination would be Cleveland.

I continued observing and, whenever possible, discussing local, state, national, and the world situation with teachers, students, police and firemen, grocery-store clerks, truck stop mechanics, several hookers, librarians, druggists, doctors, restaurant waitresses, shop owners, fellow RV travelers, road-repair crews, park rangers, town councilmen, a couple of mayors, a few vagrants, and many others. The number of journal entries grew, and I had begun to collect news articles from the local and national papers purchased along the way. The commonality of the problems was evident. To be fair, there were some good comments, but not many. Numerous times I heard variations of the old adage "If it looks like a duck, walks like a duck, and quacks like a duck, you'll never convince me that it's really an elephant (or a donkey)." It became more and more evident our social and economic problems could no longer be chalked up to minor leadership neglect; it was an epidemic and was growing! Why in the world didn't our government, our congressmen, our senators, our business and financial leaders see what was happening, what John Q. Public was going through? Or if they did see it, why weren't they reacting? Even the entertainment industry and religious leaders were evading the obvious issues.

I had a memorable experience refueling at a truck stop in New York, a short distance south of Buffalo. I accidentally (it really was an accident) stumbled on what I'll describe as a mobile house of ill repute.

After refueling, I parked in the designated RV area and started across the parking lot to the restaurant for a late lunch. I saw a young woman under the hood of an older model Jeep. She seemed to be in distress, so I asked if she needed some help. When she turned around, I noticed how attractive she was. She appeared to be in her late twenties and stated she did indeed need some help. She was trying to check her oil but didn't know how. Boy, good old naive me jumped right in there. I was ready to save the day. Next thing I know, the damsel in distress was joined by another attractive gal who had just exited a large RV parked next to the Jeep. I still didn't smell a rat. I was busy checking the oil level in the Jeep. "Hello!" We were at a truck stop, dummy! They have mechanics on duty twenty-four hours a day who are ready, willing, and able to perform this task. I informed her the oil level was where it should be. She expressed her thanks, and the two of them offered me the opportunity for a thank-you drink in the motor home they were delivering to a guy in Chicago. That's when the alarm finally went off in my dull-witted brain. These gals were truly entrepreneurs of the open road. After my mind started working and I introduced myself, I explained my reason for taking the trip and plans to write about my experiences. They asked me a couple of questions about what I was going to do with the information I collected in my journal. I was pleasantly surprised when they introduced themselves (Lois was the spokesperson) and offered to have a frank discussion with me over lunch (in the restaurant) as long as their identity wasn't revealed. Here's their tale. (Would have been a really great place for a pun.)

There were five of them in the group, but only three of them joined me for lunch. Apparently, the others were working. All were attractive. They were their own boss—no pimp involvement. Their ages ranged from twenty-three to thirty-one. The thirty-one-year-old was the chairman of the board. The large RV and the Jeep belonged to the two sisters. They cruised Interstate 90 with both vehicles, between Buffalo and Chicago during the summer months and then, during the winter, dropped south to Interstate 10 where they cruised between Houston, Texas, and Jacksonville, Florida. None of them were married, and there were no children involved. They had been doing this for almost three years. Their objective was to make as much money as possible as safely as possible and stay under the radar (causing no problems for anyone). They might go back to school, start another business, or settle down if the right opportunity (or the right man) came along. So far, they had done very well. Beyond their normal traveling expenses, their only other expenditures were kickbacks to the truck stop managers for the use of their facilities. Apparently, the girls were well respected and gave value for dollars spent. Most of their clients consisted of long-haul truckers, and quite a few of them were repeat customers. The truckers and the workers at the truck stops watched out for them.

They described their exes as members of "the 3 L Club"— lazy, losers, and leeches. The RV was part of a divorce settlement from one of the exes who happened to have it because his daddy had left it to him. The original threesome decided to take the RV for a trip across the United States, planning to earn money for expenses, along the way working as waitresses. The sisters, now in their early twenties, had been in college when their mom died suddenly, and a boozing father blew their tuition money, the mom's insurance money, and then tried to raise money by pimping out the girls. They were running away from good ol' dad when the other three found them hitching a ride at a truck stop in Illinois. The thirty-one-year-old had been an attorney in Ohio. She had gotten mixed up in some kind of illegal activity because of her relationship with a married politician and decided to leave the area before the ax fell. That's all anyone knew about her.

She had become their business agent.

They invested and paid their taxes. I listened to the stories about trying to find decent jobs, trying to borrow money to finish their education, getting hit on by lowlifes, being taken advantage of by the boss or coworkers, etc. They finally said enough already and decided to take matters into their own hands. They formed their own "company" and became independent businesswomen. They had an organization chart with responsibilities outlined for each member. They conducted weekly operating meetings and monthly financial reviews. They were succeeding and doing so without any government intervention or financial assistance. It was one of the good entries I'd make in my journal. I truly hoped their story had a happy ending. Maybe they would relocate to The Villages after they retired.

These recent experiences, along with several more over the following days and weeks, caused me to rethink the purpose of my road trip. Did I want to accomplish more than just a taking a vacation? I wasn't committing to making a change, but I decided it was time to gather more detailed facts and figures about what was happening in our world, both good and bad, then decide if I wanted to do something with my research like writing a travelogue or posting informational articles online.

That's what I did. I turned west and headed toward Cleveland. En route, I added stories to the journal, reviewed/edited previous entries, and continued collecting newspaper articles. I spent hours online, gathering information concerning conditions in the USA, Canada, and the world in general. As my review progressed, it became more and more evident that significant change was needed. It was easy to identify what needed to be changed. To determine who would make the changes and how they would accomplish them was more difficult. I had no idea what potential impact, if any, my involvement could possibly have on the situation. Could publishing an article or a series of them about my trip be of any benefit? My confusion about what the plan should be continued, but I was determined I would do something. My philosophy was no longer *C'est la vie*. I decided it would be prudent to continue gathering information still following my original route. Perhaps I would find things weren't really as bad as they seemed. Hopefully, I'd find answers to these questions and resolve any commitment issues I had before I reached my self-imposed point of no return, Chicago.

CHAPTER 5

A CHANGE IN PLANS?

Here are a few more stories I gathered in the Cleveland area as I continued traveling west.

The part of the city adjacent to Lake Erie was well kept and fairly busy, especially in the downtown shopping / business-office section. The local shop owners didn't mind telling me that business was down roughly 50 percent, and they had no choice but to terminate quite a few employees in the last eighteen to twenty-four months. Bankruptcy was in the near future for several of them. The folks in the financial sector weren't as forthcoming. The only info they wanted to share with me was how to apply for a loan.

Most of the folks I spoke to continued to hold out hope that the poorly performing Browns (their NFL football team) and the Cavaliers (their mediocre NBA basketball team) would regain their long-lost status as top performers and bring some pride (and tourists) back to the area.

While touring many of the cities, I now found it beneficial to wander off the usual scenic routes and visit the less touristy areas. I wound up seeing things and finding people in situations that would pull at your heartstrings or turn your stomach. In many cases, the people I met had given up. There were a few who still had some spirit left and often used it to participate in protest marches, but they were in a small minority. Most were tired fighting a no-win battle. Some of the individuals I spoke to never had a chance from the get-go. They were fifth—or sixth-generation welfare professionals with absolutely no education, training, or delusions of becoming anything else. In Cleveland, Maybell was such a person. She was black. She wasn't married. She hadn't graduated high school. She thought she'd finished ninth grade, could barely read or write. She didn't have a job, moved about once a month, and spent a lot of time in homeless shelters, soup kitchens and, during the warmer months, in cardboard boxes under highway or railroad bridges. She had never voted. What she did have were four kids aged two to eleven, following her around. Every time she met a guy that liked her, she thought life was going to change. Invariably, the man disappeared in a couple of months, and Maybell wound up with another child. When the kids got sick, she took them to the hospital emergency room. One saving grace for Maybell, she didn't do drugs. Her dream was for her kids to grow up and take care of her. Maybell was one of many women I'd talk to with similar stories.

To explore suburban areas south of Cleveland, I parked the RV in a secure campground and set off on the Honda. I managed to get into a few areas I exited as fast as my bike could go. The Honda didn't have a GPS or a 9 mm onboard. I headed farther south and wound up in the Rubber Capital of the World, Akron, and visited the Firestone Country Club.

In actuality, Akron is the ex–Rubber Capital. Almost all the rubber manufacturing facilities have disappeared. They've been torn down, revamped, or replaced by upscale shops and restaurants. The University of Akron has taken over some of the buildings. The city's claim to fame now is "the Rock and Roll Hall of Fame" and just south of Akron, in Canton, is "the Pro Football Hall of Fame." Driving around Akron, I stumbled across a construction site with about sixty workmen, building a new medical complex. I thought it was lunchtime when I parked the bike next to a pickup truck that had been converted into a mobile kitchen. I figured this would be a good spot to interview some of the workers.

Unfortunately, the crew had eaten an early lunch and were already back on the job. Fortunately, this allowed me to step right up to the window and order a Philly cheesesteak sandwich, fries, and a Coke. It cost me $5, and it was delicious. That's how I met Frank and Carolyn, restaurateurs.

They were from Detroit, had been married for almost ten years, and had a six-year-old son who was playing with his toy trucks in a pile of sand next to their restaurant. Frank had been laid off as a machinist/welder from one of the auto plants almost four years ago. Carolyn had worked as a secretary (administrative assistant) for an electronics firm that had gone bankrupt about the same time Frank was laid off. Both of them were in good health, but their son wasn't. He was autistic, required special ed, and suffered from childhood diseases and allergies. He needed to see a doctor frequently and prescriptions refilled monthly. When employed, their insurance had taken care of these expenses. The coverage ceased about three months after they lost their jobs. (The federal government's 65 percent subsidy for COBRA premiums for laid off workers didn't take effect until February 2009). Without this subsidy, the Joneses' COBRA payment would have been $1,107 a month. This was hardly affordable even before their unemployment benefits of $1,303 ran out. Both were well educated with good work history and had vigorously looked for work. Nothing was available. They refused to ask relatives for help. Frank was embarrassed when he told me about not being able to even file an application for McDonald's or Walmart. Both had stopped taking applications when their backlog reached two hundred. With a mortgage, living expenses, medical bills, and no income, they decided to do something about it. Here's their story.

They loved to go camping and fishing. Their son was a year old when they decided to give up tenting and acquired a used three-fourth-ton pickup truck with a self-contained camper on it for their weekends and vacations. After the loss of his job, Frank spent a couple of months (and not much cash) converting the camper into a mobile kitchen. He and Carolyn both love to cook and figured they could make a living cooking breakfasts and lunches for construction crews at building or highway construction sites outside the city limits. Frank made a great cheesesteak sandwich, but his real specialty was cheesecake. No matter how bad the economy was, there always seemed to be some construction in progress in Ohio but not in their hometown of Detroit. Frank called Detroit "the junkyard of the United States." They had managed to sell their home in Detroit, and even though they had taken a loss on the deal, there was enough equity for them to put a down payment on a small ranch house in suburban Cleveland. After converting the camper to a mobile kitchen, they were able to find willing customers at several long-term building sites. Most construction work was scheduled Monday through Friday. This gave them a financial break-even point, which they were very thankful for. They found a medical center they were able to service on the weekends. This gave them a small profit, but it meant working seven days a week. This is what they'd been doing for almost two years when I met them. The good news was they were keeping their heads above water and putting away a few bucks. The old pickup truck still ran OK, and customers were happy with the food and service. They had acquired the proper vendor licenses. Medical coverage was still not available because of their son's preexisting condition, but they were able to cover the expenses themselves but not much else. The bad news was there had been no camping or fishing trips for almost three years, and they missed it very much. What they were doing to earn a living was hard work, but both felt it was nice being their own boss. Their dream was to open a small restaurant or expand their mobile food service when the time was right. They had applied for an SBL but had been turned down twice. As I said good-bye to them, I had a good feeling that someday their wish was going to come true.

I decided to continue to head west. After listening to Frank and Carolyn's tale of how bad things were in Detroit, I wanted to witness the situation firsthand.

CHAPTER 6

THE JUNKYARD

I said adios to Cleveland and continued my westward journey. I entered the Detroit city limits on a Saturday afternoon. The weather was warm, but it had been raining off and on for two days. I hadn't noticed an RV park or campground on the way into the city. Fortunately, using my RV guidebook for reference, I had phoned ahead for a reservation at a park about fifteen miles west of the downtown area. Driving through the city, my RV was very conspicuous and seemed out of place in this ghost town. The Honda was covered by its traveling tarp, so no one could tell I was hauling around a perceived foreign-built machine. To be on the safe side, I knew that touring Detroit would have to be on foot, by bus, by taxi, or in a rental car (one made in the USA). I drove straight to the RV park, checked in at the office, and set up camp for three nights. The hookups were nice, and there were a lot of vacant spaces even though this was peak tourist/travel season. I walked to the small grocery store/restaurant/office at the entrance to pick up some supplies and maybe do dinner. It was still raining, and I thought it would be a good night to just kick back, log my journal entries, and relax for a change.

There were a few road-weary travelers in the restaurant area. A couple of them actually looked like they were on vacation. The others appeared to be in a hurry to get somewhere else.

Sitting at the counter, waiting on my burger and fries, I struck up a conversation with two older gentlemen. Herb and Gary were originally from the Detroit area but moved away to a trailer park in Florida, with their wives, about twenty years ago after taking an early-retirement buyout from one of the auto plants. Recently, their wives had passed away, and the two widowers decided to visit their old neighborhood up north. Herb told me that taking the buyout had been the smartest thing he'd ever done. Gary agreed. They both felt like the US government had let them down by allowing foreign competition free access to the US markets while our cars and other goods were taxed to high heaven when sold in those countries. They commented that "First, the steel industry vanished in Pittsburgh. Then the rubber plants closed down in Akron. Now the auto industry is dead in Detroit. What's next?" Of course, the auto companies they worked for didn't help the situation. They started to cut corners (reduce costs) to meet foreign competition (and UAW wage demands) and caused quality problems with the vehicles they manufactured. Gary stated, "For some reason, our 'glorious leaders' just never learn! Do they?" Both went on to tell me they were scared to death their pension checks would stop coming in the mail someday. "There's just no loyalty left anymore." The guys finished their meals and said good-bye. They were going to stay overnight at a Days Inn just a few blocks from the RV park and then get an early start, touring their old neighborhood. Our waitress,

Holly, who had joined in on our discussion from time to time, told them to be careful. "Things have changed, and a lot of the old places aren't safe anymore." I'm not sure if Herb and Gary listened to her warning, but I took it very seriously.

Holly and I shared a few more moments of conversation be-fore I excused myself and headed to the RV for the night. After catching up with journal entries, cutting a few articles from the newspaper, and watching the TV for about thirty seconds, I retreated to the shower and called it a night.

The next morning just before breakfast, I called the Enter-prise Rental Car agency. They weren't very busy and delivered a new Ford to me about an hour later. While waiting for the car to arrive, I ordered an omelet, toast, and coffee, and I continued last night's discussion with the day shift waitress. She seconded what the other gal told me about being careful while in the city. A young man with a cane limped into the restaurant, sat down on the stool next to me, and ordered breakfast. His name was Randy. He didn't have a lot to say, but he did add a few useful tidbits to the conversation. He told me to "just pick up a newspaper and try to find job openings in the classified" if I wanted to see how bad the employment situation was. He added, "Be careful if you decide to call or go for an interview. There are a lot of con artists out there who'd love to steal your money instead of getting you a job." Just before I left, he gave me one more tip: "When you call about jobs, pretend that you're a disabled vet and see what happens."

I finished breakfast about the time the rental car showed up. After dropping off the guy who had delivered the rental Ford, I made a few notes to help avoid what he suggested as "do not go into" areas. I hadn't considered taking the 9 mm, but I made sure the gas tank was full.

The Ford and I explored the Detroit area for the next three days. Any signs of the automotive industry had all but disappeared. It was the same across the border in Windsor, Canada. Just like Frank had stated, Detroit truly had become America's junkyard.

Like some of the other cities and towns I'd driven through, there was an accumulation of trash and grime. I recalled a comment someone made at breakfast: "It's almost like the city is rusting"! There were a lot of abandoned cars parked along the streets of Detroit, even on the main streets. There were entire blocks of vacant homes and bulldozed lots. Some of the homes still standing had been vandalized and even burned out. Broken windows and doors added to the unsightly piles of dented and rusting appliances on bare lawns. The same was true of vacant factory buildings, shops, and boarded-up strip malls.

In talks with longtime residents, I found most believed that Detroit would someday return to its former glory. The neighborhoods I visited appeared to be affected by a blight brought on by unemployment, crime, or people just giving up and abandoning their nearly worthless homes. By accident, I met Earl and Joyce, an elderly African American couple. It was a warm morning, and they were weeding their small front yard. We struck up a conversation when I stopped to ask directions. The street I was on didn't match my map. Earl told me they had lived in the same place since 1964 and enjoyed talking about "the good ol' days." Although only six homes were still occupied on their street, they were still proud of their little bungalow. The home was well kept and the postage-stamp yard was neat and trimmed. Earl had worked for one of the automotive giants for thirty-five years before they closed up shop. Joyce had raised two sons and a daughter. They hated what had happened to Detroit, to their neighborhood, and as Earl put it, "To the G—d—country!" We sat on the front steps, reminiscing. Joyce brought out some Cokes and a bowl of pretzels. She had tears in her eyes when she told me they hadn't sat out front and talked to anyone for months. She sure missed passing the time with friends and neighbors, but it was "getting too dangerous to sit on the porch." Earl said, "There's nobody left to talk to anyway!" Joyce told me their TV hadn't been working for a couple of weeks, but they couldn't get anyone to come to repair it. One fellow told her on the phone he'd come if she could arrange a police escort for him! Earl didn't have any qualms telling me about the loaded 12-gauge shotgun he kept just inside his front door. He cautioned me to visit downtown only during the daylight hours and always lock the car doors. They didn't own a car anymore. He said it wasn't worth the hassle of going out to the garage and finding tires or the battery had been stolen. When they needed to go to the market, they called a taxi. Apparently, the cabbies didn't have the same fears as the TV repairmen. Their oldest son had moved to California and worked at one of the ports. The daughter was an RN in Pittsburgh. They didn't visit home very often. The youngest son managed to get mixed up with the wrong crowd and had three years to go on his prison sentence.

Earl had served in the army in Korea. We talked a little about his time in the service. The thing he remembered most about Korea, besides getting shot at every day, was it had been cold—"a lot colder than it gets here!" Somehow, we got on the topic of the VA and benefits. WOW! That certainly got his attention. He let me know in no uncertain terms exactly what he thought about the way the United

States treated the folks who had served in our military. He told me that he had met a few nice folks (mostly nurses and orderlies) at the VA hospital/clinic he went to "only when he had to." For the most part, the doctors acted like they were doing you a favor when they saw you, and the facilities stunk—literally. He told me that he was much more fortunate than the guys that had been sent to Vietnam and the young soldiers returning from Afghanistan and Iraq. The things they were exposed to and the damage to their minds and bodies was much worse than in Korea. Earl hadn't been to the VA hospital for quite a while and had no intention of visiting one unless it was a last resort. "It's just too depressing, seeing all those young men there" was all he had to say.

They pointed me in the right direction. We said our good-byes, and I started looking for the next story. I noticed that there were no Help Wanted signs anywhere. I stopped at a 7-Eleven for gas, a newspaper, and a Diet Coke. A clerk wearing a turban took my money but didn't appear willing to engage in conversation. I think he was in a hurry to get back to the book he'd been reading when I interrupted him. I'll bet his story would have been an interesting one.

I drove around for a bit but didn't see any place that looked safe or even worth visiting. I returned to my home at the RV park to look through the newspaper, watch TV, or check online, hoping to find some good news about what was happening in the world and to browse the classified ads. I intended to make a list of the calls I'd make when I went looking for a job. At the RV café, I had a plate of pretty good spaghetti and meatballs for dinner. I borrowed the phone book from behind the counter and looked up the address and phone number for the closest VA facility. Day one in Detroit was over except for a shower and making my journal entries.

The next morning, I decided to skip breakfast at the RV park, jumped into the rented Ford, and headed directly into the downtown area. I went searching for an eatery where I could get breakfast and, hopefully, some stimulating conversation before calling about jobs or visiting the VA hospital. I found a place called Mel's Diner. Mel's place looked like an Airstream travel trailer on steroids. The outside was shiny aluminum with red neon trim. There wasn't a blade of grass or a bush in sight. There were plenty of parking spaces, and they all came with a meter. I found a quarter in my pocket and plunked it into the meter. I had just purchased fifteen minutes of legal parking. I entered the diner, and before I had a chance to ask for change, the waitress smiled at me and handed me four quarters as she took my dollar bill. Apparently, this happened all the time. I put three more quarters in the meter (now I had an hour) and went back inside the diner for breakfast. That's where I met the cops, Rick and Judy. I promised to use aliases for these two police officers. That's the only way they would agree to tell me their story and what was happening in their world. By the way, they were having scrambled eggs, toast, and coffee—not doughnuts!

First off, they made sure that I understood what real law-enforcement officers experienced every day was nothing like the *Law & Order* shows on TV. The two of them had been in the department for thirteen years and had been partners for three years. They took turns driving their customized cruiser, a battered-up six-year-old Ford with almost 250,000 miles on it. Rick told me that he and Judy knew every nook and cranny of the neighborhoods they patrolled and the people who lived there. They informed me there were some pretty bad folks in the metropolitan areas: dealing drugs, stealing anything not nailed down, pimping out both guys and gals, vandalizing homes and what few businesses that were left. They felt sorry for most of the residents who were law-abiding citizens. "A guy steals food and goes to jail. Another guy steals a billion dollars and goes to a fenced-in country club. How fair is that?" It was no wonder the citizens felt the government had let them down and were mad as hell! Sometimes they took out their frustrations on the police, an easily accessed symbol of government authority. Judy's broken nose gave testimony to this. Sometimes they resorted to what the cops called frustration violence. There weren't any jobs. No one had a dollar to spend. The neighborhoods were falling apart. No one was helping them. They had no idea what to do to get out of a hopeless situation.

Rick told me, "The 'breadwinners' are ashamed to go home empty-handed and broke. So they do the only thing left to survive—they steal. When possible, they steal things they can use, but often, they steal things they can sell. Go check out the local pawnshops, and you'll likely find some good deals." Judy stated that she had shopped at a couple of the places and got some really great deals last Christmas. She was concerned about the increasing number of automatic weapons turning up on the streets. Neither cared much for the NRA, but they did think citizens had the right to own guns—just not automatic assault rifles but bazookas or grenades!

They told me the crime rate was still high even though the number of violent crimes had declined. They never left the patrol car without notifying dispatch first, making sure their vests were in place and checking to see their weapons were loaded. Two bullet holes in the trunk lid gave testimony to the kind of lives these officers were subjected to. Rick had been divorced for several years. "The old lady couldn't take it. She hated my job, and she hated this city. She took the two girls to live with her folks in Virginia. I think she's dating some local politician." Judy was married and reasonably happy. Her husband was an attorney, and even though they lived in a safe suburban area (outside the city limits), they didn't want any kids. I was told not to even think of asking to ride along with them. A year ago, their captain had sent a reporter along to "observe and write an article about the men/women in blue."

The assignment was for a week. He never wrote the story; he quit after four hours (that was the day the two bullet holes appeared in the old Ford's trunk lid while they were trying to arrest a guy robbing a convenience store).

They took advantage of moonlighting to make a few extra bucks. Their philosophy was they needed the extra cash, and there was always someone ready to pay them to provide better security. Turns out, liquor stores, bars, Walmarts, and shopping malls were willing customers. Bars apparently were the least desirable (the most dangerous) for this after-hours work, but the pay was better. Both of them were trying to put money away, hoping retirement would become a possibility after they'd put in the minimum twenty years. "This morning we only had 2,555 days to go." These were two reasonably intelligent and very nice people. I didn't envy their chosen profession.

I sincerely wished them good health and good fortune as I headed to the Ford.

On my way around town, I passed by a middle school and a high school. Neither one was in session (summer vacation), but both seemed to be very busy. Kids were everywhere. They were playing basketball (no nets on the hoops and with cracks in the asphalt), Hacky Sack, hopscotch, jump rope, stickball, and just sitting around with rap music blaring from an oversized boom box. Later I asked Holly the waitress about what I'd observed. She informed me, "They don't have anyplace else to go. The playgrounds and pools are closed. No money to open them. The malls let them spend money but won't let them just hang out there. The Y is always at capacity. No one wants to get involved with organizing sports. The politicians look the other way and leave to police to keep order. If you were one of these kids, what would you do all day? Watch TV, play video games, or what?" I had no answer.

While looking for my next story, my mind must have wan-dered, and I managed to get lost. I found myself in what I'd call a bad section of town. I followed the street signs and obeyed the one-way and stop signs, but no matter which way I turned, I seemed to wind up back in the same place. I really didn't want to stop and ask for help, but I had no choice. The problem was, there didn't seem to be anyone around to ask for directions.

I turned a corner (it seemed like the tenth time around this same block) and noticed graffiti, garbage, and a bunch of young black kids wearing what looked like Lions jackets standing there. I pulled up to the curb, wound the passenger-side window down to ask how to get out of there, and *bam*—there was one of them standing next to my door with his hand out. I wasn't sure what to do: hand him my wallet, hit the gas pedal, or ask for directions. He looked at me and said something I didn't understand. I just looked at him, so he said it again. This time he had a small baggie in his hand with two red pills in it. He said something that sounded like, "Twenty dollars or git lost." Uh-oh! What had I gotten myself into? I decided to be direct with him (he looked like he was only about twelve). I told him I was lost and only wanted to know how to get to the interstate.

He looked around, hesitated for a second, then smiled and said in a very clear English, "Go straight for two blocks and turn left at the light. If I were you, I wouldn't stop for anything." I didn't! In the rearview mirror, I could see the gang laughing as I accelerated down the road. Eight blocks later, I was back in civilization and hoped never to get into another drug-buying situation. A half hour later, I was still shaking, so I pulled over and parked at what looked like a safe Super Walmart. I walked next door to an Arby's for an overdue lunch. I must have looked a little nervous after getting lost in the asphalt jungle. The guy in line next to me asked if I was OK. I told him I was all right. He looked at me again and told me it looked like I'd seen a ghost. I started to feel a little better and decided I'd share my experience with him if he were interested. He was.

So we sat together, ate our sandwiches, drank our milk shakes, and I told him my tale. He was a good listener and appeared to get a kick out of my story. His name was Sam, and he was from Detroit. As a matter of fact, he was the assistant manager at the Walmart next door. He told me that I should consider myself very lucky to have met a reasonable drug salesman instead of a hyped-up teenage junkie or gang member who would have thought nothing of robbing me, if not worse. Sam told me about his life in Detroit. He was an ex-marine (we shared a couple of war stories) and lived here all his life (he was thirty-eight).

He was happily married to Sandy and had two teenage sons. They lived in a reasonably secure, gated community, and his two boys went to a private school "out in the country." His wife never left their compound alone. When she did venture out, it was always with him or at least three other women, only during the day and only to the good sections of town. His home had an alarm, and he had an "adequate supply of arms and ammo" on hand. His folks and his brother's family lived west of Detroit in the small town of Jackson. They owned the franchise for the Ace Hardware Store. Sam enjoyed his job, but he and Sandy couldn't wait until the boys went off to college. Then their plan was for him to quit and to get out of Detroit as soon as possible. Sam believed Detroit would recover someday but not in his lifetime, and he wanted to enjoy life, not worry about his family's safety every minute. He didn't know where they would wind up, but it would be someplace "safe and warmer."

Sam and I said our good-byes. It had been an interesting lunch and another enlightening conversation to add to my archives. Not only that, I had finally calmed down, and my knees had ceased shaking.

I walked across the parking lot to the Walmart and did some grocery shopping. Then it was back to the RV. I prayed not to get lost this time.

CHAPTER 7

THE VETERAN'S ADMINISTRATION

After an uneventful night and a quick breakfast at the RV park, I decided to follow the advice of folks I'd interviewed over the last couple of days and went to visit the local VA Hospital. Dressed in slacks and a sport coat with a white shirt and tie, I arrived shortly about 10:00 a.m. at an aging campus-style building well outside the city limits. At one time, the place had been surrounded by walking paths, groomed lawns, trees, benches, and ponds. Not anymore. The grounds were not being kept up, and the lawn needed cutting. The parking lot was cracked, and a number of potholes were visible. I parked in a slot with a *visitor* sign attached to a post by a twisty. My first impression wasn't a good one.

Passing through the double glass doors, I immediately encountered the ever-present ammonia/Lysol/Clorox smell of hospitals and nursing homes. A receptionist was seated at a cluttered desk in a sparsely decorated entry foyer. She said hello, pointed to a guest registry, and asked me to sign in. I entered my name, put NA under "rank," and listed the address and phone number of the RV park instead of my actual home information. Having completed this task, I turned to find my greeter busily engaged in a phone conversation with what I guessed was her daughter (maybe one of the kids on the school playground from yesterday?). About five minutes later, she smiled at me and inquired how she could be of help.

I thought the best way to approach a fact-finding mission without possessing any credentials was to use "honesty is the best policy" and see if it worked. I explained to Dorothy (from her red, white, and blue name tag) I wanted to talk to the administrator about care for our returning wounded veterans. She politely asked if I had an appointment, which I informed her I did not. She seemed to be at a loss as to what to do with someone who just showed up on her doorstep without any warning, wanting to talk to the boss. Finally, she asked me to have a seat while she checked to see if anyone was available. I pushed her a little and informed her that I didn't want to speak to just anyone; I wanted to speak to someone in charge. I don't know if it was the shirt and tie or my attitude, but she consulted her directory and made a phone call. I couldn't hear the conversation, but I could tell Dorothy was a bit irritated by the person on the other end of the conversation. After a few minutes, I was informed that Mrs. Sanchez from the administration office would be down to meet me. (I wondered where she was coming "down" from since we were in a one-story building.)

A few minutes later, Mrs. Sanchez came down the hall, walked up to me (I was the only person in the waiting area), and we proceeded with introductions. Naturally she wanted to know exactly what kind of information I was looking for and why. Again, I tried the honesty route and told her of my concerns regarding the rumored lack of care for our wounded warriors. Roberta (name tag) seemed to be evaluating me and my request. After a few seconds, she told me my inquiry was a little unusual. "The only 'outside' people who seem interested in what we do here are family members, government auditors, or a politician who needs some publicity," she said with a halfhearted smile. I assured her that I wasn't any of those, and my interest was purely patriotic. I firmly believed our wounded soldiers deserved more than the Purple Heart; they deserved the best care our country could provide.

This statement proved to be "the key to the kingdom." Roberta led me down a long hallway (very clean and not at all cluttered) to a cheery cafeteria. The two of us sat, had a cup of coffee, and conversed. The cafeteria wasn't very busy. Lunchtime had passed (they ate early), and the kitchen crew was preparing for dinner. There were 116 residents being treated at the facility. Nine were females. The facility had a capacity to treat 150 patients and a few years ago had been able to cope with 166 residents. At present, nineteen required psychological help, and the rest suffered from a variety of physical wounds.

Most of the doctors and nurses were military personnel. The nonmedical staff were a mix of civilians and military personnel. When necessary, outside medical experts (consultants) were brought in to assist. These outsiders entered the picture when eye surgery, amputations and/or prostheses, skin grafts, or plastic surgery was required. Both military and civilian personnel were used for these services. Roberta told me, "Our soldiers get the best possible care here. They've been through hell, and we know it. I've worked at three VA hospitals in the last fifteen years, and this one is the best. The people who work at these places really do work hard. Their pay is only fair, but they have a job, and most appreciate that fact. The budget allocations for the VA have improved dramatically in the last ten years, but they're never enough. It took a lot of negative publicity, a few vote-seeking politicians, and celebs to get involved, but we do get the necessary funds."

I didn't just sit there and listen. I asked pertinent questions and received spot-on answers. Roberta didn't shy away from any of my inquiries. I was surprised at her answer when asked what was lacking in the program. She informed me they had first-class in everything except one category. "After we put them back together and through rehab, they face the really tough battle. Getting back into normal society and finding a job. Some of our 'graduates' have technical training provided by the military like pilots, mechanics, on computers or in electronics. These usually have no problem finding a decent job. The grunts (infantrymen and support people) aren't as fortunate. After leaving us, 30 percent of these young people will be jobless for as long as two years. There isn't any demand for the skills they acquired in the service except maybe in some type of security. The government has to realize these 'kids' need to receive job-skills training so they can survive. There is nothing so frustrating as watching a young person's wounds heal, a smile come back, and then *wham*, they can't find a job. It's a shame! Our politicians know about this problem. Hell, it's been around since the Vietnam conflict. Yet nothing of any substance has been done. Why not? Of course, the handicapped vets are another problem altogether. Some of them may never be able to hold a job. What do we tell them?"

Wow! I believe if Roberta had the opportunity to talk to Congress, our vets would have a job-training bill passed in a week. Money was allocated for veterans to go back to school, but it was largely for academics, not for job/vocational training. (I did some checking later on and found money was set aside specifically for vocational job training, but it was far less than necessary. I also found employers had very little incentive to hire and train our veterans.)

We finished our coffee, and Roberta took me on a tour. She'd guessed I didn't want the VIP treatment, and I really wanted to visit some of the patients and hear their stories. Roberta was a very perceptive woman. We walked around for a bit and then stopped at a set of double doors identified as Meeting Room no. 5. Before entering, Roberta told me to remember that the troops I would be meeting were all young, were all wounded in combat, and were all undergoing multiple surgeries and/or rehab. Her advice was, "Take it slow, and I'll be back to get you in about an hour." With that, she opened the door, and we entered a bright and airy atrium. It had a wide-screen TV, shelves full of paperbacks, four computer consoles with Internet access and printers, eight round tables with four comfortable chairs at each, and a double glass-door refrigerator full of juice and soft drinks. There were fourteen young men and one young woman in the room, talking, reading, or watching TV. Roberta apologized for the interruption and introduced me to them. I noted all of them were in pajamas and robes. Some were wearing casts. All had bandages on some part of their body. A few were missing limbs. Two were in wheelchairs. She explained to the group why I was visiting; I'd asked to talk to them for a short while if it was OK with them. They responded positively, so she introduced each of them to me. The first intro was to Corporal Raymond Sanchez, Roberta's youngest son!

Corporal Sanchez, Raymond, had been in the infantry in Iraq. Eleven weeks ago, while being transported to a secure outpost in a Humvee, they'd hit an IED (improvised explosive device) that blew the bottom out of their truck. Half of the occupants died instantly. The remaining half had survived but with major wounds. Two were amputees, two were severely burned, and one was permanently blind; all the survivors had broken bones and suffered some degree of hearing loss. Raymond lost his left foot just above the ankle, had severe burns on his left arm and the left side of his face. Two members of his team were at this VA hospital with him (I'd meet Tom and Laverne later). Ray wasn't sure where the rest of his team had been taken after evacuated from Iraq via Germany. He told me it was pure chance he'd wound up at the hospital where his Mom worked, but I could tell he was grateful for it. He had no complaints about the care he had received either in Iraq, in Germany, or here in the States. He did have complaints about some of the equipment his squad had in Iraq. The vehicle they were riding in was only partially armored! It was basically like any Hummer on US highways except it had bigger tires, smaller widows, gun mounts, and a different paint job. When the bomb went off under the truck, there was nothing to protect those inside. With clenched teeth, he told me that "a piece of one-half-inch armor plate bolted under the bottom of the truck would have prevented this." (He pointed to his missing foot for emphasis.) I thought to myself, "This isn't right. If we knew how to prevent something like this from happening, why didn't we?"

Ray was in the process of multiple skin grafts for his face and being fitted for a replacement foot. He knew that he'd be able to walk again and play golf, but he didn't think tennis, basketball, football, or mountain climbing were in his future. The doctors had told him they'd be able to repair his face to "almost normal," but it would take five or six surgeries spread over three years. For now, if he wanted to hide the scars on his left arm, he'd wear a long-sleeved shirt. It would be a few more years until those scars were taken care of. "I only have so much skin they can take off my butt," he joked.

Ray was twenty-two years old, was facing multiple surgical procedures for at least the next five years, and was wearing a fake foot for the rest of his life, yet he actually smiled frequently. I'm not sure I would have under those circumstances. I didn't bring up the subject of his looking for a job. It was too soon for that discussion. Ray and I spent a few minutes talking about sports (He was a Michigan football fan and of course, the Lions), Iraq, Afghanistan, and even the best TV shows. Knowing that my time was limited, Ray wheeled over to one of the tables and introduced me to his friends, Tom and Laverne. Tom was listening intently to something playing on an elaborate set of Bose headphones, and they were both reading. Tom had what looked like a children's book, and Laverne had a *People* magazine.

Ray exchanged a few words with Laverne and then, speaking very loudly, filled Tom in on my mission. Ray explained to me I needed to speak up since Tom's hearing was shot. He wasn't totally deaf, and his temporary hearing aids were helping, but he still had a ways to go. Tom's real problem wasn't his hearing; it was that he was totally blind. I'm sure I would have realized it at some point, but he looked normal. He had no bandages over his eyes and seemed to have no problem locating the can of Coke in front of him, and he was reading a book! On closer inspection, I saw that the book was in braille. He explained to me that he was learning (very slowly) to read braille and, so far, had made it through several "Dick and Jane" stories. He found he could learn faster if he could find an audio tape to listen to (with his hearing aids set to full volume) while he "let his fingers do the reading." His biggest problem, so far, was trying to wear the calluses off his fingertips using fine sandpaper so they would be sensitive enough to feel the dots. He was also aware that everyone had to speak very loud so he could hear them and was concerned that when he received his new hearing aids, people would continue yelling at him!

Tom had been in the seat next to Ray when they hit the IED. All he remembers was a *whoosh* followed by a loud bang and a burning light. He woke up hours later in a medical tent. He wondered why it was so dark and so quiet. It took awhile for him to understand that he was blind and almost deaf. "Pretty scary" was the way Tom put it. "Everyone's been great. I know I'll never be able to see again. I just wish I would have seen more of the world before this happened. I'll learn to read, and I'll get most of my hearing back, but they tell me I'll have to use my imagination to 'see' things. I play poker with the guys, but they won't let me deal. Braille poker cards have some side benefits."

Tom was from suburban Pittsburgh and told me he loved the Steelers and the Penguins. He'd given up on the Pirates years ago. We talked about his family. He had two younger sisters who just started college. His girlfriend visited several times when his parents made the trip, but she was working, and it was hard for her to get away. I looked across the table at this young man and wondered what would become of him over the next fifty or sixty years. I prayed he would be able to keep his positive attitude throughout what undoubtedly would be a lifelong ordeal for him.

Laverne was another story. She had been sitting right behind Tom when the explosion happened. She'd been slammed against the roof of their vehicle. She had seventeen broken bones and a concussion as a result. Three of the bone breaks had to be joined together with stainless steel pins. She told me that the doctors had told her she would be back to normal in about three months. Laverne planned on resuming her military career. She only hoped that she wouldn't be sent back to Iraq or Afghanistan.

My mind drifted away from the conversation for a few seconds. I was thinking why this had happened to them and how strange it was that none of these young people seemed bitter about what their futures were going to be like. They had accepted their fate. I was pulled back to the discussion when the other young man in a wheelchair joined us at the table. He asked if I minded answering a couple of questions for him. I told him I didn't I mind at all. His first question caught me by surprise. "Why do you think the United States sent troops to Afghanistan?" The obvious answer was we were out for revenge. Afghanistan condoned terrorism, trained terrorists, and terrorists had attacked the United States on 9/11 much like Japan had done at Pearl Harbor. He accepted this and stated, "The troops I meet coming back from the fight in Afghanistan agree with you, and so do I. Whatever happens there, they deserve it for what they did." Three more of the guys joined our discussion group.

His next question was "Why did we invade Iraq?" I told him the US intel agencies had information that Saddam had WMDs, was manufacturing chemical weapons, and planned to use them, and had actually used them on an entire village of his enemies. Our wealthy oil-rich "friends" in Kuwait were also under attack. He said, "OK, I'll buy that, but what happened after we went in, chased the Iraqi troops out of Kuwait, and found that Saddam didn't have WMDs, that our billion-dollar intelligence agencies had screwed up or lied to us? Why didn't we just admit that we made a mistake? We eliminated a murdering dictator and his two sadistic sons. That could have been a good enough reason. We should have loaded up, moved out, and left. It wasn't until much later we were forced to tell the world there were no WMDs, but we were staying to help the Iraqis build a democracy. Hell, those folks had no idea what a democracy was. When we told them they were free, they wandered around in circles, waiting on someone to tell them what to do. They didn't need troops. They needed businessmen and people to teach them how to do things, not shoot them. We all know the real reason we're still in Iraq. 'It's the oil, stupid.' They have it, and we need it. Everything else is just 'window dressing.' You may or may not agree, but we know, we were there. The Iraqis don't want us there. Maybe they did at one time, but not anymore. We aren't accomplishing a thing except this (he pointed to the soldiers gathered around the table.) Look at us! Yeah! We're being treated well, but if we hadn't been in that hellhole to begin with, we wouldn't be here." Nods from the others supported his statement. "We need to get the hell out of there and fast!"

Just then, Roberta "rescued" me. I thanked them for sharing, told them I wished them the best, and followed her down the hall to her office.

Her space was pleasant, with large widows and the usual equipment you'd expect to see. Roberta wasn't the boss, but she was no. 2 on the organizational chart. She knew where the bodies were buried and could recite statistics from memory. She told me disability claims with the US Department of Veterans Affairs has doubled in the last seven or eight years. I was very surprised to find most of this increase came from veterans of Vietnam and the first Persian Gulf conflict. These vets accounted for $35 billion or 85 percent of the total year's spending. She confided to me that she was worried Ray and Tom would become part of a growing backlog of disability claims (now at about two hundred thousand) that could take as long as two years to process. "They're getting the care they need now, but what's going to happen to them long term depends on when and how their disability claim is handled. The VA is trying but at a snail's pace. In this modern age, the VA is still largely 'paper based' with an admitted 17 percent error in initial ratings for individual vets! The older vets' claims for chemical (Agent Orange) and PTSD (the 'invisible illness') have been joined by another 25 percent in claims for diabetes. Claims are growing faster and faster. One of the problems was the government and the VA grossly underestimated the number of disabled veterans we would be contending with from Afghanistan and Iraq. Our troops are much better equipped today, and field medical facilities have improved dramatically. Soldiers who would have died from their wounds ten years ago are now surviving, creating a backlog for hospital care and disability claims."

I could tell Roberta's feelings and her frustration wasn't solely for her son. She was thinking about "them all," all two hundred thousand of them. We talked for quite a while, and at one point she told me one way to stop the problem was for the United States to stop trying to be the "police force for the world." When attacked (like 9/11), find the culprits and eliminate them with lethal force, including nukes if necessary. She said that it sounded a little brutal, but not only would this policy reduce the number of US casualties, it would reduce the number of terrorists and future conflicts in the long term. She told me, "I think Harry Truman proved this when he decided to end World War II with the atomic bomb. The bleeding hearts today claim that the 'collateral damage' would be too great and the United States would be seen as a 'bully.' Who cares? Would being called a bully really matter? We're sitting on our hands while Iran develops nuclear capability and Syria (and others) continue to supply and train terrorist groups intent on annihilating us. Walk through this hospital, look at these young people, and then talk to me about 'collateral damage.' When you cut through the rhetoric and media inspired BS, we're in Iraq because we wanted to save face over a tactical error (there were no WMDs) we made long ago, and there's lots of oil under the sand dunes. It's time our troops were taken out of Iraq and brought home. Let's finish in Afghanistan! We need to start getting ready for Iran!"

I said good-bye to Roberta and thanked her for allowing me to visit and for sharing her insights with me. I wished her luck and told her I'd pray for Ray to recuperate and do well for himself. I think she knew I sincerely meant what I said, but she also knew I felt as hopeless as she did. When I told her my next investigation would be to check out employment opportunities for veterans, she just smiled and wished me good luck. Roberta was the first person I had spoken to who asked me what I intended to do with the "facts, figures, and BS" I was gathering. I told her in all honesty I really didn't know what I was going to do, but the information would not be wasted. She seemed OK with that answer. While we only met for a few hours, I felt like we parted as friends.

I drove back to the RV park, realizing my time-out vacation was turning into a mission of some kind. Some of the things our political, industrial, financial leaders condoned or implemented were wrong, and in quite a few cases, they were aware of that fact! I wasn't sure what I could do about it. It was obvious to me we were headed in the wrong direction, but what chance does one guy have, even a highly motivated senior citizen, to do something to change our world for the better? After dinner at a local steak house, I spent several hours recording my notes in the electronic journal, took a shower, and watched TV for a while. Then I hit the sheets. I needed my rest. The next day I'd be going job hunting.

NOTE: I would continue investigations at two more VA facilities over the next three months with more or less the same results. Our wounded troops were being treated well. They weren't sure about their futures. After rehab, they needed job training and social integration, but very little of it existed. They were sure our government, our leaders, were wrong in what they were trying to do in Iraq. On the other hand, these young men wondered why we weren't "trying to win in Afghanistan" or going into Iran now instead of waiting until they actually had nukes. Here's a good question for our intel folks: "How many lives is the oil in Iraq worth or the nuclear material in Iran?" One of them was a little prophetic when he told me, "It's like Yogi said, it's déjà vu all over again!"

CHAPTER 8

JOB HUNTING

It had been a long time since I went looking for a job. My intention wasn't to actually go to work; I wanted to see what types of employment were available and what considerations were given to our returning veterans. After looking through the classified ads, I made a list of available jobs I planned to inquire about. It was an easy task; there were only nine ads to pursue. Those I selected stated they were an "equal opportunity employer" and had a phone number listed; none mentioned being veteran friendly. There were other ads stating applicants needed to submit a written résumé for consideration. Then, if your qualifications met their needs, they would contact you for an interview. This would consume a lot of time and was not the method I wanted to use.

I intended to complete my job search over the phone. I expected to be able to speak directly to a person in charge, and after providing my tailor-made pedigree, which should get his or her interest, I'd try getting the particulars about the job opening. That would be step 1.

Then I'd inform them I was a returning veteran from Iraq and see what the reaction was. This part would be step 2. I rehearsed what I would say to the interviewer or the employment agent who answered my call. If successful with step 1 and the continuing conversation from step 2 was mutually acceptable, I'd drop the bombshell; step 3 would ask how they felt about hiring a disabled vet. I had no idea how these contacts would go, but I guessed they could get a little tricky when we reached step 3.

The necessary materials sat on top of my desk in the RV. I had a legal tablet, several pencils, a glass of ice water, my classified ad list, and a cell phone. I made sure I visited the potty and dressed comfortably. I had another cup of coffee, and at 10:00 a.m., it was time to begin. By then the person at the other end of the conversation should have taken care of any overnight chores, morning contacts, coffee, and pastry. I would be his or her first challenge for the day.

For all contacts, I would use an alias: Robert "Bob" C. (Claytor) Fuller ("like the brush"). I was twenty-seven years old, single but engaged, born and raised in Ohio (suburban Cleveland). The company I worked for had gone out of business.

Cleveland held no job prospects for me. From that point on, I would provide a verbal résumé that would fit the requirements for the position advertised. The résumé would include the necessary education and associated work experience specific to the open position. After establishing a dialogue with the interviewer and providing qualifications for the position, I would move on to step 2 to see what would happen.

For step 2, my cover story was that I had been in the National Guard and had been called up and sent to Iraq for eighteen months. When I returned home, I found my employer had gone belly-up, and I was unemployed. If the interviewer accepted this and the conversation continued, I would wait for the right time to ask about their hiring policy for a disabled vet. If I got this far, my "disability" would be the loss of my right foot. If my disability presented a problem, I'd thank him or her for their time and hang up. If the disability wasn't a problem, I'd complete the conversation, say thanks, and I'd promise to consider the position and get back to them for an interview.

On paper it looked like a good plan. During a dress rehearsal in the RV and frequently referring to my notes, it actually sounded like a good story. Hopefully, I'd find employers were receptive to hiring veterans, and maybe one would even consider a disabled vet. At 10:00 a.m., it was time to find out.

The first advertisement was for a customer-service sales rep. I dialed the number and waited three rings for a receptionist to answer. I gave her the extension number listed in the ad, and she asked me to "please hold while I put you through." So far, so good. A few seconds later, I was greeted by a professional-sounding woman who introduced herself as Maxine Turney. After the introductory pleasantries, we got down to business. The opening was at the corporate offices for an office-supply company. The candidate needed a pleasing appearance, had to be a good communicator with the ability to greet customers, possess basic computer skills (record-keeping function), and understand and be able to explain company benefits to other employees (making sure procedures were followed).

A forty-hour week was necessary, the hours were somewhat flexible, but would involve some evening and weekend work. It was an hourly position starting at $14 an hour for the first six months. The rate would go to $16 an hour, assuming performance was adequate for the next six months. At the end of the first year, the rate would be $20 an hour. They provided standard benefits with large copays for medical, no dental, and no eye-care provisions. A 401(k) was available to full-time employees after the first year. It would be possible to move into direct sales later with a salary, commission, and bonus structure. I seriously thought about applying for this job!

We reviewed my qualifications, which I made sure were more than adequate for the position (according to my fictitious résumé). Step 1 was completed, so I moved on to step 2.

I explained about being in the Guard and getting called to Iraq and having no job when I got home. Maxine informed me they had hired several veterans in the last two or three years and were happy with their performance. That's when I hit her with step 3, being disabled. After a brief silence, Maxine asked what the disability was. I explained the loss of my foot and clarified that I had no difficulty walking or standing and that it did not affect my appearance. She thoroughly surprised me with her next statement. "Why don't we set up an interview for you? I think you have the qualifications we need, and it sounds like your disability won't be a problem. How's your schedule for next Wednesday?" Wow! We agreed to 10:00 a.m. on Wednesday and said our good-byes. I would phone Maxine the next day, thank her, and tell her I had accepted another position, but I might know of another candidate. While thinking about this conversation, I realized

I had found the perfect job for Cpl Raymond Sanchez. I contacted a very grateful Roberta the next day. I hope an interview was arranged.

My next contact was for the position of a long-haul trucker. The ad said, "Experience preferred, but willing to train the right person." I spoke to a gruff-voiced man named Jerry about the position. He explained that I'd be driving a boxed 18-wheeler from Detroit to LA and back every week. The pay and benefits sounded pretty good. It was a nonunion job. After I covered my previous work experience with him, we agreed I had the proper qualifications, but I would need to take a driver's test. When I brought up step 2, Jerry told me he didn't have a problem with veterans. His nephew had a similar situation and now drove truck for him. Jerry seemed like a nice guy and I hesitated to bring up step 3, but this was research, and I needed to follow through. He told me there was no way he could hire someone with my disability. "I'm truly sorry, but my insurance company would drop me like a hot potato." I thanked him, and he wished me luck. I decided to take a break and have some lunch before making the next call. So I raided the RV's fridge.

Call no. 3 was in response to an ad for a full-time line cook for a well-known country club. After reaching the proper person in charge, (she sounded like a teenager over the phone) I proceeded with my introduction. The young lady then informed me that I'd have to "come in for a face-to-face interview" as the next step. I agreed, but before wasting our time, I needed to know if they had a problem hiring a veteran (step 2). Her answer was really a question. "Are you disabled?" She had jumped ahead of me and gone directly to step 3. I asked her if that made any difference, and without any hesitation, she answered, "Yes, it could make a difference!"

Another question quickly followed. "What is your disability?" When I explained about my missing foot, she told me there was no way I'd be able to handle a job requiring long hours standing and walking. She thanked me for my interest, wished me good luck, and hung up.

Over the next three months, I would continue the job-hunting process fourteen more times in three different states. There wasn't an abundance of work listed in the classified ads anywhere. (There were a lot of employment agencies claiming they could find a job for anyone. I phoned one of them and found they could actually guarantee me a job for $11 an hour but with no benefits. The up-front fee for this service was $500. I wonder how many desperate folks paid for this service.) The results for the fourteen contacts were similar. For the most part, employers would hire a vet if he/she had the education/ work experience required. Most hesitated when confronted with my disability. Some seemed genuinely concerned about my ability to handle the job (standing for long periods, climbing or walking a lot). A few told me flat out that they didn't think I'd be able to do the job and wished me good luck. At the end of my "job search," I drew some conclusions. Qualified people really looking for work could probably find a job. Vets could find a job if they had the proper skills (training!). Disabled vets would have difficulty. If the government offered an employer some type of incentive (dollars/tax break) to hire and train a disabled vet, it would make a difference. We already have the Americans with Disabilities Act but need much more emphasis regarding our disabled vets.

I was satisfied I had fulfilled my self-imposed obligation of looking into the VA, job availability in general, jobs specifically for our veterans and in finding what problems there were with the system. I'd found some interesting facts regarding employers, being exposed to some of the veterans' insights, VA staff input and what the VA and our government leaders needed to correct. I guess I'd sum it up this way: the system wasn't broken, but it needed a tune-up. It became clear what our soldiers were supportive of and what they opposed. Also, "the politicians need to get their heads out of their a— and take care of Iran and North Korea before nukes become an issue." Many of the veterans I spoke with stated they would be willing to return to Iraq in a civilian capacity as trainers.

I guessed my "work" in Detroit was completed. My planned three days had stretched into five. It was time well spent, but I was ready to move on. Without realizing it, I'd begun making a transition from taking a vacation to volunteering for a mission, possibly a long one. The journal entries continued to grow. The news articles were piling up in a box next to my desk. It was interesting reading, and I finally began to see a theme emerging.

I pondered a change in my schedule. In three days, my fourteen-year-old granddaughter, Amanda, was to meet me in Chicago. We had planned for her to join me for a week before she returned to school in late summer. I phoned her with the intent of canceling her trip, but before I could broach the topic, she informed me that I was the only man in her life; she was all packed, looking forward to seeing me and visiting the Windy City. I found out later that she had an ulterior motive: she planned to write an article about her summer with Grandpa and her tour of Chicago. It was an extra credit assignment about "How I spent my summer vacation." After our conversation, I set off for the Windy City. There was no way I could disappoint her. I had three days to get to the Midway International Airport.

CHAPTER 9

THE WINDY CITY

The weather is beautiful, and I'm on my way to Chicago, looking forward to my granddaughter's visit. Amanda and I planned to tour Chicago, the Old Town section and the Lake Shore. I could make it to Chicago from Detroit in a day. I had plenty of time to check out a few of the popular casinos en route. I'd also take a day for some investigative interviews before her arrival. We had a reservation at an RV park on the Lake Shore. It was close enough to downtown to allow us to check out the tourist traps and, maybe, do some shopping. I had no intention of sharing my journal entries or my potential mission with her. This was going to be a fun time for both of us. I knew she wanted to ride on my motorcycle. Amanda had informed me she didn't have a romantic interest at home, so I'd have her full attention during our visit. Hopefully, she would enjoy the scenery and not spend her time on a cell phone or texting her girlfriends.

I bid farewell to Detroit, entered the destination into my trusty GPS (Betsy), and headed west. I transitioned from I-94 onto 912, refueled, and found my way to the casino district in East Chicago. It was about six o'clock in the evening when I parked the RV at Harrah's Casino. I cleaned myself up, locked up, and made my way to the casino and joined the buffet line. An abundant dinner over with, I "visited" with a slot machine for a while and then made my way to the poker room. After checking out a few tables, I decided to sit in at a table with six other Texas Hold 'em players for a couple of hours before calling it a night. I didn't win, but I didn't lose much, either. All in all a successful night!

At eleven o'clock, everyone decided to call it quits. Two of the card players, Steven and Ben, asked if I wanted to join them at the bar for a drink. Earlier, I had briefly explained my mission to them, and they wanted to hear more. I accepted their invitation. A few minutes later, a couple of gals, Gwynn and Betty, joined them (us) and were introduced as their wives. Turned out Steven and Gwynn were couple no. 1 and Ben and Betty were couple no. 2. That was the beginning of a very interesting tale. All four had served as cooks in the navy and finished their tour together aboard an aircraft carrier. That was about eight years ago. Two or three drinks later, after sharing a few war stories and a couple of jokes, they confided to me that the four of them had been participants in the "don't ask, don't tell" military philosophy. They were gay!

This revelation really floored me! Steven and Ben didn't fit my mold for a couple of gay guys. Not having been exposed to lesbians, I had no idea how to size up Gwynn and Betty. They were pretty and well-spoken. The four of them had a good laugh at my expense. They explained that yes, they were married, conventionally, but only for insurance and tax purposes. After receiving an honorable discharge, the four of them pooled their savings and started a small restaurant in what was considered an upscale area of Chicago.

Their business was doing well in spite of the down economy. The four of them lived together in a nice residential section of the city. Only their most intimate friends and a few relatives knew their secret. In the privacy of their home, the public persona changed to the real relationships. They laughed about the arguments they had over who would cook meals or what color to paint the walls. Quite a twist! Publicly, as two conventional couples, they were able to get a mortgage, a small business loan, decent medical insurance, and acceptance in a nice neighborhood. As it was in the navy, they firmly believed their lives would be very different if they came out. Since I had zero experience in this social area, I accepted their rationale. I would have loved to see the way their home was decorated. We had one more for the road and said our good-byes. I wished them continued good luck. Then I walked to my "house," took a shower, and slid into bed. I'd look for the RV park by the lake tomorrow morning, set up camp, visit a café or two for some interviews, make a couple phone calls "looking for a job," and begin preparations for Amanda's visit.

I spent the next two days repeating the phone job search and meeting some Midwesterners who wanted to share their opinions regarding the state of our country and the world. With few exceptions, the results of both endeavors were carbon copies of my previous experiences.

The next morning, I took a taxi to the airport (I had learned my lesson) to meet granddaughter Amanda. The taxi was much easier than taking the RV, and using the Honda was out of the question (luggage and other stuff). Her flight was on time, and we had a minifamily reunion at the baggage claim carousel. I was thankful I hadn't tried to bring the Honda as we loaded her two large suitcases and a carry-on bag into the taxi. Our cab driver was from India but knew the city well. He gave us a few tips on places to visit, and we added a couple of them to our list. We arrived at the RV and unpacked. A couple of hours after Amanda's plane landed, we were off to begin exploring Chicago.

The third night of her visit, after another busy day, we decided to take a break, stay at home, and order pizza. We were having a ball, but I was worn-out (I almost didn't make it through our trip to the zoo) and we still had two days to go. Thankfully, the weather was warm and dry. I was watching the news on TV while waiting on the pizza guy to show up. I don't remember what depressing piece of news the anchorperson was reporting, but I made a comment about "the sorry state of affairs Congress kept getting us into."

Amanda put down the magazine she was reading and said to me, "There's no sense getting upset, Grandpa. It's always been that way!" This simple statement from a fourteen-year-old shocked me into realizing something I'd never considered. To Amanda and millions of kids in her age-group, today's world really is "the way it's always been." They'd never experienced a world without war, one without the threat of a terrorist or a nuclear attack looming every moment. I'll bet the history they study in school includes many important historical events, but I wonder if they ever hear about the peaceful times our age-group has experienced.

Amanda and I spent the next couple hours discussing this topic while enjoying our pizza and Cokes. It was a learning experience for both of us. I shared comments about the many good times and the good years I'd had during my life. Amanda showed great interest and even said wow a few times and asked questions frequently. She loved the stories about my being in the Marine Corps. I made a mental note to reconsider writing my memoirs as soon as possible. I'm sure some of my memories would be interesting to the future generations. I began to understand why our teenagers and probably the young-adult generation and even the toddlers of today did some of the outlandish things we've seen over the last thirty years. They're coping with the everyday stresses of life today, not the life we knew yesterday or what we hoped life would be like tomorrow! Their best-case scenario was the world would remain as is. Their worst-case scenario was terrorists would win, or a nuclear war would annihilate the planet. We need to think about what these kids have been exposed to their entire life and what it's doing to them and to the future of civilization. Where are the shrinks when you need them? We can't allow this to continue! Our children, grandchildren and great-grandchildren, future generations deserve better than this!

As I said, this was quite a revelation, more so for me than for Amanda. This conversation, more than anything else I'd been exposed to in the past few months, caused me to willingly consider changing my life's purpose. First and foremost, I had to prioritize what needed to be changed and then develop a plan of action that would allow me to do something about it. I had no idea what I could possibly do to bring about needed changes, so future generations wouldn't have to live a life full of fear and anxiety, so my children would never hear their grandchildren tell them "that's just the way it is."

After two more interesting (and exhausting) days, we reversed the trip to the airport, and Amanda caught her flight home. We'd had a great time together, took lots of photos, shared some fond memories, and made a few new ones. I doubted we would ever have this opportunity again.

I stayed in Chicago a few more days and took my time debating what I would do next. Would my route continue to follow the original vacation trip as outlined? Did I want to accept the fact the USA, maybe the whole world, was headed in the wrong direction? If that were truly the case, what would I do about it? It was totally out of character, but I procrastinated again. The next two days were spent on R & R. I took time to, again, review the journal entries, newspaper clippings, and to check the latest news developments on TV. (Even though I remained skeptical of their "fair and balanced" reporting, if nothing else, they were entertaining. I still believe media personalities fall in a category somewhere between porn stars and politicians.) I reviewed the latest online entries to see what new and pertinent details I could find. My commitment was to make a decision on the third day. If I decided I could actually do something about the world situation, my decision would, by necessity, be ambitious. If the decision was arbitrary or ambiguous or I wasn't totally committed to it, it would be easier to just pack up, go home to The Villages, and enjoy my life. Which would it be?

CHAPTER 10

CAUSE AND EFFECT

After hours of rereading hundreds of news articles I'd gathered over the weeks and my electronic journal entries, my vision began to blur, but I completed the review. While in this process, I started to keep score. At first there was one scorecard, but it grew to three. The deeper I dug into complex facts and figures, the information began to provide evidence of a lack of understanding and action by our so-called leadership and not just politicians. Society, in general, appeared willing to accept their fate no matter how much they bitched and moaned about it. This was unacceptable! It's not just the economy, stupid! It's our lives! One thing became very clear: the biggest danger to our planet is human complacency! Here's a summary of the primary causes for the potential demise of our world and a list of those responsible entities who would eventually become targets for change!

Big Oil interests were the no. 1 cause. Big Oil spawned about a dozen subcategories (no. 1-As) responsible for another three dozen (no.

1-Bs). These included everything from pollution and global warming to financial skullduggery to blocking the growth of alternative reuseable energy sources or hindering development of electric cars or blatant corruption of the political process or—the list just kept on going! When it comes to Jerry McGuire's show me the money, Big Oil did it better than anyone else. They bought our government representatives and any legislation they happened to want passed. I guess it's fair to state that Big Oil included the Seven Sisters and OPEC but involved others as well.

I listed Congress as the no. 2 cause. I argued with myself that Congress should be given the no. 1 label, but Big Oil won! Whoever has the keys to the vault is in control, and that was Big Oil. Our elected leaders were supposed to do what the people wanted, what was required to ensure the continuance of our free and democratic society. Members of Congress were corrupted, largely by greed or power. The corruption of elected representatives wasn't isolated to the federal government. The public needed to open their eyes and witness what was happening in our country and in each state or city! The corruption came in many forms, but campaign contributions were the main driver. Major contributors such as Big Oil ("we want offshore drilling and the Arctic opened up"), the big financial institutions (Congress was supposed to keep an eye on them and had done such an outstanding job as the trillion-dollar bailout showed!), drug companies (where was the FDA?), etc. The list of corruptors filled more than two pages. What happened to campaign finance reform or ethics reviews or term limits? What these elected officials were getting away with was a national disgrace. The media leads us to believe there is wholesale corruption in other countries, but they neglect to "find" it here at home. We, the constituency, allowed it to happen.

Some of the worst offenders got elected and reelected time and again by us because we thought of them as good ol' boys, and in many cases, the media fostered that illusion. We had several ancient senators who couldn't stay awake when supposedly voting on important issues. An aide was positioned near them to wake them, so they could cast their vote. Imagine how they participated in debates leading up to a vote. Congress had done nothing with the oversight of the big banks. They had done nothing about illegal immigration. They did almost nothing to fund reuseable energy development. Think about this: if Congress would encourage/fund alternative energy growth, Big Oil political contributions would cease and what would replace the billions of tax dollars paid into the federal, state, or local agencies? They haven't figured out how to tax us for wind, water, battery, or solar power—yet! Congress did succeed in giving us an almost worthless health care program. They bailed out Wall Street and mortgaged our lives for the next fifty years. Need I go on? I think not. Without a doubt, Congress was the no. 2 cause.

Terrorism had to be the no. 3 cause. Congress and the administration both had checkmarks on this one. They doled out billions of dollars to our intelligence agencies and then ignored the reports they received. They neglected to listen to our military leaders and displayed "armchair general" philosophy when making decisions with detrimental effects on our troops. They exerted very little pressure on our allies for assistance in stopping terrorist activities, supporting a weak NATO and an impotent United Nations. As bad as our Congress was regarding terrorism, most other foreign governments were worse. While some did not directly support terrorist activity, they had no qualms about looking the other way ("see no evil"), which was actually supporting terrorism! Terrorism yesterday was Japan and the Nazis. Today it's the

Taliban and Al-Qaida. Tomorrow it will be Iran and North Korea. It's as if there is a never-ending supply of these misguided religious zealots and a couple of bleeding-heart liberal organizations like the ACLU or the Center for Constitutional Rights helping to keep them alive and out of prison. Cyberterrorism was in its infant stages but would become one of the most prolific causes of mayhem in the years to come.

Pollution is the no. 4 cause: Big Oil; Congress; state governments; various industries including the chemical, aluminum, and automotive giants; power generating utilities; timber companies; surface mining—even some stonewalling American Indian Tribes—all have a share of the blame for pollution.

There are many more causes, but I believe I'd identified the major players. After reviewing the facts and deliberating with myself for a couple of days, I developed a summary listing, as promised, on day three.

The direction the world leaders were following led me to fear we would not survive the Armageddon the media and religious leaders were forecasting. This fear, unchecked, would drive every person over ten years old in industrialized nations to therapy where they'd undoubtedly become addicted to tranquilizers or drugs of some kind in a few years. Every ten year old living in a third world country would join a terrorist group by age eleven or die before his or her twelfth birthday. If something didn't change the course we were on, by 2020 no one would be interested in stopping pollution or developing renewable energy sources. Survival would be at the top of everyone's list. The United States and any remaining allies would be engaged in a limited nuclear war with Iran and North Korea. Russia and China would not participate; they would sit and wait until it was over, then easily conquer whoever "won." By 2030, without the United States to intervene, Russia and China would engage in their own nuclear conflict. This would ultimately result in the destruction of our planet and mankind. The often quoted translation of the Mayan calendar, telling us that our world would end 12/21/12, was in error. The current (intellectual community) interpretation of the data showed the date as 12/21/32. My conclusion, based on "today's information," was either Iran or North Korea would create a nuclear holocaust. We were running out of time, and if we hoped to survive, someone had to make the local, national, and world leaders listen and, if they didn't, do whatever was necessary to motivate them or their successors to take immediate and decisive action. My vacation was over. I'd made my decision—my commitment. My life was about to take on an entirely different purpose.

Before leaving Chicago, I decided it would be appropriate for me to visit several of the larger metropolitan areas in the United States instead of continuing my planned vacation through the western United States, Canada, and Alaska. The Palin family would have to wait for my visit! The actions I found myself considering were drastic and the consequences more than a little scary! I guess I was looking for some positive reinforcement, some sign telling me I was making the right choice and about to do the right thing.

The new route took me through Denver, San Francisco, LA, Phoenix, Dallas, Atlanta and, finally, to DC. I could write another hundred pages about my experiences in those cities. The cast of characters changed, but my conversations and observations at these destinations confirmed my earlier findings, some worse—some better. It was a time consuming yet worthwhile trip. People everywhere were mad as hell! Passivity was rapidly being replaced with a real passion for change. Tranquility could soon become chaos and anarchy. People were tired of hearing leadership singing the same old song and absolutely nothing changing. Folks were losing their jobs, their homes, their retirement benefits, and were not the least bit bashful telling me how stupid and greedy the bank managers and Wall Street gurus had been. Employer/employee loyalty was nonexistent. They were dumbfounded when our government leaders allocated a trillion dollars to keep these firms from going under, permitted the same executives to keep their jobs, and give themselves million-dollar bonuses. This was happening right under the noses of the government oversight officials who did nothing about it. These trillion-dollar programs would turn our heirs into indentured servants who'd donate twenty years of their income to pay for these expenditures.

Everywhere I traveled, things that should not have been allowed to happen were happening. Things that should have happened didn't. Ninety-five percent of those I spoke with were frustrated; they demanded change and were determined to make it happen, but they had no idea how! The Tea Party movement, militia groups, and others would soon join together with a cry for a national uprising if something didn't change! This was definitely the failure of a government bureaucracy that had grown beyond realistic limits and was out of control and out of touch with the public it was supposed to represent.

Since DC was my final destination, I thought it would be appropriate to visit my representative in the House and/or my senator. Perhaps

I could share some of my concerns with them. After spending about twenty minutes online, tracking down their phone numbers, I contacted both offices. I was informed that my representative was "out of town on business" but that "an aide would be happy to speak" with me. My senator was "in an important legislative discussion and would be tied up for a few days. An aide would be happy to speak" with me. I declined both opportunities to talk with an aide. I considered stalking one or both of them to see if what I'd been told was truthful or if this was the normal runaround unannounced visiting constituents received. Then I had an idea; I'd call back to see when they had time available and make an appointment. So I did. The receptionist informed me the congressman would be returning in three days. "Would I like to be 'penciled in' for a 10:00 a.m. or a 3:00 p.m. meeting?" If I wanted on the schedule, she needed to know what the meeting would be about. I explained I wanted to discuss some domestic issues and see what the congressman's position was. I found out that "penciled in" meant that I had a fifty-fifty chance of actually meeting with him, and if he had to cancel, "an aide would be happy to speak with me"! I declined being "penciled in." I repeated this process with the senator's office with almost the identical results. The only difference was the senator wouldn't be available until the following week (at least eight days hence). While they hadn't told me to "buzz off," I felt like that's exactly what had happened. Apparently, the folks who got to see these guys (or gals) either contributed lots of bucks to their campaign chests or had nothing better to do than hang around DC for three to eight days (like lobbyists) and take a chance they would actually get to talk with a duly elected representative. I didn't!

I decided that I'd leave DC the next morning. I wasn't getting anywhere gathering the information I thought I needed, so why waste my time?

Sitting in the RV, the local news was on the TV, and the commentator credited "inside sources" for a report he was delivering. I thought to myself, "I could sure use an inside source." That's when I remembered Roy. We had been friends in high school and for a while in college but lost touch after graduating. Several years later, while on business in DC (I was working on the development of aluminum composite materials for NASA, military applications, and "downweighting" the automobile), we crossed paths again. Roy was a staff member for a Massachusetts senator serving on an oversight committee for military spending, and we wound up attending several meetings together. After our reunion, Barbara and I became very good friends with Roy and his wife, Becky. We exchanged visits over the next five or six years, and then as family duties increased, we drifted apart.

I grabbed my cell phone and asked information for a listing. Ten minutes later, Roy and I were reminiscing about the good old days. That evening, we had dinner together. Roy and Becky had divorced. His job with the senator was very demanding, and he was traveling 50 percent of the time. The more we talked, the more convinced I was that I'd found my "inside source." Over the next six years, Roy and I would spend quite a bit of time together. Unknowingly, Roy became my confidential informant. I'll never forget a quote from Roy: "If you want to know where the bodies are buried, ask the gravedigger—not the mortician." I left DC two days later with a wealth of insider information. It was time to check on the old homestead; inform neighbors, friends, and relatives I was still alive; and to recharge my batteries. I was sure the neighbors would be happy to listen to my travel tales while drinking the Lake Erie wine I'd brought back as souvenirs from my trip. I also needed to decide if I intended to restart the flea market eBay business. I still had a garage full of junk to do something with. It wasn't until later that I realized I made the right decision to keep the business operating: it made an excellent "cover" for the business of The Lists!

I'm including the following for information and, perhaps, comparison. Years before retiring, I'd been granted entry into East Germany for a potential business opportunity. While there, I witnessed the pathetic situation fifty years of communist rule had brought to this country. The citizens led a drab existence. They shuffled through littered streets like slumped-over zombies in gray work clothes, coughing in the smoke-filled, polluted air. No one smiled. No one talked, and I heard no laughter. They looked scared. When I spoke to them, they kept their eyes focused on their feet; they would not look me in the eye. They hated their government and their leaders. They led a hopeless existence with no means to improve. Of course, when the wall fell and East and West Germany merged, this all changed. But I could not help thinking, if my world continued on today's path, we could all be facing a 1960s East Germany existence! If we didn't act soon, this could be our future. Could I help prevent this?

Here's what I asked myself. Did I believe, as some others did, that divine intervention would save us? Should we wait for Superman to appear? How about "it's part of the evolutionary process"? What do I believe in, and could I make a difference? Do I want to live and see my grandchildren and future generations survive? I needed to open my eyes and my brain to the reality of what was happening and try to convince others to help, or there may not be a tomorrow. We have very little proactive leadership. Be honest with yourself and take a look at who is representing your interests. It's a difficult situation to accept, let alone participate in correcting it. We must accept the fact there are alternatives.

It's up to us to stop what's going on and mandate the needed changes occur before we run out of time. We could just accept our fate as *que sera, sera*! Sorry—that's not in my DNA! I remembered a quote I'd read: "The only people who can change the world are those who try!"

I had the validation I'd been searching for. Now, all I had to do was figure out what an individual, no matter how highly motivated, could hope to accomplish. Hundreds of protests in front of the White House have accomplished little. I'm no Dirty Harry or Rambo, and I don't have a death wish. The job of making the needed changes would be like trying to pull the *Queen Mary* with a piece of dental floss while swimming against the tide. I needed to find something tangible to motivate leaders all over the world to recognize the need for change and to inspire them to "do it." If I were in their shoes, what would motivate me to do this?

In an instant of inspiration, I found the tool I needed: survival.

The more I thought about it, the more I was convinced the secret to successfully motivating politicians, industrial leaders, financial leaders, religious leaders—anyone in a responsible leadership role—was the fear of not surviving. Survival would furnish the motivation. For this method to work, I would need to be totally committed to enforcement. Was I? After thinking about it (again), my answer was yes but only if the leaders received the proper guidance (assignments), understood the task, and were given a chance to implement it. Unfortunately, time would show me I was naive when it came to judging the character of some of these bad actors.

Their guidance would be furnished by a detailed written explanation of the task, with any required documentation, for the individual assignment involved. In order to provide the explanations and the proper documents for each assignment, I'd need to do a lot of research and formulate an intricate plan of action. That's why The Lists were born. The Lists would be a prioritized compilation of individual assignments developed from the months of in-depth research and analysis. Individual communiqués would be issued and leave no doubt as to what the assignment was and what the consequences of failure would be. Simply put, failure would result in termination. This method will undoubtedly be much more effective than marches around the Washington Mall, protests in front of the Capitol Building, or boycotting the giant oil companies.

The Lists and motivating techniques will be reviewed next.

CHAPTER 11

EXPLAINING The Lists

If I were going to make change happen, I'd require a detailed plan to follow, something I could use as a guide. It would be somewhat flexible, and it would need to define the various categories to be addressed. So to begin the process, I compiled four separate lists dealing with what, who, when, and how. The Lists were born when these four lists were finally summarized and became my life's work.

I selected The Lists as a means for communicating the changes world leadership would need to make. Why? *Webster* provides multiple definitions for the word *list*. You can take the time to look them up if you want to, but it's easier to just review the following. Lists are nothing new. They're simple and they work. We've been exposed to them during most of our lives. For me, a list is a written reminder of things I am supposed to do or not do. Often, topics are itemized and prioritized. When things are written on a list, we generally don't forget them, or if we do, we feel guilty about it, or we're made to feel guilty by others (guilt trip).

My first exposure to a list was as a young child when I sent my wish list to Santa Claus. Then I went to Sunday school, and there were the Ten Commandments, a two-thousand-year-old list we still refer to today. Next came a to-do list of chores provided by Dad or Mom (take out the trash, feed the dog, rake the leaves, clean your room), teachers (homework assignments), and then your mate (take out the trash, feed the dog, rake the leaves, cut the grass, wash the car, clean the garage). I've always had a to-do list of the things I wanted/ needed to take care of (leaky faucet—check the oil/tires/ battery, polish the clubs, oil the hinges). Then, at work, it was Post-its, maybe a tickle file on the computer, and a job description (a list of responsibilities) provided by the boss. If you were lucky, you had a bucket list of things you wanted to do or places you wanted to visit during your life: usually after retirement.

The Lists followed the original four-part analysis: (no. 1— what) definition of correctable items, (no. 2—who) identify the individual responsible for results and (no. 3—when), the timetable for completion of each activity, and finally (no. 4—how), the method used to accomplish a task (a.k.a. assignment). Items 1 through 3 were spelled out, in detail, by The Lists. However, item 4 of an assignment was left up to the individual.

The responsible person could check off the item when com-pleted or they could feel guilty if they ignored the assignment. I didn't want anyone to have a legitimate claim they hadn't been informed of their duties or responsibilities. The Lists would also serve as a sort of report card for annual performance reviews and, when required, subsequent motivational actions. If an individual completed his/her assignment, no action was taken. For those who did not comply, did not achieve the desired result, they became a target for elimination (a.k.a. termination). It's like when Donald Trump says "You're fired!" but with more feeling! Lists are a great tool to get a job done and done properly. They don't leave much room for interpretation, and they eliminate the need to micromanage.

The Lists might turn out to be an exercise in futility. But since nothing else seemed to be working, I felt it was worth a try. Below is the master list' of international issues (no. 1—what) to be dealt with. See what you think.

MASTER LIST OF INTERNATIONAL ISSUES

Global warming
Global economy/financial regulation/inflation/poverty
Positive/negative impact of oil on society Pollution
Unemployment/job training
Immigration/civil rights
Population control
Terrorism
Health care/physical fitness
Nuclear threat/WMD/waste storage
Alternative/renewable energy
Restoration of infrastructure
Drugs/crime
Food supply
Potable water supply
Education
Individual and social security
Military service and recognition
Space exploration/threats from space
Religious/cultural differences

CHAPTER 12

MOTIVATION, AKA TERMINATION

The motivational technique I plan to use is fear, fear of not surviving, the fear of being terminated. This technique will be used for individual leader(s), staff member(s), or family member(s). If my research showed it was an impossibility to get to an individual, a more accessible yet valued person was selected. In most cases, if a family member perished, it was unintentional collateral damage caused accidentally by the motivational method used (wrong place, wrong time).

Every human being has some kind of a weakness. Some have medical problems requiring medications. Some are greedy or power hungry. Others are sex addicts. There are cigar aficionados and chocolate lovers. Of course, all humans need oxygen to breathe, water to drink, food to eat, and TP.

A general rule of thumb regarding security is the higher on the organization chart an individual is shown, the more security provided.

The strategic targets selected for termination were mostly high on the charts. They were considered the movers and the shakers. They were the decision makers; they could make things happen or not. As stated previously, the original list included four hundred candidates, comprised of national and world political leaders, oil magnates, financial gurus, entertainment and media moguls, industrial giants, security providers, quite a few "bleeding heart" advocates, legal "eagles," community activists, union leaders, professors, etc. One hundred sixty-one of those identified were deemed totally corrupted, beyond saving, and marked for elimination in early 2012. Their replacements would receive assignments during the year. Others would receive assignments during November each year.

The law-enforcement community knows if you desire to kill someone, in most instances if you have an IQ over twelve, you'll accomplish the task. If someone realizes they will be killed unless they adapt (in this case comply with The Lists), a fear of dying becomes the tool for motivation. Early on, those who received an assignment obviously felt secure; they hadn't implemented change, and nothing bad had happened to them. It's like a parent who continually threatens a misbehaving child with punishment but never actually does so. There could be no future delays for terminating the nonperformers.

It was difficult deciding what to use as a tool for termination. I didn't have a death wish or suicidal tendencies, so I needed to select a method that provided the desired result (death) without my actually being anywhere near the target area. This ruled out guns, knives, or a bow and arrow. I didn't want to deal with explosives. Electrocution or drowning seemed out of the question. So did a hit-and-run (CSI always finds the vehicle that was used). I used the Net for much of my research, and while doing so, I stumbled across the perfect method to eliminate nonperformers: poison.

I found more than sixty poisons listed that would do the job. The list (another one) contained fourteen natural lethal poisons, not including venom, and eight of these met my selection criteria: they were readily available; they were easily acquired (not traceable when purchased); a simple delivery system could be used (ingested and/or absorbed); they had a long shelf life; and once used, they were virtually undetectable, and death would probably be diagnosed as natural causes. They posed no risk to me during packaging or to others during transport (I had ruled out anything airborne). Four of those on the list could be made from readily available, natural ingredients. As it turned out, because of varying security methods in use at the target sites, I elected to use four types of poisons. Different security measures required different applications. The habits of each target were a prime consideration when selecting a delivery method. Remember the earlier statement regarding ingested or absorbed? For obvious reasons, I won't provide the details of what I used. I can tell you they did the job. While I expected some collateral damage, I didn't think the toll would be nearly as high as it was. Most accidental deaths occurred when the absorption method was used (poison was absorbed through the skin by anyone who handled an object with the poison on its surface).

Selecting a way to deliver a poison to a target wasn't difficult. Just think how many items you come into contact with or swallow every day. Items ingested such as toothpaste, breath mints, salt, pepper, aspirin, chewing gum, chocolate, cheese, wine, bottled water, coffee or tea, antacid tablets, etc., are easily acquired, untraceable, and can be readily laced with the appropriate nondetectable poison. For the entitled gourmet, there's always the expensive delivery method like champagne, cigars, chocolate, or caviar. Contact items (absorption) were aftershave (or perfume), deodorant, keys, door handles, CDs, DVDs, cell phones, miscellaneous containers, toothbrushes, hair brushes, golf clubs, shoes, belts, steering wheels, remote controls, coins, cotton swabs, and a thousand others. A splash of poison that would be absorbed through the skin was easily applied to any of these items. Fortunately, most of these applications can be applied at a remote location and well in advance. This provided me with the security I wanted. These methods were not infallible, but I was very surprised when they achieved an overall 84 percent success rate for the 161 incorrigibles. Since my objective was to achieve results without being caught or killed (I had no desire to be the next Booth or Oswald), 84 percent was very acceptable.

I spent a few months acquiring the poisons and evaluating delivery systems. The expenses to purchase gift items wasn't excessive, except the gourmet items. Most of the targets possessed a large ego, and when they received a gift with a card congratulating them for something, they wasted no time unwrapping it and sampling the contents. Delivery accomplished! Other daily-use items could easily be dropped into a bag of groceries being delivered to the target. I just needed to be certain that the thousands of big-brother cameras were pointed in another direction when I was making the arrangements. On several occasions, I used a disguise when I needed to make a personal delivery.

In order to make certain the target received the item (not an underling or a child) via mail or courier, it was important to know the target's habits and cravings for the finer things in life (champagne, caviar, cigars, cheese, coffee, tea, or chocolates) and then select only the best.

It wouldn't have been very smart to send an expensive bottle of wine to a recovering alcoholic or chocolates to a diabetic! When observation wasn't possible, the Net proved to be very valuable. Another problem was making sure deliveries couldn't be traced back to me. Without revealing details, I can tell you again that it's much easier than you might think. National and worldwide delivery services are readily available, reliable, and relatively inexpensive (with the exception of a few dictatorships and/or third world countries), especially the USPS, UPS, FedEx, or independent courier services. Developing a chain of multiple mailing locations for the packages was a problem that had to be handled well in advance and carefully, but the solution was only a matter of timing and dollars to the right people.

I set up several of these temporary organizations during eighteen months of vacation/research travels. For security reasons (my security) each system would be used no more than twice. The delivery systems were not time sensitive, and I maintained sufficient control over them, so timing could be changed or even stopped depending on circumstances. If a target met his or her obligation, as spelled out in The Lists, the planned noncompliance action was stopped. It didn't happen very often the first couple of years, but there were a few instances when late compliance was noted and I was able to stop a delivery.

During this planning and development phase, I continued to lead a normal life. I kept dental appointments, golf dates, attended birthday parties, graduations, and funerals. I didn't want anyone to suspect me of leading a double life. Postal services in many countries delivered the assignment letters. If a postal service wasn't reliable, a courier service could be used.

My garage or basement didn't offer the security or the space I needed. Even though I remembered my wife's words of wisdom when buying stuff for the eBay business ("Never buy volume—always buy unique"), space was becoming a problem without considering my second business: The Lists.

I needed a secure place away from my everyday life, large enough for eBay merchandise, where I could print the assignment letters, store termination gifts, poisons, mailing supplies, files, etc. I figured I would need a place for about five or six years. A portion of the termination packages would consist of freshly baked goods, meats, and fruits. These items required the quick response of a courier service. The majority of packages would be delivered using an existing mail system. Personally preparing the assignment letters and the packages was a necessity. Each package would contain a reward item, appropriately treated with the selected poison in a very attractive (and expensive-looking) gift box complete with a handwritten card of congratulations, inside a mailing box, inside another preaddressed mailing box containing a separate envelope with the agreed to amount of cash for the transferee as payment for remailing the package, inside a second preaddressed mailing box containing another envelope with the agreed to amount of cash, and so on. These termination mailings would consist of between three and five preaddressed containers, each with a fictitious return address: like Russian matryoshka nesting dolls. One hundred sixty-one termination packages (for the incorrigibles) were prepared and distributed starting in November 2011. This was a lot of work when added to the almost four hundred assignment letters being prepared for delivery.

My space problem was easily resolved by renting a storage shed from one of the larger chains. It provided the space I needed. My cover story was that I had an eBay business my wife had started years ago, and I'd decided it was time to expand. The shed was reasonably secure, available 16/7, with lighting and electricity. I would add shelving, a worktable, and other items later.

I rented it for a year and even got a discount for paying in advance. It took me two visits to see George, my friend at Home Depot, to get the shelving, a worktable, a fan, and a chair for my new office. Then I made a visit to the local Staples for more supplies. An economical way to get boxes and the best pricing for the first—or second-phase deliveries of the packages came by using the USPS. I managed to obtain several hundred boxes of various sizes from thirteen different USPS locations in six states. Of course the final expensive-looking gift boxes came from various department stores, or I bought them online. After the second week in my new space, I decided to buy a minifridge and keep some refreshments available. I was quickly running out of room. A two-drawer filing cabinet was purchased at a garage sale. My business records would be kept in it. Records associated with The Lists were transferred to secure flash drives that I kept well hidden. They were destroyed every three or four months.

It was about time to conduct two or three trial runs to verify my package-delivery system worked. Two sets of packages were prepared (minus the poison) and mailed through preselected drops with me as the final destination. I anxiously waited for the deliveries to arrive.

Trial package no. 1 was the domestic package. It began its journey as a twelve-inch box routed through four locations in the United States and a four-inch box reached me nineteen days later. Trial package no. 2 was the foreign-system test. It had been routed through Mexico,

Canada, France, and finally the United States. Twenty-seven days after mailing, a four-inch box was delivered to me. The system worked! It was time to get busy preparing the first batch of packages.

During the second month of preparing the termination packages, which required about one thousand different-sized boxes, bubble wrap, packing tape, a scale, etc., I decided my ten by sixteen space wasn't going to be big enough. I asked the facility manager if there was another unit available. There was. The only problem: it wasn't next to my unit. It was in the next row, about one hundred yards away. The manager promised that he would move me to two side-by-side units as soon as possible. So I rented no. 2 for a year (got the same discount). A few months later, my units were side-by-side. My plan was for storage unit no. 1 to be used for supply storage and act as my office. No. 2 would be the package prep area with shelves, a table, and a minifridge. My warehouse, production, packaging, and delivery system was ready to go in September 2011.

Even though the two trial runs were successful, I still had a nagging doubt.

What would happen when I sent the real thing? So I decided it was time to fully commit myself to The Lists. There would be no turning back after this next step! I selected two termination targets, one domestic and one foreign. I picked high-profile individuals (a corrupt member of the House and a Pakistani politician no one would miss), knowing the media would report the deaths (hopefully as natural causes) and I would have confirmation that my system worked. I sent the two packages and began preparing forty termination packages from the list of 161 identified by The Lists. The remaining 159 packages would not be mailed until I was thoroughly convinced the entire system worked. It took seventeen days for the representative's obit to hit CNN and twenty-six days to read about the "untimely demise" of the Pakistani leader.

The system worked; the trials were definitely a success! It was time for the rest of the packages to be delivered, beginning Christmas 2011. Over eight years, more than one thousand assignment letters and four hundred termination packages would be prepared and sent from this location. That's commitment!

CHAPTER 13

The Lists

(A Domestic And Foreign Summary)

Everyone should realize that in the United States, if the president, the cabinet, Congress, HEW, INS, the Federal Reserve, and other government officials and agencies— including the Supremes—had been doing their jobs instead of trying to win reelection or popularity contests, avoid conflict, add to their bank accounts or gain more power, The Lists wouldn't have included many of their names or many of the domestic assignments. The same is true for most of the foreign governments. Nothing in The Lists should have been a surprise to anyone. The problems existed for years, and it was past time for world leaders, in all areas, to deal with them. Complacency was not acceptable! You were expected to do your job or be replaced by someone who would.

Originally, I envisioned The Lists as something I'd get published: a summary of my journal entries and news reports. This would raise public awareness and, hopefully, begin motivating negligent, irresponsible leaders to do their jobs for a change. The early entries made in 2007 and 2008 grew in detail and content in 2009 and 2010 as a result of my continuing research. Conclusions were listed along with conditions I'd witnessed in much of the United States and several foreign locations. Discussions with concerned citizens in the United States and abroad became part of the entries. There was a ton of online info and media reporting to be sifted through. Many injustices were long overdue for major changes, and a slew of environmental issues needed immediate attention if we were to survive.

After completing my analysis, it became more and more obvious something well beyond just publishing facts and figures would be necessary to force those involved to act responsibly. If there was any hope to actually make change happen, a motivational technique far more punitive than public disclosure or public humiliation would be required. The idea of termination surfaced. I wasn't in a position to fire these people, but I could arrange for them to be replaced. It took awhile for me to accept this responsibility. Once I started, I knew there could be no turning back.

Using an intricate and time-consuming process, I selected candidates who'd receive an assignment. How many bad guys could there be? More than I thought! Early research identified 225 domestic and 175 foreign persons. Further analysis found 119 domestic and 42 foreign (politicians, CEOs, COBs, union bosses, industrialists, financiers, entertainers, lobbyists, etc.), all in positions of power and responsibility, had been corrupted for years and were easily defined as incorrigible. They were not sent an assignment letter. Instead, each of the 161 was sent a termination package. The packages were sent at carefully selected times. Some received a Christmas gift. Other packages arrived in the form of a gift recognizing a promotion, a successful business venture, or reelection. Still others opened their package on a birthday or an anniversary. The remaining 239 potential targets had not been identified for termination—yet. They received individual assignment letters in late 2011 and 2012. The objective of the first 161 terminations was to remove the bad actors and also to get the attention of their replacements and other leaders: maybe even motivate them to "do the right thing" without further intervention from The Lists.

By mid-2012, the first batch of termination packages had surprisingly scored an 87 percent success rate: 140 targets had been terminated. Unfortunately, 21 more died as collateral damage. In December individualized assignment letters (domestic and foreign) were sent to the 140 replacements. All assignment letters were sent directly to the selected individuals in very expensive, official-looking envelopes labeled "Personal and Confidential."

I would use this same method for communicating The Lists' assignments over the next seven years without detection. No one received a copy of The Lists. This allowed the recipients to concentrate on their assigned task and not become embroiled in the big picture. Reactions varied from incredulity ("just another nutcase") to immediate dispatch of law-enforcement agencies with orders to find and eliminate this threat to national security or international stability. Initially (and fortunately for me), the recipients felt they had been singled out as targets and neglected to compare notes with others for almost a full year.

Each letter contained a full explanation of what receiving an assignment meant and a specific task to be performed. It also explained the consequences for noncompliance would include their elimination, a.k.a. termination, and possibly others close to them. Recipients were told what was required, not how to accomplish their mission. An example of the assignment letter and an assignment were included earlier.

It's really a shame nothing, to that point, had moved these people to act responsibly. The Roman leader Publius Syrus stated, "None should govern who are not more virtuous than the governed." Perhaps The Lists and the consequences for noncompliance would accomplish this. The Lists contained reasonable, attainable, no-nonsense, common-sense objectives. Those receiving an assignment had only to make up their minds to "just do it"! To keep those in the security business from finding me, I made the copies of The Lists' assignments for 2012/2013 in eighteen different stateside locations and in nine foreign locations over a two-year period (2011/2012). They were then snail mailed from many different locations throughout the United States and overseas. It really wasn't as difficult as you might think. The law-enforcement community had almost stopped monitoring snail mail, placing most of their surveillance emphasis on electronic mail.

The selection process for assignments was fair and reasonably simple. Use of the Internet was very helpful. The rest of the procedure was a bit more complex.

What was the infraction defined by the List?

Who was the entity responsible (with authority) to make the change?

If he/she chose not to act, was there a legitimate reason for inactivity?

If compliance did not occur, when should a termination package be sent?

What should the package consist of and how should it be delivered?

Lastly, a list of the viable replacements was included.

As I stated, it was a fairly simple process. The real difficulty was keeping track of all the assignments, deciding if/when termination was justified, and how it would be accomplished. This system was used many times over the years, so keeping it simple was an imperative. I did not keep hard copy records of transactions. Every piece of information pertaining to The Lists was kept on duplicate flash drives in two very secure locations. They were reviewed and destroyed every two or three months.

Our world leaders had promised us "change is coming" or "things will get better" so many times! They continually dangled the "change carrot" in front of us, and we just kept trudging along like jackasses, trying to get a bite of the carrot. We were continually brainwashed by a media no longer bound to unbiased, truthful reporting. They were after ratings and advertising dollars.

How did we wind up in this mess? It didn't happen overnight. It took years for greedy, power-hungry leaders all over the world to "blossom" and we let it happen. Most of the people in the industrialized world have enough sense to know when we're getting a "snow job," but most were content "not to make waves." We avoided confrontation. We were the silent majority. We permitted a large number of very vocal and highly publicized minority groups, special interest groups, or ruthless individuals with hidden agendas to take control of the political and financial processes. Quite a few leaders became well-paid puppets, and we were guilty of complacency. We didn't pay attention to what we saw. We believed what the "fair and balanced" media told us. Remember the "sincerity" of Blitzer? What a name! Then there was Glenn, King, and Limbaugh when we wanted the "real scoop."

It seemed practical to tackle the items listed for the home front first ("The Lists-domestic") since these should be the easiest for monitoring compliance. After all, the good ol' US of A was considered the world's remaining superpower, at least until China figures out what's what. Please remember, these were the minimum requirements and, when initiated or in place on schedule, avoided consequences for those who were responsible for the assignment.

The contrived shortage of oil (short supply versus high prices) and the consequences brought on by this one item affected the entire world and was listed as a priority 1 for both the domestic list and the foreign list. Oil suppliers and processors were high up on The Lists' assignments. There was several more priority 1s requiring equal attention in the United States, so I assigned priority 1 items additional status designations. Oil became "1 A." Auto, truck, and bus exhaust emissions was listed as "1 B." Industrial air pollution was a "1 C" and industrial water pollution a "1 D." This included coal-fired and oil-fired electrical producing facilities throughout the world. Most world leaders recognized increasing shortages of food were a high priority today, but how many leaders do you think realized that tomorrow's shortages would be oxygen to breath and/or water to drink? I believe they were aware of this, but none of them had the balls to take responsibility for changing the situation. Unless immediate corrective action was initiated over the next ten to fifteen years, it would have resulted in chaos, anarchy, and possibly extinction. Recognizing this made the death of a few irresponsible leaders bearable.

Was it too late to get governments working on The Lists? In the United States, the government needed to put people to work, not on welfare! The increase in homeless citizens was frightening; dangerous subcultures were forming. We needed to find an alternative supply of potable water for a couple of our major cities. At the same time, we had to work on reducing harmful emissions or water pollutants from industrial complexes being dumped into rivers or streams and reducing or eliminating our dependency (and major indebtedness) to foreign oil suppliers (most openly hostile to the United States).

Naturally, we should try to get the biggest bang for our buck by utilizing BAT (best available technology) and also multiple-construction activities (i.e., assembly-line philosophy but on a grander scale). Thousands of jobs would be created instantly. Since Congress mortgaged our futures to provide $900 billion to bail out the smartest bankers and dumbest businessmen in history (while allowing them to take exorbitant bonuses) and then pass more than a $3.8 trillion operating budget, I was certain these same bureaucrats would find the necessary funds to pay for these jobs The Lists projects would create. (Bonds, anyone?) Hell, why not just use the billions they still hadn't handed out from the bailout funds and then the billions in repayments due to come from the banking institutions? Pretty easy to figure that one out, huh? Of course, ordinary folks would get really upset if the money didn't get repaid! Or would you rather future generations face a welfare state (no jobs) and, in all probability, continuous wars being fought over everything from a lack of energy, starvation, or a scarcity of sanitary water. These wars would be unlike anything from the past. There would be global wars with the "haves" versus the "have nots," and survival of the human race would be at stake. Pleasant thought, isn't it? Maybe not, but it was REALITY!

The first thing needed for successful implementation of The Lists-domestic was for the US government leaders to act responsibly as a bipartisan group and pass the needed legislation. Also, the Foreign Policy Advisory Group (the real power behind the throne), state or local governments, along with bleeding heart organizations like the ACLU, NAACP, NRA, AARP, AMA, the RNC and the DNC, union leaders, and a host of others—you know who you are—need to assist in implementing change and not sandbag as in the past. I hope recipients of an assignment from The Lists read it thoroughly before jumping to conclusions as to why they didn't want to do this or why it was a bad plan. I wanted them to understand the assignment as outlined. I didn't really care if they agreed with it or not. If they started out with a negative attitude, they needed to know there would be drastic consequences. Fewer of them would be around to resist in a very short time. This wasn't a threat. It was a commitment.

Based on exposure to what was happening to our civilization and life's realities I'd witnessed firsthand, I adopted a new set of core beliefs and values that transformed me into an instant activist. This is what drove me to develop The Lists and accept the fact there would, by necessity, be casualties. I came to believe in this cause with every bone in my body!

You will find a complete copy of The Lists, both domestic and foreign, next. This is for your review, and hopefully, you'll understand what actually occurred because of The Lists. Please note that abortion, stem cell research, "don't ask, don't tell," or gay marriage didn't even make the cut. That doesn't mean there won't be another List, including these topics and others, at a later date.

CHAPTER 14

The Lists: A DOMESTIC SUMMARY

(Domestic assignments were based on these assumptions)

This is not an attempt to cure all the social inequities or economic ills the United States has developed beginning in 2008. At the outset, only issues requiring immediate corrective action negatively affected our lives, and our planet was included. Every item on The Lists was designed to improve the quality of life. This was a common sense reality approach, not BS. Those assigned were advised to carry out their task and avoid consequences. As stated earlier, a selected individual was responsible for a specific activity. It will be interesting to see how an almost socially unconscious public reacts to The Lists if ever published!

1. The seven largest oil companies in the United States, beginning January 1, 2013, and on this same date for the next seven years,

will contribute 15 percent of profits to an escrow fund, which will be used for development of wind turbine farms, solar-generation complexes, hydroelectric generators on existing flood-control dams, electric-powered vehicles and pollution cleanup. The funds will be managed by a group of five college graduates, all must be US citizens. An electrical, civil, mechanical, and computer engineer, accompanied by a senior-level accountant, will immediately be appointed by the president. They will receive $250,000 annually. Each will have the authority to hire ten qualified assistants at a salary of $75,000 annually. No elected representative, past or present, is to ever serve on this board! If oil company executives attempt to manipulate pricing of their products, reaction will be swift. Gasoline, diesel, and fuel oil prices are NOT to exceed $3.50 a gallon throughout the seven-year period. Oil company executive salaries and bonuses will be "capped" at $250,000 annually.

2. Congress will require the building of four fifteen-million-gallons-per-day saltwater desalinization facilities with distribution network(s). These will be completed and operational in the State of California no later than January 1, 2014 (funded by the federal government). Two of these plants will supply potable water to the Los Angeles area, and two will supply the San Francisco area. BAT and assembly-line methods will be used. Do not attempt to take shortcuts.

3. Additionally, two fifteen-million-gallons-per-day saltwater desalinization facilities, with distribution network(s), are to be completed and operational not later than January 1, 2015 in the NYC area (funded by the federal government). BAT to be used (no shortcuts).

4. Six hydroelectric generating facilities are to be installed adjacent to six of the US Army Corps of Engineers flood-control dams already existing on the Ohio River and near major metropolitan areas (i.e.: Pittsburgh, Cincinnati, Huntington, Marietta, etc.). Each power plant is to be capable of furnishing a minimum of 20 percent of the residential requirements of the adjacent residential area not later than January 1, 2016.

5. Three windmill-powered generating farms will be erected in lightly populated areas of Arizona, New Mexico, and Texas. They will include a distribution network capable of furnishing 20 percent of the residential power requirements for at least three major metropolitan areas. Completion will be by January 1, 2016.

6. Two large municipal solar-powered generating facilities are to be built in either Arizona, Nevada, New Mexico, Arkansas, or other states where solar power has been deemed feasible as an energy source. These systems, with distribution networks, are to be completed before January 1, 2018 and will have the capability to furnish 20 percent of the power requirements for two municipalities (i.e., Las Vegas or Albuquerque, New Mexico).

7. Three large generating plants are to be built, utilizing thermal high-stack technology along with an adequate distribution network. This project is to be completed by January 1, 2017. Stacks will be a minimum of 1,800 feet tall and 200 feet in diameter with multiple wind-driven turbines around the base of the stack and capable of supplying at least 10 percent of the power requirements for three large Midwest cities.

Please, don't screw up and locate these units in glide paths or near airports! Note: As the above energy suppliers come online, we will begin a reduction of nuclear-powered generators to eliminate the "waste storage" problem. Coal-fired generators will be taken off line to reduce the pollution problem. Employees in both of these industries will be trained to work for the new energy providers.

8. Congress is to immediately pass legislation stating hybrid— or battery-powered vehicles will be the only powered vehicles permitted inside any city limits after January 1, 2015. A hybrid, by definition, will be a vehicle capable of running on battery power, hydrogen, or natural gas with a gasoline-powered backup motor with a minimum 50-mpg capability. This includes a proven 70 percent reduction in emissions based on 2010 standards. Gasoline or natural gas units will be required to pass an annual emissions test at a registered/licensed state-testing station with no fee. All delivery vehicles required to enter city limits will be powered by battery, diesel, or natural gas. Diesel—or natural-gas-powered delivery vehicles will be required to pass a state–administered annual emissions test at a cost of $10 per unit. "Over the road" vehicles used outside city limits (gasoline, diesel, or natural gas powered) will be required annually to pass a federally mandated/administered emissions test at a registered/ licensed and properly equipped station (designated highway truck weigh stations?) for a fee of $10. Failure to acquire the proper emission-test decal will result in a $1,000 fine for the first violation and confiscation of the vehicle the second time. Confiscated vehicles by either state or federal government agencies will be modified, as necessary, to meet the emissions/mileage requirements and then sold at auction. If the cost for the modifications are deemed to be prohibitive, the

vehicle will be scrapped/recycled. This procedure will provide additional funding for the program.

Note: I have deliberately left the issue of "localized" mass transit off The Lists. This item is an important one that individual municipalities need to address in a timely manner. Compare notes with each other to avoid duplicating efforts.

9. A uniform packaging program will be developed by the appropriate governmental agency to drastically improve recycling. This is to be in place by January 1, 2014.

10. Spending for space travel/exploration will be placed on hold for a period of fifteen years from 2013 to 2028. Maintaining the existing space station and the Hubble Scope is to continue. All other resources, including funds, will be diverted to the following: improving transportation of people and goods throughout the nation. The rail system will be drastically improved in order to reduce the number of large trucks necessary for long-distance hauling (reduction of damaging emissions, highway damage, and fuel consumption).

   a. A large portion of these diverted funds will be used to restore the integrity of our highway system, especially bridges.
   a. Additionally, 25 percent of the diverted funds will be used to develop tracking of and developing the ability to destroy meteors or asteroids that threaten our planet. This is much more important than practical missions or a manned flight to Mars.

11. Immigration issues will be addressed as follows: effective January 1, 2012, anyone found to be illegally inside the borders of the United States will be deported immediately. They will not be eligible for health care, welfare of any kind, education, or Social Security benefits. All children born in the United States from illegal-alien parents will be considered illegal aliens. Any individual, family or corporation found employing illegal aliens will be fined $1000/day per illegal employee. Aliens wishing to become citizens of the United States must meet the requirements for citizenship, which will include demonstrating proficiency of reading, writing, speaking, and comprehending the English language at a sixth-grade level. The US Department of Immigration will double the size of its workforce by January 1, 2011 and reduce the processing time for legal-immigration entry to ninety days or less.

12. Health care will be addressed as follows:

    Effective January 1, 2015, a national health care system will be in place for all citizens of the United States. This includes senators and congressmen/ women who will no longer have a separate system of their own. It's unimaginable that our elected representatives have procrastinated so long on an issue so important to the citizens of this country. The influence of the "band of doctors," better known as the AMA, and lobbyists for pharmaceutical companies on our government leaders can't be underestimated. I would have thought that organizations like AARP would have had more influence in rectifying this problem. This is no insurmountable task as Congress and the pharmaceutical sponsored media have led us to believe (watch the nightly-news sponsors to verify what I've stated). All they needed to do was to tell the AMA leadership to shut up, the drug company gurus to close their political contribution checkbooks, and then look at the Canadian system. Yes, the Canadian system has some problems, but it is 100 percent better than what we have today, and we can quickly duplicate it. Who cares if it's "socialized medicine"! At least it works! Improvements can be made over time. But let's get started, NOW! As stated previously, illegal aliens will not be able to use this system, but all government employees and all members of Congress must use it! (The "good for the goose, good for the gander" philosophy will apply). Drastic improvements in health care and disability benefits for our military personnel will be included in the national health care program. Adequate provisions for "eldercare," for those over eighty-five, will begin no later than January 1, 2015.

13. Forty-seven percent of Americans pay no federal income tax! A 20 percent flat tax with absolutely no loopholes will be instituted no later than 2015. There will be zero tolerance if this does not happen! This will be the responsibility of the president, the treasury secretary, the Senate majority leader, and the Speaker of the House. NO MORE EXCUSES!

14. Term limits are to be addressed. This is another lingering sore spot that has been ignored for too long! Congress will pass legislation no later than January 1, 2013, stating the following:

    a. A president and vice president will be eligible for two terms of four years each.
    b. A vice president will be eligible to serve two terms as president (no change).
    c. Senators will be eligible for a maximum of four terms of six years each. Representatives will be eligible for four terms of four years each. Members of Congress will not receive a full pension unless they serve three terms. The above limits will

also apply to state governments. There will be no "grandfather" provisions allowed. Anyone who will exceed these provisions as of January 1, 2014 will be replaced within six months either by legal appointment or an election.

    d. Future members of the US Supreme Court will be appointed for a period not to exceed twenty years. Those now seated on the Supreme Court will be permitted to remain there until they are eighty-five years of age. No one will be permitted to stay in any of these positions after their eighty-fifth birthday.

    e. Retirement benefits for those who served in these government positions will duplicate benefits given to members of our military at the rank of colonel.

15. As for education, there are several issues the general population demands be addressed. Proficiency tests for all teachers at all levels, including college professors, are to be developed and administered to everyone working in these professions not later than January 1, 2014. Those who fail the initial test will continue working but must retake the test and pass it within one year. A second failure will result in immediate dismissal. If dismissed, they may reapply for a testing after one year. Three test failings will negate any future testing be done. Tenure or union membership will not interfere with this program. On January 1, 2014, English will become the official language of the United States. A second-language mandate will be issued for all elementary, middle, and high schools, stating that a second language must be taken beginning in first grade and finishing in twelfth grade.

Students will be given a choice of taking either Spanish or Chinese. As time passes, HEW may determine that another language may be substituted or added to this mandate list. As of January 1, 2014, there will no longer be a policy of "pass them to the next grade level if they have failed to meet the requirements." If a student fails, they are to continue at the same level until they can do the required work. If a student continually fails, at age twelve they are to begin attending newly instituted remedial-educational facilities (boot camps?) in their geographical area. I see no need to build more large (and usually expensive) schools. Most locations have boarded-up shopping plazas with plenty of parking area. These buildings could very easily be refitted as schools. These institutes will provide useful vocational training for the below-average academic students. They will employ unemployed, trained, "journeymen/women" for hands-on teaching for trade and craft positions. These new teachers will be compensated at the same union scale/rate of pay they would receive if working at their respective trade or craft position.

16. The tobacco industry is one very close to or perhaps in front of oil for winning a trophy for "the worst of the worst." Yet because of lobbyist activity, advertising, and political contributions, their products continue to be sold and are now responsible for 1,200 deaths every day! That's right—1,200 people die every day because they are addicted to tobacco products. In three days, more people die from tobacco-related diseases than people who were murdered on 9/11. This must stop, and it's the responsibility of our government, the people we voted for, to put a stop to the manufacture and sale of all tobacco products in the United States. The projects outlined by The Lists provide jobs for the folks who will no longer work in this industry. They should be ashamed for their part in contributing to this horrendous situation. The Feds

will establish a national chain of "stop smoking" clinics for the treatment of addicts. This is to happen no later than 1/1/14.

17. Of special note: the above items are of extreme national and international importance, but there are others that must be corrected. These are included in The Lists but are a separate category. Leaders in politics, oil, industry, communications, financial institutions, auto manufacturing, government regulators, law enforcement, and others are to be dealt with. The individuals targeted were selected based on their record of greed, environmental misdeeds, and corruption. There were 119 of them selected in the United States. They are considered "the worst of the worst" for what they have done or have allowed to be done. My records show it is past the time for rehabilitation of these 119, so they will be targeted for elimination in 2012. Their successors will receive specific assignments from The Lists, and hopefully, they will "get the message." I did not wish to create chaos, but that's exactly what would have occurred if a $0.99 hamburger suddenly started selling for $5.00, a sixteen-ounce bottle of spring water for $5.00, and a gallon of gas for $10.00 (when available). That's where we were headed. It had to stop!

I have one more request. I recently found an article regarding the health of young men, eighteen to twenty-four years of age, in the United States. It's estimated that 70 to 75 percent of them are physically unfit for military duty because they are too fat! The absence of mandatory physical education programs in our schools and the elimination of the military draft (I won't go into parental neglect or TV or any of the hundreds of electronic devices and games that daily drain the physical well-being of our youth) have definitely contributed to this sorry state of affairs. Taking this into consideration and coupling it with the need for continued military intervention by the United States throughout the world, Congress needs to revisit mandatory physical education classes in our schools and reintroduce the draft for eighteen-year-olds (male and female). I would like to see this as an agenda item during the 2014 congressional session.

I sincerely hope the recipients of each of the assignments from The Lists (domestic) take it very, very seriously and understand the consequences of noncompliance. No one is exempt from an assignment: not even the members of the infamous Skull and Bones fraternity. Compliance not only ensures the responsible entity survives, it also ensures our planet and the human race continue to exist and that our lives and the lives of our descendants continue to improve over time.

The following is a listing of the specific domestic targets for 2012. These were considered the incorrigibles and were listed for termination as quickly as practical.

1. Three US senators
2. Nine members of the US House of Representatives
3. Four congressional staffers
4. Fourteen federal government regulators
5. Eight lobbyists
6. Fourteen Big Oil company executives
7. Two ACLU attorneys
8. One federal judge
9. One superior court judge
10. Five entertainment icons
11. Five communications executives

12. Six law-enforcement managers
13. Two national union leaders
14. Sixteen industry executives (four in the tobacco industry)
15. Three auto-company executives
16. Sixteen Wall Street executives including five hedge fund managers
17. Two NASA executives
18. Two pharmaceutical executives
19. One governor
20. One lieutenant governor
21. One mayor
22. Two GSA administrators
23. One pentagon official (nonmilitary)

Total = 119 domestic terminations.

Assignment letters will be issued annually during the fourth quarter.

Termination packages will be issued annually during the first quarter.

CHAPTER 15

The Lists: A FOREIGN SUMMARY

(Foreign Assignments Were Based On These Assumptions)

As with The Lists for domestic issues, The Lists for foreign issues is not all encompassing nor was anything on The Lists required to be accomplished on an unrealistic timetable. The Lists (foreign) were a compilation of actions, long overdue and demanded by civilians from across several continents. It was developed in 2008, 2009, and 2010, refined and finalized in 2011. Forty-two targets were identified as totally corrupt and were earmarked for immediate elimination. "Termination packages" were sent to each of them in late 2011. By April 2012, 80 percent of these targets had been eliminated. Thirty-four replacements received assignments shortly thereafter.

In November 2011, those not listed for immediate termination received their assignments. Afghanistan and Iraq were not included in The Lists. However, leaders in countries providing resources or safe havens to terrorists involved in the United States were included. Leaders of Iran, Syria, Pakistan, Yemen, China, North Korea, Russia, Africa, Algeria, and Lebanon are in this listing. A few others were included, but they were of less importance. The items to be dealt with were complex, but corrections were necessary for humanity to continue to exist on our planet. While several of the selected leaders had security so tight that it was impossible to get to them, copies of assignments from The Lists were sent through staff members or intermediaries who, after a review of the contents, more than likely shared it with the responsible entity. If not then, I'm sure they did so as soon as deaths began to occur in their countries in early 2012.

As a precaution, the succession lists were researched to four "deep." Individual copies of foreign assignments were made in six countries, including the United States, Canada, and Mexico. They were printed in English and mailed from twelve locations. The primary thrust of corrective actions dealt with those guilty of supporting or funding terrorist activities against the United States and our allies. The second area of emphasis was the development or sale of nuclear reactors/waste disposal/weapons. The third area was illicit trade of drugs and/or conventional weapons. The fourth was the lack of pollution controls within each location.

Human rights abuses and lax immigration enforcement were included in several parallel areas. In many of these countries, it became necessary to remind leadership that human beings cannot be trusted to have unchecked power over other humans. When they do, despotism, totalitarianism, and even slavery can result: "Man's inhumanity to man!" or "Who will guard the guards?" The countries and individuals were carefully chosen. They had the authority to make the necessary changes. They possessed the technical, military, and economic resources to succeed within the time frame allocated. Their actions were to be self-funded: the United States would not supply monetary aid to them. We would share technical information if requested.

1. The US government was required to eliminate foreign subsidies and foreign aid to all nations—except the UK, Canada, and Australia—not later than January 1, 2013. Favorable trade allowances to any nation were to be eliminated not later than January 1, 2014.

2. The United States was directed to reconsider continuing membership in the United Nations. If this group continues to procrastinate on issues and backstab the United States, we are to renounce our membership and financial support for this organization not later than January 1, 2012.

3. NATO had been rendered nearly impotent. This must change. NATO is to be developed into a military-response force, consisting of troops from all participating countries and to be used for timely and aggressive action against those who threaten member nations. NATO is to be a fully functioning entity not later than January 1, 2012. Arguing over who leads the NATO forces will not be tolerated. OPEC and the Saudis will fund this improvement. Everyone knows they have more than enough money!

4. Canada, our neighbor to the north, has always been an ally and has been usually supportive of democratic institutions and individual freedoms. They share the largest border with the United States,

and it is a border that's full of holes. They are to strengthen their border security and initiate actions to reduce border crossings of illegal aliens, drugs, and other illicit goods—including air and ship traffic—by at least 50 percent no later than January 1, 2013. If this slows border crossings to a snail's pace, learn to cope with it! Canada will enter into serious discussions with the United States in an attempt to merge into a common currency, similar to what the EU accomplished with the euro. These discussions are to begin no later than January 1, 2013. This is only a demand to explore the possibilities, to weigh the benefits for both countries—not to actually initiate a common currency unless advantageous and agreed to by all.

5. Mexico is our southern neighbor and presents multiple, major problems that are beginning to have more and more of a negative effect on the United States. Illegal aliens, drugs, arms smuggling, terrorist activities, crime sprees, murder, and mayhem are out of control, and it appears that the authorities are not capable of dealing with it. Mexican authorities must demonstrate their ability and willingness to put a stop to these activities at home and on our border not later than January 1, 2013. They will dramatically crack down on illegal immigration. They will use whatever force is required to eliminate drug dealers and roving gangs. If they can't achieve this result with the full use and support of their law-enforcement agencies and their military force by this date, the United States will offer the assistance of our law enforcement and military personnel. Mexico will have the option to refuse our assistance until January 1, 2014. If they are still unsuccessful, the United States will have no choice except to intercede on our own behalf and do whatever it takes to correct this breach of our

security. We may request assistance from Canadian officials. At this same time, the responsible Mexican authorities will become targets of The Lists. Incompetence or unwillingness are equally reasons for elimination.

Mexico will participate with the United States and Canada in discussions regarding a common currency for all of North America (remember the Euro!) before January 1, 2013. They will have the same ability to refuse to adopt the dollar, but they can't refuse to discuss the possibilities.

6. Iranian leadership, or the distinct lack of mentally competent leadership, should be a major concern for everyone on the planet. It's a wonder that the lunatic they currently have for a leader is still alive. If I ever needed to have a personal security detail, I'd want his bunch with me. What I can't understand is how the leaders of the rest of the other neighboring nations, including Israel, have stood by and watched this travesty unfold. Something must be done to eliminate this constant nuclear threat, the possibility of dirty bombs by selling nuclear waste, support of terrorist groups, and only God knows what else. The Lists' targets for remedial action for Iranian transgressions are not only Iranians; they are the leaders of other countries who have ignored this situation, and now, it is out of control. This task is assigned to the following countries for corrective action no later than January 1, 2014. This should provide you with sufficient time to accomplish this mission. Israel will lead the effort and will be assisted by Spain, England, Germany, and Saudi Arabia. (France and India were intentionally left off this list.) Participation is not an option. It is a dictate. Of all the assignments that have been given, this one is

very much needed and very easily measured to see if accomplished. The established deadline will be the kickoff point for targeting those who have failed to eliminate the Iranian threat. The United States is not assigned to this group. They already have their hands full with Iraq, North Korea, and Afghanistan. Once the current Iranian leadership has been eliminated, these same countries will be tasked to install a government/leadership with demonstrated capabilities to become a contributing member to the rest of the civilized world. I have not specified how Iran is to be liberated. As George Patton said, "Never tell people how to do things. Tell them what needs done and you'll be surprised with their ingenuity." Surprise the world!

7. Next, we must deal with Syria. While not as disruptive as Iran, Syria poses a threat for several reasons. They support the moron now leading Iran, and they have been known to conspire with Libya, Yemen, and even Pakistani activists. They continue to provide support to a variety of terrorist organizations. Syria, Libya, and Yemen have been given until January 1, 2013 to renounce support of or any affiliation with Iran and/or other terrorist organizations. The leadership in these countries does not possess the degree of security sophistication found in Iran. Therefore, leadership targets will be dealt with, utilizing methods provided by The Lists, and countries in the area can concentrate their efforts on other problems needing correction in Palestine and Pakistan. The clock is ticking!

8. Indian leaders have been given the task of cleaning up the leadership "mess" (no pun intended) in their own country. Their lack of population controls, human rights abuses, and sanitary and

environmental issues are self-evident and must be dramatically improved and quickly! There is no excuse for these conditions to continue to exist. It's a very good idea to start now.

9. France is a major problem simply because they have allowed themselves to become a passive society, more so than the United States. They have found it easier to look the other way when international terrorism occurs and not get involved. The mentality seems to be that other nations have bailed them out of trouble so often, they've grown to expect it. Their lack of timely support for NATO in stopping atrocities in Europe and not allowing coverage to expand in Africa, is appalling. Their insincere voting record and lack of financial support at the UN needs to be internally questioned and remedial action taken. Their performance on the world stage leaves much to be desired: they know it and the world knows it! It would be best for them to change, quickly!

10. Germany had its faults over the last century but seems to have rebounded once more. In recent years, their record against terrorism and support for international human rights has been very good. They need to adopt a much stronger stance in support of NATO and improve the actions of the UN. Germany will assist Israel with the problem of Iran.

11. The United Kingdom, much like Canada, has been an ally of the United States for years. They have very few issues needing to be dealt with. As far as The Lists are concerned, the UK needs to be supportive of the actions that must be taken to remedy the situation in Iran, Syria, Lebanon, and Pakistan. The UK is

expected to assist Israel, who has been given the task to correct the leadership situation in Israel.

12. Israel is to take the lead role in correcting the ills of Iran. They will be assisted by the UK, Spain, Saudi Arabia, and Germany. Israel will work diligently with the Palestinian leaders to once and for all establish a workable border between the two countries not later than January 1, 2014. Failure of the leaders to do so will result in additional "terminations" for both sides until resolution is achieved.

13. North Korea, like Iran, presents a very real nuclear threat. They're also one of the nations with terrible human rights abuses. Ever since they "beat the United States" during the Korean War in the '50s, they have tried to "buddy up" to China and Russia, either publicly or behind the scenes, with an unknown degree of success. What we do know is they have an irrational dictatorship bent on nuclear-arms acquisition, not for the betterment of society, but to the detriment of South Korea and Japan at the minimum. This is a world problem not just one for the United States to solve/change. I plan to do my part by eliminating a few of the very bad actors on the North Korean stage, but it will take a concentrated effort by all responsible nations, including the United States, Japan, China, and Russia, to permanently stop North Korea's nuclear ambitions and civil rights abuses.

14. China is a work in progress. No one knows how it will turn out! In the last ten years, China has entered the world of manufacturing, sales and marketing, and influence peddling: they're becoming a nuclear power and, in the next five years, will become a super

power. Human rights abuses still abound, but they are improving as they move more and more toward their version of capitalism. What do we do now about China? My self-educated opinion is wait and see, at least until 2015 or until they do something that we can't ignore. I have no plans to try and motivate anyone in China, but I have sent several leaders a cautionary note regarding terrorism, arms dealing, and any support for North Korea. Since the United States intervened in Panama, "set them free," and gave them the canal, China has been quietly acquiring property and businesses there. Is it too soon to wonder if China intends to establish a satellite community in Panama and why? Then the United States would have two Communist neighbors. Let's not forget Kennedy's screwup at the Bay of Pigs in the '60s and that we've had a "burglar at our back door" ever since. We all need to watch China closely.

15. The sixteen member nations of the EU are to take the necessary steps to strengthen their alliance, stabilize the value of the euro, and improve relations and involvement with the IMF. This must be done continuously to avert an international economic crisis.

16. I've saved "the best for last." Actually, Russia is second place to Iran. Russia remains an enigma as well as a pain in the ass for the entire world. Their leaders sit back and try to be as disruptive as possible whether in the business of the UN, support for NATO, or stopping international terrorism. They continue to distribute weapons to third world dictators and look the other way while atrocities are taking place, atrocities they could easily prevent. I don't know if anyone at any level actually knows what the Russian involvement is in nuclear arms distribution, but we all know that

they are involved. The directive to Russian leaders is to STOP and do it quickly. Quit being the "bully in the school yard," or we'll try it with an entirely new leadership crew. If needed, we'll repeat the process as often as necessary until you get it right, and we are not going to wait very long.

Being a realist, I didn't believe the domestic or foreign leaders would just accept these assignments as "the right thing to do" and become advocates of The Lists. That's why it was necessary to develop a method to motivate them. As you know from my earlier statements, the greatest motivator I could find beyond power and greed was fear. Remember, "Politics do have boundaries. Death is not so restricted."

Here is a listing of the specified foreign targets marked for immediate termination in 2012:

1. Four from Saudi Arabia/OPEC
2. Five from Iran
3. Four from Africa
4. Two representatives of the EU
5. Two from Syria
6. Two from France
7. Two from Libya
8. Two from Pakistan
9. One from North Korea
10. Three from Indonesia
11. Two from Russia
12. Two from Lebanon
13. One from Argentine
14. Two from Brazil

15. Three from Venezuela
16. One from Chile
17. One from Panama
18. Three from Mexico

Total = Forty-two foreign targets

Assignment letters will be distributed annually in the fourth quarter.

Termination packages for nonperformers will be issued annually, during the first quarter. One hundred one individuals remain on The Lists for assignments in the coming years.

CHAPTER 16

(LOGISTICS—MOBILIZATION)

LABOR—United States

It's well known there is a distinct lack of qualified engineering, construction personnel in management, administrative, and trade/craft positions. Every construction site will incorporate a learning center for the training of the necessary workers. At the beginning and for several years thereafter, experienced personnel will be utilized as teachers/ instructors and will be compensated at a pay rate 20 percent higher than their normal pay grade. Qualified retirees will be used as instructors. The "students" will have three pay grades: beginner (minimum wage— United States), intermediate (50 percent above minimum wage— United States), and fully qualified (the proper union-scale pay grade for the position). Increases in pay will be awarded as the result of demonstrated competence, not time in grade. The "graduate students" at the top of their classes will be given the opportunity to become teachers/ instructors with the appropriate compensation. In the United States, HEW will ensure that this happens! Everyone will work a forty-four-hour week throughout the ten-year construction period from 2012 to 2022. Unions will continue to function, but interference/strikes will not be tolerated. The Lists' research includes intimate details regarding union leadership.

Materials—United States

The lack of available materials for each job site will be an issue, especially at the beginning of construction. A lack of experienced purchasing, distribution, and warehouse personnel will exist. Fast-track training is to be included for these positions at a learning center at each major job site. Qualified retirees will undoubtedly be necessary. A central location for purchasing is to be developed somewhere in central United States (Chicago?) and will provide assistance in all areas of material acquisition. Part of the duties of those at the central location will be to identify areas within the United States capable of quickly restarting or retooling existing or mothballed manufacturing facilities to meet the necessary material needs for this huge undertaking. Through 2015, it will be acceptable to purchase 50 to 60 percent of the required construction materials from foreign suppliers. From 2016 through 2019, a maximum of 40 percent of these materials will come from foreign suppliers. By 2020, only 10 percent of the construction materials used in the United States will come from foreign sources.

Materials—Foreign

There will be a lack of materials for some projects in foreign countries, but the degree of construction required overseas is substantially less than in the United States and deals mostly with environmental projects. Each country will meet their own construction needs and will ship excess materials to the United States. There will be zero tolerance for "black market" activity.

Labor—Foreign

The major labor requirement overseas will be for law enforcement and military personnel to identify and eliminate terrorists and supporters of terrorism. While they will need to add to their current compliment of personnel, they are well positioned to provide this service. Better use of NATO will be of immense benefit in this endeavor.

Construction Management

All major construction and manufacturing firms in the United States will participate in the completion of these domestic projects, and they are expected to provide the necessary qualified personnel for management. Project-management personnel will be compensated at their normal rate of pay plus a 20 percent allowance if relocation is required. A 10 percent adder will be given to participating firms for each management person provided for the duration of each project. The executives from any firm suspected of price fixing or gouging will be severely dealt with.

NOTE:

In the United States, it will be beneficial to improving the rail delivery system by using rail to ship materials from the manufacturer to a drop point close to each construction site for truck distribution/delivery.

CHAPTER 17

LOOKING BACK: 2012 DOMESTIC ISSUES

January 2013

It's time to review what happened during 2012, but to do so, I need to review some events that occurred in 2010 and 2011 and their impact on 2012. My expectations for any changes attributable to The Lists were reasonably low. After all, assignments weren't delivered until late in 2011. Late notification could have been used as a legitimate reason for delayed response. I'd bet 99 percent of the recipients were more than a little skeptical, initially, and thought the assignment letter they received was part of an elaborate joke. That feeling didn't last long when terminations of the first batch of corrupt individuals were made public beginning in early 2012. A few positive changes were noted. Could this be coincidence, or did The Lists and the "motivation" method used for nonperformers cause the change? Maybe the unplanned collateral damage had something to do with it? We'll never know for certain, but even the smallest positive changes were beneficial to all of us. I had no doubt the security folks had begun hunting for me.

My flashback shows several major happenings starting as far back as 2007/2008. We had a Republican president, but the Democrats controlled the Congress, and for the first time in history, we had a female Speaker of the House. With a Republican president, Bush Jr., in office through 2008, not much was accomplished in Washington. Then, in November 2008, another first occurred: we elected a Democratic black president. Well, not really. His father was black and from someplace in Africa. His mother was white and from the United States. I think he was raised by white grandparents in Hawaii. He qualified as a US citizen. Where he was actually born or why the media refused to use the word *mulatto* and zeroed in on his black heritage instead were unanswered questions.

In 2009/2010, the Democrats were finally in complete charge and promised us great things would be accomplished. What got done was our government passed some of the worst legislation ever. They bailed out Wall Street, the banks, and the auto manufacturers (again) by mortgaging our future for the next fifty years. They passed an abomination of a national health care plan. They did almost nothing about unemployment, illegal immigration, or foreign-energy dependence and sent billions of dollars to foreign governments. The list goes on and on about what wasn't accomplished. Citizens began to show their growing discontent with dramatic increases in bankruptcies, foreclosures, unemployment, border violence, suicides, drugs, and crime. Politicians, bankers, and industrialists were not being taken to task for their mismanagement and ineptitude. During 2010, the media was obsessed with reporting the off-course antics of a world-famous professional golfer. The Democrats kept blaming the previous administration for our problems even though they had actually been "in charge" for four years! Since 2006, thirty-five thousand people had died in Mexico as a result of the drug wars, yet there had been no large-scale response! The election results in November 2010, proved to be very interesting.

The year 2011 began with President Obama and the Democrats (assisted by the media) blaming the Republican-controlled House for the lack of progress and "blasphemous rhetoric." Then, on January 8, a beautiful Saturday morning in Tucson, Arizona, a deranged twenty-two-year-old pulled out a 9 mm at a community gathering at a small strip mall and proceeded to murder six people and wound fourteen more before a couple of witnesses managed to disarm him. Those killed included a nine-year-old girl and a federal judge. It was alleged that his primary target was a sitting congresswoman named Giffords who had scheduled an event for her constituents to meet her and discuss their concerns. He shot her through the head at point-blank range. Miraculously, she didn't die, but her life was altered forever as were the lives of almost everyone else in the United States. It became a media circus and a platform for the Democrats who immediately set out to blame someone else for what took place. They accused Sarah Palin and the Tea Party of being guilty. After all, the TP had put a bull's-eye over congressional districts where work was needed to convert voters before the 2012 elections.

Gifford's district was one of many with a bull's-eye. Then Congress and the media shifted focus to the venomous words and accusations constantly exchanged on the floor of the House and the Senate. Then law-enforcement agencies were guilty of not enforcing the laws. Then gun control advocates got onboard with the need for stricter laws for gun ownership. Next, it became an "issue of grave importance" that congressmen/women receive more protection.

As is normal in high-profile cases like this one, the best defense money can buy was provided. (The taxpayer was footing the bill.) Of course, the ACLU was involved.

"Fairness, everyone!"

At first it seemed as though no one was interested in the actual facts of how this individual was able to do this or why he was motivated to do it. His defense claimed he was a twenty-two-year-old mentally disturbed young man. Allegations of insanity would come later. He disliked the congresswoman because she was unable to answer a moronic question he had asked her three years ago at one of her public gatherings. He'd been thrown out of college for being disruptive, twice. The army declined to sign him up because of drug use. Yet he was able to legally buy a 9 pistol, extended clips, ammunition, and kill six people. Go figure!

Another such event had taken place three days before the Tucson tragedy in Omaha, Nebraska. An assistant principal at the high school had suspended a seventeen-year-old boy for driving his pickup truck onto the football field and tearing up the grass. That afternoon, the student walked into the fifty-eight-year-old woman's office and shot her. He wounded the principal and another teacher. Then he drove out to the country and committed suicide. He had taken the semiautomatic pistol from a drawer in the house. His dad was a police detective. This news was published on page three of the newspaper and never made it to the national TV coverage.

Over the following months, gun laws would be revisited. Security for politicians would be scrutinized. Language in congressional meetings would be toned down. The Tucson assassin would be tried and tried again. Then the appeals began and are still going. A year after these attacks, we were back to "business as usual." Nothing much had changed. What a debacle!

I did notice that the DNC selected Charlotte, North Carolina, for the site of their 2012 convention. The RNC picked Tampa, Florida, for their gathering. Interesting!

The wars in Iraq and Afghanistan continued. President Obama was adamant that our troops be pulled from Iraq "no matter what." Of course, the troops pulled from Iraq were sent to Afghanistan. In 2011 there were several failed terrorist bombing attempts, one in LA, one in New York, and another in Miami. Two failed political assassinations occurred in the United States in 2012.

A "positive indicator" (media quote) was the passage of a National Health Care Bill in 2010. The legislation passed—actually, "bulldozed"—through by the Democrats was a long way from what should have and could easily have been provided for US citizens, but it was a beginning. The timing benchmarks allocated were less than desired, allowing procrastination on needed portions of the bill through 2020, and as usual, the price tag was exorbitant at more than $940 billion. Of course, the money was supposed to come from the "rich" taxpayers, and the insurance companies were clubbed over the head with a gavel, but it's fair to say they deserved it. Members of Congress did not have the same coverage as you and me, nor was the issue of illegal immigrant health care included. The RNC vowed to repeal the law as soon as they controlled Congress (in 2012?). The citizens were mad! The government mandate proclaimed everyone had to buy insurance or be penalized. Was this the beginning of socialism in the United States? More later.

A gorilla-sized "negative indicator"—the lack of legislation regarding the immigration problem—was hanging around. The president, after "winning" the battle on health care reform, stated immigration would move to the front of his list. Wasn't that a grand gesture? It was estimated there were more than fourteen million illegal immigrants in the United States in 2010. They were still here in 2011 and 2012 (just ask the part-time census takers). They were making money, not paying taxes, receiving free medical care and other benefits, and our President stated, "I'll get around to it someday." Arizona passed their own laws to deal with this problem, and the president made jokes about it! Immigration is no joke. Just ask an American Indian. At year-end, the Senate had done nothing. This demonstrated lack of leadership was exactly the reason The Lists were born and why; over the next decade, lethal "motivators" for many selected targets would be distributed.

Unemployment hovered around 10 percent. The only jobs being created were for 165,000 PT census takers in 2010 and FT IRS agents. Of course, the administration was taking credit for making these jobs available "as promised." When and if they move ahead with the projects outlined in The Lists, they could create three hundred thousand full-time jobs in less than a year and three times that many by the end of the third year. The financial markets were stagnant.

Let's take a peek at the folks our government bailed out with our tax money in 2009/2010. I used the Freedom of Information Act to see who did what. This made target selection fairly easy. Of the identified 119 top executives at the "big five" companies that had received billions of tax dollars, sixty-nine reported bonuses in excess of a million dollars! There was an established cap for their take-home salary of $500,000, but it wasn't working. American International, GMAC Financial, Chrysler Financial, Chrysler Motors, and General Motors executives obviously hadn't gotten the message, and the government overseers were still toothless. Then there was the OTS (Office of Thrift Supervision), the OCC (Office of the Comptroller of the Currency), the SEC, and the FDIC (Federal Deposit Insurance Corp.). These were the same guys who were supposed to prevent the financial disasters that happened in '08, '09, and continued into 2010 and 2011. They were either totally incompetent, or they just didn't give a damn. They had done such a fine job; they were kept on the payroll in 2011, after a trillion-dollar bailout of the companies these same regulators had been keeping watch over. The guy running the OTS had the guts to say "large bonuses for executives in financial institutions were necessary to motivate them to work hard and do a better job." Wow! In 2012, when The Lists were introduced, the alternative method to motivate them was implemented, and it was a lot cheaper. Some of them were included in the first batch to be terminated in 2012.

Then there was the saga of the American Indian tribes (there are 560 federally recognized tribes in the United States), and their impact on, of all things, renewable energy sources. Five percent of United States lands belong to various Indian tribes. Their land holds more than 10 percent of our renewable energy sources. Projects to harness the sun's energy or wind-powered generation was being hampered by tribal elders who wanted incentives (*payoffs* sounds like a better word) to permit use of their land for these purposes. The potential electrical energy would be 17.6 trillion kilowatt hours/year from solar (this alone is four times the total power generated in the United States in 2004) and about 535 billion kilowatt hours/year from wind. Of course, the matter wasn't helped very much with a federal allocation for these projects of a paltry $20 million while we continued to waste billions of dollars on oil imports and coal pollution. As stated in The Lists, it was time for a wake-up call!

Four hundred years ago, the Wampanoag Indians welcomed the Pilgrims and the Mayflower to Plymouth, Massachusetts. They were screwed so often since then, it was time to try and get even. They were opposing the introduction of an offshore wind turbine farm. Why? The tribe members said that the four-hundred-foot tall towers would interrupt their spiritual ceremony of greeting the sunrise each morning by obstructing their view. They go on to claim that the excavations made for tower foundations could possibly disturb unknown burial grounds even though the potential burial grounds would never be found since they are now thirty feet underwater. I anxiously waited to see what the elders were going to do after their chief received his assignment from The Lists and now knew the consequences for failure to comply. There was still a little time to reconsider.

Not only were the American Indians a problem for wind turbine installations, the American bald eagle was another holdup. The BLM and Fish and Wildlife Service caved in to the demands of several wildlife groups and stopped permitting installations on government lands. It seems the birds could fly into the large blades and be killed. I wonder if any of the brains running these organizations ever thought about what's going to happen when pollution from the other power sources kills the vegetation, small animals die, and the eagles die from starvation!

On a happier note, there was positive government movement for nonpolluting renewable energy sources. While the respective government agencies were still moving as slow as molasses on a cold day, they were at least showing some interest in both solar—and wind-powered generation. GE was heavily involved (guess why?), and their political "clout" was still up for grabs (it's called campaign contributions). However, just showing an interest was progress. The government-approved increase in offshore drilling was put on hold due to the BP oil spill in the Gulf. We wouldn't have seen any of this "new" oil for at least three years anyway. We could begin to see benefits from wind or solar generation in about a year if we made up our minds to "just do it" and if the bureaucrats in the BLM (Bureau of Land Management) kept out of the way.

The requirement for Congress to immediately pass legislation detailing the development and use of electric and hybrid technology for transportation was largely ignored. They did reduce spending on hydrogen fuel technology by $70 million.

There had been no congressional action to immediately cease spending on the space program and redirect those funds to domestic projects as stipulated in The Lists. The aging heroes of the space race and one ancient astronaut/senator seemed to be the largest roadblock to this change. Unfortunately, a couple of strategic terminations were needed to help move this legislation along. Returning to the moon and a manned mission to Mars would be important someday, but not for a while. There were signs private-sector investments would offset this delay in NASA's space activity. While limited in their scope, private projects would keep interest "alive" for future space exploration and save the taxpayer a bundle. The final launch took place in 2011 after five or six delays. Then the Russians took over. Of course, the United States continued to subsidize this effort, at least for a while.

Term limits were nowhere to be found as an agenda item. Campaign finance reform was set back years when the Supremes opened Pandora's box and legalized unlimited campaign contributions from industry, unions, or other special interest groups. This served as justification for preparing termination packages for several members of Congress and a few cabinet members the following year. A ninety-year-old member of the Supremes announced his retirement. Unfortunately, several ancient senators did not. One ninety-two-year-old (and very corrupt) senator passed away (with no help from The Lists). Then there was the story of corruption and condemnation of an eighty-year-old twenty-term Democratic congressman from New York's Harlem District. I came to believe the majority of the voting public casts their vote based on the media depiction of a candidate's "pork barrel popularity," not credentials.

The midterm elections in 2010 proved to be history making. With high unemployment, the financial crisis continuing, an unpopular health care bill, a significant portion of the population stunned by the administration's position regarding nuclear arms reduction, the lack of law enforcement on the Mexican border, the continuing situation in Afghanistan, very little movement regarding environmental concerns, and a host of other negative issues that couldn't be hidden any longer by a politically friendly media, the Democrats in Congress were almost wiped out! There were 37 governorships, 37 Senate seats, and all 435 seats in the House up for grabs. The exploding popularity of the Tea Party presented another variable. Prior to the election, four sitting Democratic senators announced they would not seek reelection. The November 2, 2010 election results told the whole story. "The wheels had fallen off the Democrat's bandwagon"! For 2011, fifty incumbents were swept out of Congress; Republicans took the majority of the House and state governor positions. A new Republican Speaker was installed. The female Democratic ex-Speaker claimed her rightful place as the minority Speaker. We now had a "split Congress" with a new Speaker. Over the next two years, the legislature tried to override a presidential veto six times. They succeeded twice, but we still had most of the idiotic health care legislation although we were waiting on the Supreme Court to weigh in on the subject. Many of the president's staff began to jump ship including the Secretaries of Defense and State. Everyone was wondering what the S of S had in her apron pocket. Was 2012 going to be her year or was this just preparation for 2016?

The RNC, the DNC and the TP adopted the same war cry; "Remember 2010." The mud slinging and blame game began immediately when the freshmen class took their seats in Congress. The Lists sent assignment letters to the Democratic Senate Majority Leader and the House GOP leader in 2011. The RNC favored Mitt but Jeb and Newt weren't giving up. Sarah wasn't much of a consideration.

Beginning in 2011, voters began to worry about what they had done. New blood was in Congress and they began to do as promised. Substantial spending cuts were implemented and pork barrel projects no longer received a rubber stamp approval. Projects for highways or bridges to nowhere disappeared and so did the jobs they would have provided. Voters didn't realize there was little to worry about: all Congress had to do was implement the plans outlined by The Lists. Unfortunately, implementing this plan didn't happen for more than a year.

During 2011 and 2012 the media provided the public with all of the dirt on every newsworthy topic including every politician. I've never quite understood why anyone would spend millions of dollars (some of their own fortunes at times) for publicity and traveling around the country for months to get elected to a job paying $300,000 and being roasted or humiliated in the process. This apparently has not had an impact on Nancy, Hillary, Sarah or the dozens of male candidates still actively seeking a spot on the ticket.

In 2011, Congress voted to lift the ban on gays in the military in spite of the objections of our admirals and generals. Tactically, this became another plus for the administration during the elections.

Prior to the November elections, five senators announced their retirement. Ironically, only two of them had been given assignments from The Lists. When the election smoke cleared the president had barely managed to keep his job. The DNC made him keep ol' Joe on the ticket. He didn't win because of the accomplishments of his administration. He won because he was our first black president and because Bin Laden had been terminated while he was in office.

The DNC had seriously considered dumping Joe, but decided he was the lesser of the evils available at the time. Did this decision signify the

DNC were throwing in the towel for 2016? Or were they grooming some new players? The GOP ticket for 2012 included Mitt and a new face, Chris Christie. I can't help but think the GOP had decided to use these two as sacrificial lambs and save the big guns for 2016. 'The Donald' attempted to enter the fray, but aside from the publicity he got, he really didn't present much of a threat to anyone. He found it much easier to hire celebrity apprentices and rebuild golf courses.

The GOP, with some help from the Tea Party, took control of Congress and began to pass business friendly legislation: some of the projects identified by The Lists were approved. Congress found it necessary to over ride a presidential veto on more than one occasion. For a while the GOP was able to avoid internal power struggles between the incumbents and the new members. Unemployment began to improve, financial institutions rebounded while other popular (and necessary) initiatives were implemented.

The financial Goliath, Goldman Sachs, was found guilty of double dealing. They made a ton of money investing in deals they knew to be losers. The federal oversight folks were asleep at the switch (or watching porn on their computer screens). The Lists eliminated 16 financial targets in 2011 and 2012. A GS director, Gupta, escaped termination when he was convicted of insider trading. Lucky guy!

The CEO of the defunct Lehman Brothers financial organization pocketed $530,000,000 in the 8 years prior to the firm going belly up. A well paid lobbying group continued a campaign to prevent passage of financial reforms and stronger oversight provisions. They thought giving six and seven figure salaries and bonuses to the financial crooks on Wall Street was necessary. Seven of them were removed by The Lists.

During this period, our federal taxes stabilized unless you believe the double speak commentaries delivered daily by MSNBC-they still claim to be fair and balanced! Unfortunately, the so called 'death tax' was still active and a flat income tax appeared to be buried, again. Eighteen government positions were vacated in an eight month period.

In 2010, former House Majority Leader, Tom Delay, was convicted of money laundering and sentenced to 3 years in prison. Of course his prison was actually a fenced in country club with an activity director instead of a guard. Since he had just been voted off 'Dancing With the Stars', this was quite a blow to his ego. I'll bet when he's released he applies for the next episode of 'Survivor'.

In 2011, the Chairman of the Federal Reserve attempted to force Congress into approving a $600 billion economic aid program to buy bonds. He claimed this would generate a half million jobs in two years. Unfortunately, the government didn't have the money available to pay for this grandiose scheme. They would need to contact China or perhaps the sheiks in Saudi Arabia for another trillion dollar loan to finance this program. They would be printing more money and going further and further in debt. One more time I reminded key players to start the projects on The Lists—NOW! Jobs and payback would begin almost immediately.

Leaders of the Muslim community in New York continued to create havoc by attempting to build a mosque next to the site of the Twin Towers' devastation. What are they thinking? Because of what I call "America's social amnesia," the mosque will probably get built.

There were several major man-made impacts on the global environment, including the continuing destruction of the forests in the Amazon and the Congo, two very large offshore oil spills and a chemical spill that contaminated much of Lake Erie. Nine targets were eliminated because of this.

Of special interest, 12/21/12 came and went, and the world didn't end as the ancient Mayan calendar predicted. The Mayans were great astronomers, and 12/21/12, the winter solstice, marked the end of their five-thousand-year cycle: the exact date the earth, moon, and sun would align for a complete eclipse. This event would be a bit different than other eclipses. This time the alignment would extend into the dark rift or black hole. Scientists told us when this happened thirteen thousand years ago, a major climate shift took place on earth (electromagnetic?). So to be on the safe side, I scheduled a wine (and beer), cheese, cold shrimp, and chocolate (all stuff I liked) party on my lanai. I invited twenty-six friends and neighbors to attend. The event was to occur at 6:11 a.m. in our time zone. I didn't expect many to attend, but I was really surprised when most of them showed up. I did add coffee to the menu. Since the party was held on December 21, we included Christmas as a cotheme. Everyone was back home in bed about noon.

The year 2012 did see a major shift, but it wasn't the climate; it was political. If the Mayans had been around, they would probably have started a new five-thousand-year calendar. No one has yet explained how these ancient people could be so accurate with their astronomical predictions. Could ET have visited?

The Lists were responsible for many events during the year, but there's one that had some significance for many people who'd lost money on Wall Street. It had to do with a very irritating lobbyist.

This particular influence peddler was functioning as a specialist for the House minority leadership. His specialty was undermining the efforts to overhaul the ineffectual regulations for Wall Street and financial businesses. In spite of the efforts of the Republicans and Tea Party, new legislation was repeatedly voted down. This lobbyist, let's call him Jack, and his cohorts were largely responsible for the failure. Jack had a close working relationship with highly placed members on "the Hill," but his paychecks came from several large financial institutions.

Over the Christmas break, I arranged for Jack to receive a holiday basket with fruit, cheeses, chocolates, and a specially prepared bottle of very expensive booze (his favorite, according to a local bartender) on a Friday evening. A note was attached and read "Dear Jack, Thanks so much for your assistance. Have a Happy Holiday." It wasn't signed, but it was initialed "NP." No matter what his background, Jack had to be impressed with a $200 bottle of whiskey and a note from "you know who!"

I figured Jack would immediately open the bottle and have a well-deserved libation. Then, be found dead from a heart attack. That's not what happened. It took almost a month, but after several news reports, I was able to piece together what probably happened.

The second Friday of each month, Jack played host to a poker club. The seven members gathered in Jack's well-appointed and provisioned game room, complete with a fully stocked bar. The players arrived promptly at 6:00 p.m. for drinks and finger food (supplied by Jack). The buy-in was $1,000, and no-limit stud poker was the only game played. The charter members were Jack, a federal judge, two congressmen, a three-star general, a cabinet secretary, and an officer of the Federal Reserve.

I sure would like to have been privy to some of the conversations around that poker table. Two lower-level government officials were alternates and usually called on at the last minute.

Fortunately, for the alternates, all members showed up on this Friday night. It seems that Jack took pleasure in bragging about his conquests, and he chose the poker game to share his good fortune (the $200 bottle) and to read to the players the personal note he'd received from "you know who." They must have been impressed. I have no idea who won the card game, but over the weekend, Jack and three of his poker buddies were found dead in various locations in DC from natural causes. The other three players didn't care for hard alcohol and had survived. Even with this successful intervention, the legislation demanding the overhaul of regulations controlling the financial community didn't pass until 2013, after the Republicans gained control of Congress.

Our secretary of state, Hillary Clinton, spent most of the first half of 2010 as a wedding planner for Chelsea's wedding. Her most difficult task was keeping Bill sober and away from the bridesmaids.

Do you remember an Internet site called Wikileaks and its founder, Julian Assange? This guy was the epitome of a cyberspace terrorist. Using his computer skills and input from a spy in the Pentagon, he managed to copy thousands of US government, military, and diplomatic encrypted/ secret files and began publishing them on the Net for anyone to read (about three thousand hits every second!). He fled to Switzerland and managed to hide from the authorities for months in a vacated military underground bunker we couldn't seem to locate. How many underground military bunkers are there in Switzerland, or was it Sweden? Once again, our billion-dollar intelligence agencies were hard at work! Apparently, Wikileaks had attained cult status with its followers branching out into cyberspace and vowing to carry on, claiming "freedom of information" no matter what! Julian fled to London where he was arrested. He was finally deported to Sweden for, of all things, sex crimes. He is still in jail, awaiting trial. He might wind up in the United States someday to face charges. Homeland Security and other organizations wanted to get their hands on this guy! His informant was found and is in big trouble. Treason is being discussed.

Our earth continued the warming trend, and it was getting dryer.

Termination packages were mailed in late 2012 to strategic targets based on poor performance for the year. Assignment letters were mailed to the replacements the following April. A few "bad actors" popped up in 2012 and were added to The Lists as future targets.

Keith Olbermann, the controversial host of a very combative and extremely liberal TV show on MSNBC, surprised everyone when he resigned. He gave no explanation, but I like to feel it was because of the assignment letter he'd received from The Lists. His name was removed from the target list.

Our Ambassador to China, Huntsman, resigned his position in 2011. He was a Republican appointed to his post by President Obama. He had been a Mormon missionary in China, was the former governor of Utah, and was deemed eminently qualified for his posting. Political strategists were all very surprised by this move until they realized this allowed the ambassador time to develop a strategy to run for the presidential election in 2012 or maybe in 2016. It was going to be a very crowded field!

Two financial crooks gained attention during this period. A notorious lobbyist named Abramoff and an equally hated financial con-man named Madoff surfaced. Both were dealt with, but not by The Lists.

A Senator from Alaska was convicted of corruption and 'dethroned'. He died in a plane crash a short time later. The Lists had no involvement.

There were nine underground natural gas line explosions in three years. Two interstate highway bridges almost collapsed. A two lane bridge near Cincinnati did collapse on a Sunday morning in April. One hundred and twenty six people died from these failures. Yet, the federal government continued to procrastinate when it came to allocating the funds to correct these infrastructure issues.

Unemployment continued to slowly improve, but the trade deficit continued to grow. The plans outlined by The Lists, when implemented, would quickly reverse the trade deficit and continue to improve employment. Nine government officials received a wake up call in the form of an assignment. We'll watch what happens.

The final Space Shuttle missions were planned for 2011. The Shuttle Discovery had covered more than 143 million miles in thirty years. It would complete its last trip in May. The Endeavor and the Atlantis would also take their final flights in 2011. NASA didn't consider this the end of the space program, but future explorations will be accomplished without the shuttles.

In early 2011, the president took another quiet step toward vote gathering. He shutdown federal enforcement of a law stating that marriage was only recognized when between a man and a woman. In reality, this act endorsed same sex marriage and got more votes from the very vocal gay and lesbian communities. This act was reported on page 3 and I'm not sure if anything was reported on a national news broadcast.

The media reported an abnormal increase in what was called 'hate mail' directed at prominent figures. I found it odd there was no mention of the mysterious and untimely deaths of more than one hundred prominent people who may have received an assignment (they could have called it 'hate mail'). I still felt secure for the moment.

During 2011, more than eight hundred tornados pummeled the US in April. Never have we experienced anything like this. About a thousand people died and billions of dollars in damage resulted. Scientists and meteorologists tried to convince the rest of us that pollution and global warming were responsible for the dramatic changes in our weather.

CHAPTER 18

LOOKING BACK: 2012 FOREIGN ISSUES

January 2013

Similar to expectations for the domestic portion of The Lists, positive movement on foreign activities would have been nice but were not expected. One hundred years of trying to motivate foreign leadership to "do the right thing" had been in vain, so I hadn't anticipated that The Lists would accomplish very much early on. There were a few positive signals. Here's what I remember as the highlights for 2010, 2011, and 2012.

In 2010, the first thing to hit the foreign news was a multimillion-dollar corruption case in the United Nations. What a surprise? Yeah. Right! Over the past twenty-five years, there has been so much corruption exposed in the UN that it would take a team of accountants fifty years to sort it out. Yet we kept our membership and kept on supplying most of the funding for this worthless organization. Originally envisioned as the manager of an international governing body, the UN turned out to be an ineffective bunch of posturing diplomats out for a long-term romp in NYC. The Lists planned to adequately address this problem. It was a surprise to me when it was announced that sanctions against Iran were being considered, but then absolutely nothing worthwhile happened. Starvation and genocide continued in several third world countries without any UN intervention.

Throughout 2010, China stayed on the path to an improved economy, riding on the coattails of human rights abuses, out-of-control pollution, and an artificial (undervalued) exchange rate. Every major Chinese city was covered by a dirty brown haze threatening to bring about climate changes (just ask the Olympic athletes who spent weeks in Beijing). Medical and agricultural experts tell us this will eventually have a detrimental effect on health (350,000 deaths a year due to cardiovascular and respiratory disease in China and India) and food supplies for the entire planet (blocking out the sun and changing weather/rain patterns). Yet, China is the world's leading manufacturer of wind turbines. Chinese leaders continue to ignore the pleas from the UN responding in so many words, "You got yours, now we want ours!" Sanctions, what few that have been tried, have had little effect. Bribery, in the form of foreign aid, hasn't worked. China wants our technology and we give it to them freely. Why? The US already owes China billions of dollars and the Chinese keep buying US Treasury securities. It's going to be up to something like The Lists to influence 'Kim and Company'.

The cold war has been officially over for years, but the US and Russia continue discussing nuclear arms reductions. Mostly it's the US reducing our inventory thanks in large part to the wayward thinking of a lame duck president seeking to leave us with his major legacy while the Russians have no qualms about selling hardware and no how to the highest bidder. This is happening while Iran, India, Pakistan and North Korea continue to work to develop nuclear capabilities. It's little wonder the Democrats are losing credibility at home. I continue to hope The Lists aren't too late!

In other news, Bin Laden was found and eliminated in May, 2011. It only took us ten years, millions of dollars and the combined security resources of the world to accomplish this. Who's next? Libya and Iran are at the top of my list.

The US is still trying to negotiate a peaceful settlement between Israel and Palestine in Jerusalem and the bank. The Arab League of Foreign Ministers met in Libya where Moammar declared support for Hussein loyalists in Iraq. The Iraqi minister walked out. A lot of posturing was going on, but very little was actually accomplished. The OPEC ministers still smile all the way to the bank.

I didn't expect any major changes in foreign attitudes, but then the uprisings began. First it was Tunisia. Then Egypt exploded and Mubarak was thrown out after 30 years of iron rule. A domino effect began. People in Libya revolted and the government forces began killing their own civilians. NATO forces finally intervened and an internal revolt continued for years. Moammar was finally killed in raid reminiscent of the one that killed Bin Laden. People in mid-eastern countries were demanding freedom and democracy. They wanted poverty eliminated and the ability to share in the wealth of their country. Many died in the process. They were doing this without the historic US intervention. Leaders in Israel, Jordan, Syria, Algeria,

Yemen, Iran, and even Saudi Arabia watched this development very closely, wondering who would be next. Of course, the United States was concerned about the Suez Canal, oil shipments, and military bases. Egypt had accomplished this revolution in eighteen days! It would take me ten years of my life to just get things started! For obvious reasons, I needed to rethink my edict for gasoline pricing.

No one of importance was assassinated (except for several individuals identified by The Lists) although there were a few attempts. The Lists sent twenty-three packages to foreign targets. Israel demanded the world stop Iran's march to nuclear weapons. They hinted this better happen before they had to do it themselves. My research did point out Iran does have one redeeming attribute: they are known as "the nose capital of the world." Apparently, more nose jobs are done in Iran than in Hollywood! Another worrisome political marriage seemed to be taking place. Chavez of Venezuela and Ahmadinejad of Iran were becoming buddies. What now? The United States revoked the Venezuelan ambassador's visa when Venezuela refused to accept our ambassador to their country. Tit-for-tat diplomacy!

Chile gave the last of their weapons-grade uranium to the United States before it wound up in the hands of some terrorist group. It only takes fifty-five pounds of HEU (highly enriched uranium) to make a nuclear bomb, one that could level Washington. There is still more than four thousand pounds of HEU, mostly from Russia, unaccounted for. Sleep well!

Our neighbor to the south continued to be problematical. Mexico's efforts to curtail illegal immigration and drug smuggling were totally ineffective. Increased violence had spread on the US border and was spilling over into Central America with a vengeance. The Mexican government, law enforcement, and military could not cope with the situation. Hundreds of Mexicans and dozens of US citizens had been murdered. The United States had to get involved. In the meantime, The Lists used other means to "encourage" change on both sides of the border. Twenty-six Latino targets were eliminated along with nineteen collaterals.

We all remember the stories about the Somali pirates. While at first it seemed like something from Disney, this band of mischief makers in small skiffs and motorized canoes began to capture cargo ships passing through their area in 2009. Several high-profile episodes were reported, with large-dollar ransoms paid for cargoes and crews. Apparently, the pirates used their earnings to purchase newer and better equipment (from whom?). In 2010, they stepped up their efforts and began to be more than a nuisance. In the absence of UN intervention, warships from several countries were dispatched to the area, and piracy quieted down for a short while. The "skull and crossbones" were back at it before the end of 2011.

France and Spain continued with their military assistance in Afghanistan, and it was greatly appreciated. However, their involvement in other world trouble spots was nonexistent, and NATO support was lukewarm.

Hillary Clinton and the idiot leader from Iran got into a bit of an argument on the floor of the UN regarding nukes. Syria acted as a cheerleader for Iran. By the way, the United States announced that we had 5,113 nuclear warheads in our warehouses, enough to blow the planet apart.

Hillary and the Chinese leaders met and got nowhere regarding what to do with North Korea or Iran. (North Korea actually torpedoed a South Korean naval vessel and shelled a small island off the South Korea coast).

The royal family, actually most of the UK, spent the first three months of 2011 preparing for Prince William's nuptials. It was an extremely difficult situation due to the deteriorating British economy. The Queen actually had to kick in a few bucks (pounds) from the royal checking account to pay for the extravaganza. There were some tense moments when terrorist activity was detected near the cathedral (two "bag bombs" were found) and, again, when about three thousand unemployed Englishmen gathered in the courtyard and, for some reason, chanted "we don't want to eat cake."

Palestinians and Israelis continued their face-off over the Gaza Strip. Hezbollah said, "Don't forget about me!"

Greece needed a $30-billion bailout from their friends in the EU. Ireland asked for $135 billion! Was a massive financial crisis in Europe starting?

Our Arab allies questioned when we were going to sanction Iran but didn't offer to pay for anything! They were probably saving their money for the upcoming battle with their own countries.

Muslim extremists tried several times to murder a cartoonist in Belgium because he drew an unflattering characterization of Mohammed.

Moscow blamed Islamic militants when a suicide bomber killed 40 and wounded 180 at the Domodedovo Airport in 2011.

It became very evident that Pakistan continued to contribute to extremist groups like the Taliban and al-Quida. Attempts were made to blow up Times Square and Union Station. Fortunately, these attempts failed.

North Korean leaders made several secret visits to China. Think about that!

A million French students continued to riot and protest that the retirement age had been raised from 60 to 62. Most of these students hadn't worked a day in their young lives, but they still rioted. Those Frenchmen who actually did work still enjoyed a 35 hour week with five weeks of paid vacation each year.

The Dutch pulled their troops from NATO and Afghanistan. Canada plans to do the same thing in 2013. Poland will follow. Germany, the UK and the US will continue.

The US and some of our Central American friends became aware of China's growing interest in acquiring property, businesses and government assistance in Panama. Bill Clinton pulled all US bases from Panama years ago. Was the Canal in jeopardy? Only time will tell.

Climate experts warned low lying coastal cities and several island nations to begin to formulate plans for rapid evacuations and permanent relocations. Global warming was accelerating glacial melting and in about ten years, predictions were the ocean level will rise as much as two feet.

A major volcano erupted in Iceland in 2010 and continued to effect air traffic to/from Europe for months.

Five major earthquakes hit the US during this time. They ranged from 6.1 to 7.3 on the Richter Scale. Chili experienced a devastating 8.8 and New Zealand was hit by two quakes over 6.5. Then the grand daddy of the quakes, a 9.1, hit northern Japan. A fifty foot tsunami hit the island with such force that four nuclear reactors were severely damaged and harmful radiation was released into the air and the ocean. 200,000 people were evacuated. 300,000 were homeless. It was estimated that 25,000 to 50,000 were killed and $60 billion in damages and lost revenue resulted. The clean up will take years. Many nations are re-evaluating expansion of nuclear power plants vs. solar, wind or hydro plants.

The tsunami impacted the Hawaiian Islands, Oregon and Northern California, but only minimal damage resulted. To add insult to injury, a volcano on the southern tip of Japan erupted. The combined results of these natural disasters would impact the world's economic well being for years.

The scientific community published documents showing that the 'Pacific Ring of Fire', an underwater fault stretching from Antarctica to Alaska, was becoming more active and posing a threat to everyone on the planet. Nuclear power plants all over the world were structurally evaluated and disaster shut down scenarios reviewed.

The debris washed into the ocean by the tsunami floated across the Pacific and began to pile up on beaches in Hawaii and the coast of Vancouver, Washington, Oregon and California. Millions would be spent on cleaning up the debris. The islands of debris actually became a navigation problem in the shipping lanes. Some of the trash showed low level radiation contamination.

A heart warming human interest story developed during the massive clean up along the US coastal areas. Japanese Americans in California set up an operation to gather reclaimable items and return them to their owners in Japan. Many items found their way back to the owners while others were given to surviving relatives.

Getting back to The Lists; at some point the news media picked up on what they considered a newsworthy scoop and began to publish articles about prominent citizens receiving threatening letters. I was happy and a little surprised the articles made no mention of suspicious activities connected to the untimely and, in many cases, mysterious deaths of quite a few foreign notables during this time. So far, so good! I figured if they were unable to find Bin Laden for ten years, I was pretty safe.

2013

CHAPTER 19

LOOKING BACK: 2013, DOMESTIC

January 2014

The year 2013 was a good example of the adage that time flies when you're having fun! We had a lot of fun. I felt much better about the fate of the United States since we had a Republican-controlled Congress as a result of the November 2012 election. There were signs improvement in the economy was accelerating. The Republicans were unable to repeal the idiotic National Health Care Bill in 2011, but it was quickly repealed and new, much more "friendly" legislation passed in 2013. Financial regulations were strengthened. Conditions on the Mexican border were showing signs that we were gaining control. Afghanistan and Iran were still thorns. NATO's involvement was to cease in 2014, but that looked very unlikely. We still had quite a lot of work to do in every sector.

I decided it might be a good time to take some time off. Since I'd spent most of 2012 busy with restarting the eBay "business" (remember the flea market stuff?) or in the sheds preparing letters and packages. I'd had very little time to just enjoy life. So I managed to get caught up on everything and took a well-deserved vacation during a lull in the action. The vacation was to be different than the one I took through the United States and Canada four years ago: the one that started the idea for The Lists. First, the RV and the Honda came out of storage. Provisions were stored onboard. For the next two months I drove around the United States. I visited Walter and Diana, dear friends of ours, at their home in Georgia. Walter and I compared notes about our Corvettes, and Diana informed me she still planned on relocating to The Villages as soon as they sold the Georgia house. I visited daughter Laura and grandson Michael in Virginia. I attended grade school commencements, a high school graduation, an old friend's funeral, and another one's wedding (his third). I even played a few rounds of golf. All the while I suffered from paranoia: "They're coming to get me!" Once the planned terminations began, this thought never left my mind. I was certain the FBI, NSA, Interpol, and other agencies were out looking for me.

While in Ohio, I visited daughter Kim, son-in-law Chris, and grandsons Christopher and Joshua in Uniontown. I went a little south to sit in the front row in church next to son Buddy and family while grandson Jeremy said "I do" to Kristen.

Next I dropped in on son Rick, his wife Renee, granddaughter Brittany, and grandson Johnny. I spent two nights with son Jimmy, his wife Trina, granddaughter Amber, and grandson Taylor in Cincinnati. I even managed an overnight stay in Lexington, Kentucky with nephew

Steven, his wife Gwynne, Rebecca, Kayla, and Eric. Niece Lisa, her husband, Lance, and daughter Kyra dropped in. We enjoyed a great game of "trains." Then I had to hustle home and pack for my trip to Europe.

I had decided to visit a few picturesque areas of Europe (bucket list, again) and maybe spend some quiet time on a beach. After returning the RV and the Honda to storage, I secured the house and boarded a cruise ship to Italy where I "jumped ship," rented a car, and toured parts of four countries on my own. I stayed well away from the rioting going on in Egypt, Syria, Lebanon, and other Arab countries. I found the people in Italy, Southern France, Southern Germany, and the Costa del Sol region of Spain complacent when compared to US citizens. They weren't nearly as worried about their safety (terrorists) or even their economy. The French were still unhappy that their retirement age had been raised from sixty to sixty-two. The English were unhappy with the cuts to social benefits. Most showed only modest concerns about the world situation since they hadn't been directly affected by the dozen or so attacks that took place during the year. (They were convinced their country had minor internal issues and the major problems could be attributed to the United States, Iraq, Russia, Afghanistan, Pakistan, Israel, Russia, Iran, North Korea, and China.)

Pollution, food shortages, oil prices, terrorist activity, immigration, even the fluctuating value of the euro or the condition of the EU didn't seem to be a huge concern. A "this too shall pass" mentality prevailed. When pushed to think about Iran getting nukes, they did admit it was nice to see that someone had bombed a nuclear facility in Iran and eliminated a couple of their scientists. It could become a problem for them, but they didn't think the rest of the world would let it happen. Talk about rose-colored glasses. During this trip, I managed to squeeze in time to set up a few more postal drops for future foreign-package deliveries. Language is no barrier when dollars are involved.

After an enjoyable six weeks, I flew home. On the return trip, airport security wasn't nearly as diligent as when I boarded the cruise ship. Leaving the United States for my cruise, as I passed through the ship's security, they opened all my bags and actually looked in them (probably looking for bottles of wine). I wasn't concerned about clearing security: I hadn't taken any wine, my Glock, or packages for foreign delivery. When returning, I cleared airport security (in Europe) where they x-rayed everything (including me, my shoes, belt, etc.) but didn't open anything except my carry-on bag. When I landed in the United States, all I needed to do was fill out a nothing-to-declare form, show my passport, claim my bags, and walk straight through the customs counter. No one even groped me! Oh well. I made it back home safely. I was well rested and sporting a great tan. Now it was back to the business of political intrigue and saving the world!

There was still a lot of anger over immigration. The majority of US citizens wanted stronger immigration laws and enforcement. This view was shared by civic, police, and union leaders. Unfortunately, there was the noisy minority to contend with, which included a lot of the illegals, media personalities, and more than a few Hollywood celebrities. Several media personalities and celebs had already been given assignments, but after a review of what was happening, I added four targets to The Lists. Other states had fought through the storm of controversy and were adamant that illegal immigration was not only wrong, it was expensive! Fourteen states were in the process of copying the Arizona legislation. The natives were getting restless! The

Feds attacked the Arizona law, and Arizona sued the feds. The lawyers said *ka-ching*!

The new GOP Congress was finally demanding a much stronger and more active role in the Mexican immigration / border / drug problem. The military was directed to become involved. The oil spill in the Gulf had been stopped, but the devastation to the Gulf Coast from Louisiana to Florida was catastrophic. BP, the oil company responsible for the damage, was still paying the cleanup costs and making up lost income to the fishing and tourist industries out of the mandated $20-billion fund set aside for this purpose. BP had served notice they were going to stop funding when this escrow account was emptied or the cleanup deemed complete, whichever came first. When that happens, I have no doubt there will be leftover litigation, and you and me (our tax dollars) will pick up the tab for additional cleanup or to provide loss of income. Seven states still had pending lawsuits against BP. No one knew what position the feds were going to take. After all, Big Oil was still a main source of campaign contributions, whether Democrat or Republican (Tea Party?).

What caused the spill in the first place? Turns out, once again, our federal watchdogs, the Minerals Management Service (MMS), had managed to screw up! They had not required BP or their contractor to file a detailed plan of how to deal with a blowout, which they were supposed to do. The investigation of this failure to comply with safety regs found two MMS officials who were responsible for oversight of this specific safety procedure. Both saw a fairly large boost to their incomes in the previous year, and both mysteriously took early retirement four months after the initial investigation began. About two months later, they both received retirement congratulatory packages courtesy of The Lists. I'm sure their families, after a suitable bereavement period, will begin to enjoy life without them.

The remaining oil companies continued to take in massive profits with little government intervention. It's quite interesting to think that we have laws preventing excessive profiteering by utility companies (because their goods and services are "essential" for the public good) yet do absolutely nothing to prevent oil companies from raking in billions in excess profits. ("It's the campaign contributions, stupid!") The oil-company executives had begun contributing 15 percent of their annual profits to a new escrow account as demanded by no. 1 on The Lists. (The "contributions" began arriving after eighteen oil execs "bit the dust," having missed the initial payment deadline.) The new National Energy Research Foundation (NERF) seemed to be working very well. After the presidential announcement regarding the formation of NERF, a fellow by the name of Bill Gates volunteered to help oversee the organization. Money began flowing to the proper projects. The commitment that no new offshore oil rigs would be given permits was short lived. The interior secretary had lifted the ban in late 2010. Existing rigs were being thoroughly inspected to ensure compliance for emergency equipment and procedures. MMS officials were finally doing their jobs, probably because they were a little scared not to. This problem would go away or at least become negligible as time goes by and the demand for oil diminishes. I've never received a straight answer to one of life's mysteries: "If it costs the oil companies less to manufacture diesel fuel than gasoline, why does it cost more to buy diesel at the pump?" Where are the Teamsters on this one?

Development of the electric car was moving along but slower than anticipated. lithium-ion batteries were available, but mass production levels wouldn't be reached for two more years. The auto industry was finally tooling up for fabricating aluminum tubular frames, steel-drive trains, and lightweight, attractive, composite bodies. GE was smiling from ear to ear with a huge contract for electric motors. Word leaked out they were in prototype development for chargers that would be required by the millions. Outdoor installations for inclement weather seemed to be the only safety issue. Anyone familiar with potential stock market "winners" was probably investing in GE stock. Chevrolet was developing the "Volt"; I think Ford was working on a "Fusion" or something. Honda and Toyota were "hybrid happy." They were tooling up for two, four, and five passenger cars that would soon become available. More jobs!

Wind turbine farms began to appear along the northeastern shores even though the initial cost per KWH was higher to the consumer. More turbines and new huge solar collector "farms" sprouted in four western states. The need for American Indians to build casinos on their land was offset by the revenues they were raking in from these renewable energy installations. Two coal-fired generating plants had been shut down, and the output of one East Coast nuclear plant had been cut by about 10 percent. Two of the listed six Ohio River Dam generating stations were under construction in Ohio and West Virginia. This project was on time. More jobs!

The saltwater conversion project was gaining momentum. I assumed several missing government leaders and lobbyists may have provided the motivation for others to increase their interest in these new facilities. More jobs!

It appears a number of the engineering obstacles facing the high-stack generating stations were being dealt with. Two locations had been identified for installations, and negotiations were underway to procure the property. Groundbreaking could be scheduled in another year or two.

Now, it's time to review a most unpleasant subject: Congress. The Lists demanded that Congress pass several immediate pieces of legislation. They acted on reducing and closely supervising offshore drilling (they really had no choice), financial assistance to develop the electric car, and improvements for our highways and bridges. They continued dragging their feet on stopping space exploration and diverting the money to other, more immediate projects like developing ways to deal with meteors or asteroids that may be heading for the earth, diesel truck and bus emissions, improvements to the rail system, immigration (already mentioned), revising the National Health Care Bill, term limits and campaign-finance reforms, improved financial oversight of Wall Street with "teeth," modifications to the education system including improvements for our veterans, getting out of Iraq and Afghanistan, and getting into Iran. Nineteen targets were identified. They had previously received assignment letters but neglected to react. It was time for some of them to receive a motivational package! Additionally, assignment letters were sent to the White House chief of staff and the director of the National Economic Council to help "stimulate" response.

The administration attempted to reduce overall spending. The budget was established at $1.46 trillion, a reduction of 18 percent from a record $1.79 trillion. The intent was good, as long as they didn't eliminate funding for other items on The Lists. I wonder if they planned to honor all the IOUs ($2.5 trillion in treasury bonds are still considered an IOU) for the money they had already "borrowed" from the Social Security funds?

I made the mistake of sending a special communique to executives at the six big oil companies, thanking them for their 15 percent contributions to the energy escrow fund (BP was exempted from this contribution as long as they were absorbing the Gulf cleanup costs) and informing them of my displeasure with gasoline prices at almost $4 a gallon. I warned them, "Your name could appear on The Lists next year!" Apparently, one of the executives leaked the letter to the media, and it became an overnight sensation. A witch hunt began to find the originator of the document. Even with my many precautions, I really didn't want or need publicity, and someone could get lucky. About two months later, a courier delivered a case (four bottles) of expensive champagne to the executive. It was accompanied by a congratulatory note, allegedly from the editor of the newspaper who published the exposé. A special ingredient had been injected through the corks of two bottles. He, his latest love interest, and two other couples were found dead on his '85 yacht three days later, following one of his famous private parties. The media reported foul play was suspected.

It wasn't bad enough this extracurricular communique prompted several police agencies to accelerate their involvement; it also caused a tenacious investigative reporter to get interested in finding the alleged culprit(s) in these deaths. According to the reports he filed/published over the next several months, he actually got close on one occasion (even though he didn't realize it). After about four months, his search seemed to peter out, so I didn't need to send him a special congratulatory package. I took this as a bad omen and never sent out 'thank you' notes or follow up last chance warnings to targets. It made no sense to tempt fate.

I'm glad the security/intelligence agencies were spending time and resources gathering evidence to convict 'Wikileaks' founder, Julian

Assange, of espionage and not hunting for me. He'd fled to the UK, wound up in Switzerland and finally back to the US where he was confined to the same country club prison as Tom Delay. If they ever catch me, I doubt I'll be as lucky.

While doing some research on line I found an interesting ar-ticle that accused the military of using mind control techniques to convince several high ranking senators to approve military budget requests for the wars in Afghanistan and Iraq. Joe Lieberman was one of those mentioned. The program must work. Joe keeps voting to give them the money.

In June, 2013, a 7.8 quake hit about 25 miles north east of LA. This wasn't the 'big one', the mega-quake, everyone knew was coming eventually. The weather was getting more unpredictable. 17 hurricanes hit the US coast and more than six hundred tornados developed in April.

NASA and other agencies responsible for allocating taxpayer money were not responding very well to The Lists mandate for deferred spending on the space program. They had shifted some of the financial burden for flights to the space station to Russia but continued to spend $3 billion for another Mars mission and a new Rover. This unacceptable performance would be dealt with as specified by The Lists.

I almost forgot to mention Cuba. Mid-year we found out that Fidel was on his death bed. As part of his legacy, he declared Communism was still the best form of government for Cuba, but he also felt that diplomatic relations should be established with the US. Tourism and 'show me the money' were undoubtedly his motive. His replacement, his brother, wasn't in favor of this change, but agreed to it because of the 'mucho dinero' that would undoubtedly find its way into his personal offshore account. Of course the US government was happy to oblige. After all, the Cubans in Florida and throughout the US were voters who wanted to visit the old country and see old relatives and friends. Havana would be rejuvenated and the Cubans would be able to scour US junkyards for parts to keep their antique cars running. The rich and famous would now be legally able to buy Cuban cigars. Perhaps this new political arrangement would keep Cuba and Venezuela from teaming up against us.

The mistake I made in communicating with the oil executives prompted the authorities to continue their hunt for whoever was responsible for the threat. (It's still the contributions!) Then, following the "leaker's" demise, the search became a top priority for law-enforcement agencies throughout the States. Of course, the media had a field day with it: it became front-page news with every anchor person spouting how a terrorist organization was being hunted. I was amazed these same agencies had still not put two and two together, relative to the more than one hundred mysterious and untimely deaths in the past two years. True, not all the targets died immediately after eating, drinking, or handling something. A few of the items used as the "delivery system" (wine, cheese, chocolate, etc.) caused a time delay for the poison to take effect. I found this out much later in the process. Some of the delays were as long as five or six hours before death occurred. This explains why several of the targets died while driving, swimming, skiing, or jogging. One guy fell down a flight of stairs, one keeled over while delivering a speech, and another when blowing out candles on his birthday cake. Where is the NSA?

CHAPTER 20

LOOKING BACK: 2013, FOREIGN

January 2014

International results for 2013 were a mixed bag: some good, most bad! Unbelievably, the French were still PO'd about the retirement age being changed! They retained a multitude of benevolent compensation packages, compared to those in the United States, but were still unhappy. The UK, Greece, Spain, and Ireland experienced similar uprisings due to government cuts in domestic spending and services that began in 2010. It appears world economies were going through an elongated period of adjustment. Unemployment or immigration did not appear to be an issue in most of Europe, but terrorism was on the rise.

No one had anticipated the magnitude of the increased terrorist activities in Europe. The revolt in Egypt shattered years of complacency and quickly spread to Libya, Algeria, Jordan, and Syria. By media count, seventeen acts of terrorism in eight different geographical locations had occurred (not including Afghanistan or Iraq). A Muslim cleric, who supported killing US tourists, was assassinated during riots in Sanaa, Yemen. I have no idea who was responsible for the bombing of what the media called an alleged nuclear test facility in Iran, but I considered it an act of friendly terrorism. Other nonfriendly acts included the bombing of an American military hospital in Germany, a shopping complex in Russia (on Red Square, no less), a mosque in Spain, another mosque in France, a large chemical facility in England, a NATO installation in Prague, a government office complex in Pakistan, etc. The total death toll was more than 1,700 people, with many more injured. The good news was nuclear devices hadn't been used. About fifteen organizations claimed responsibility for these acts.

It seemed as if they were asking someone to award them a trophy for their efforts. Of course, the media obliged. These actions are what prompted Russia to stop their delaying tactics with NATO in developing a missile shield for Europe. NATO was also pressured to rethink their plan for troop withdrawal from Afghanistan.

When the United States reduced and then began to cut off financial aid to most of Europe, a substantial number of problems developed. Threats were made to throw out US military bases even though we still paid (actually we overpaid, considerably) rent for them. Of course, no one kicked us out. They had too much to lose. If we left, they would suffer financially and reduce their security at the same time. Not an attractive position to bring on themselves. It was interesting to note the International Red Cross stated they would continue to furnish first aid training and first aid kits to the Taliban fighters in Afghanistan. Yet the United States continues to fund the International Red Cross!

The Israelis slowed down (not stopped) their military efforts in the Gaza Strip and construction in Palestine. They claimed no involvement with the Iran bombings. (Ha!) I do know after a Somali pirate ship (a well-armed thirty-two-foot cabin cruiser) attacked a cruise ship with three hundred Jews onboard, six hundred pirates and thirty of their ships were obliterated in the next twenty-four hours. I wonder if "Captain Hook" got the message? The Israelis informed us they would do more but only if the United States agreed to provide them with more weapons and financial assistance. (Blackmail? Money well spent, if you ask me.)

North Korea and China appear to have grown closer following their fifth secret meeting. No one, including our multibillion dollar intelligence agencies, can find out what happened, what's happening, or what's planned. Even the Russians seem surprised by this turn of events. In UN meetings, China continues to side with other nations regarding keeping nuclear arms out of North Korea but continue to vote no when it comes to imposing sanctions on Iran. Is it because "junior" took over in China? Go figure!

The Chinese are beginning to take advantage of the power being generated by the US-built (and financed?) Three Gorges Dam on the Yangtze River. The distribution network (a "grid" of towers, transformers, and wires) is not yet completed, but power lines have made it to about 50 percent of the designated sites. The Chinese are becoming more competitive with the West every day. In a few more years, all countries are going to be competing with this new industrial giant. I found out the wind turbine industry is "owned" by the Chinese. Solar is probably next! They do have one problem: Chinese factory workers are committing suicide in record numbers. The high-speed manufacturing processes and frequent demands for overtime work is alleged to be the cause of more than twenty-five suicides a year. In 2011, a company called Foxconn, where they make popular electronic devices in great demand in the United States and other countries, had the worst record. The Chinese government refuses to openly comment on this situation. Inflation is becoming a major worry in China but has not become a crisis yet. Pollution has!

Central America, Brazil, Chile, Venezuela, and Argentina are becoming more and more involved in world affairs. Previously, little effort had gone into developing these countries. This all changed when mineral deposits the rest of the world craves were found here. Currently, large-scale construction activities are going on in many virgin areas, creating havoc with the ecosystems, and the "greenies" have begun to retaliate. More violence is being reported on a daily basis. Now, we have to consider international ecopolitics.

The Mexican problems had reached mammoth proportions. Thirty-seven thousand died in drug-related deaths over the past five years, and the Mexican authorities seem powerless to do anything to stop it. Illegal immigration seemed less of a problem for the United States, but drug cartels moved to the front of the "trouble line," followed closely by a different kind of terrorist activity on our southern border. All states bordering on Mexico are being targeted for drug activity and have experienced hundreds of deaths. Of course, the criminal element on the US side of the border is aiding and abetting the Latino enterprise. Some states have brought in their National Guard units to assist in halting this spreading disease, but even the Guard was being outgunned. US federal intervention is long overdue. It began in 2012, but 2013 needed to see a massive US retaliatory effort, and it could not be half assed. If the Mexican officials didn't like it, that's tough. They had their chance, and many of them became very rich by delaying action. The deaths of forty Mexican targets identified by The Lists had no effect on this problem. It was just too big! US military intervention has become a mandate.

In Russia, the missing four thousand pounds of HEU (highly enriched uranium) has not been found. They are diligently searching for it but with no results. We (the United States) vigorously began our own search. Iran was a good place to start. We, the public, will probably never know what goes on behind the scenes.

Iraq and Afghanistan are status quo. Nothing much has changed, except our military is officially out of Iraq. Pakistan continues to deny supporting terrorist groups in spite of the fact Bin Laden had been hiding in their back yard for more than five years before he was discovered and eliminated by US forces. On several occasions, American Muslims have been arrested or killed in Pakistan while attempting to detonate bombs. American-born Muslims, using their US passports, can easily cross borders in most countries and have become targets of Al-Qaida for conversion to radicalism when traveling abroad. According to NATO, Iran has jumped on this bandwagon and attempting to convert American Muslim travelers into terrorists. The ACLU continues to scream, "No profiling allowed!"

Internationally, there were sixty-one targets on The Lists for 2012 and 2013, but only forty-four deaths can be directly attributed to termination packages. Seventeen targets escaped for the time being. However, the packages were delivered and opened by nontargets. Twelve died accidentally. It appears these "accidental" deaths triggered a wave of additional killings. There were a number of terrorist factions affected, and some of them must have assumed these innocents had died at the hands of their internal enemies. So they retaliated by killing more than 150 others. Coincidently, several of those eliminated had been scratched as targets of The Lists because they were too difficult to get to. The Lists came out ahead in this situation. I thought of trying this tactic again at a later date.

The massive and sometimes violent protests in Egypt, Libya, Jordan, Yemen, Algeria, and several other Arab nations continue. Civilians are still demanding long-overdue reforms, and government officials have been replaced at all levels. In most instances, the military is not participating in or stopping the protests. The United States is remaining very quiet, at least publicly.

Nissan, a Japanese automotive giant, had great success marketing its all-electric automobile, the Leaf. Unlike the offerings from GM, Ford, Honda, or Toyota, the Leaf was truly an environmental breakthrough. The batteries on hybrids provide power for about forty miles, then a gasoline motor takes over. The battery-powered Leaf had a 250-mile range between charges. No gasoline, no pollution, no contest! They are now working on a sports car called the Esflow. Watch out, Tesla!

BMW continues its quest to become a key player in the all-electric automobile market. Their plant in Hungary now employs about three thousand people exclusively for building the new A—and B-class cars.

My vote still goes to the Tesla. It's a beautiful California all-electric sports car with extended range and speed. Unfortunately, it's still priced way above what's in my checking account. I'll just have to wait for a while to buy one. The years 2012, 2013, and 2014 are the years requiring the most dramatic changes according to the timetable in

The Lists. Obviously, there will be resistance, which will be met with promised motivational techniques. I doubt I will be taking much time off until late 2014 or early 2015.

FOLLOWING THE PERFORMANCE REVIEW FOR 2013 FOREIGN ASSIGNMENTS, MULTIPLE TERMINATION PACKAGES WERE SENT TO NONPERFORMERS. THEN, IN EARLY 2014, ASSIGNMENT LETTERS WERE MAILED TO THEIR REPLACEMENTS.

2014

CHAPTER 21

LOOKING BACK: 2014, DOMESTIC

January 2015

In 2014 I had my first brush with the law. In January, during a routine visit to storage room no. 1, the manager stopped me on my way in and told me the local police had been by inquiring about suspicious activity he may have noted. They were looking for possible illegal-drug distribution points. He told them all was well at his location. He was telling me about it, so I'd know what was going on in case they came around when I was there. Whoops! I hadn't anticipated anything like this happening. If the police decided to search my sheds, the boxes, eBay goods, or gift items were not a concern, but the vials of colored potions or the small canisters of powder (poisons) I kept in a locked box would be difficult to explain. I needed to find a way to improve my cover as a business as a buyer/seller on eBay. What would justify the need for two sheds? The inventory I had on hand wouldn't do it. I also needed some way to disguise/hide the dangerous stuff.

I had been doing quite a lot of traveling. Buying/selling items acquired at garage / yard sales, flea markets, and auctions provided a reason for my need to travel. I would need to expand my "business" and inventory to add legitimacy for the amount of space I occupied. I remembered years ago making golf ball "pulls" for the beaded chains on our ceiling fans and lights (we lived on a golf course). It was a pretty simple process requiring golf balls, beaded chains, snips, an electric drill, and two sizes of drill bits. I bought the needed supplies and took them to no. 1 shed and began making and selling the pull chains. Unbelievably, it wasn't long until I sold several hundred of them and had orders for about a hundred more. Home Depot actually bought a bunch of them. These "pulls" and my eBay items would not justify the need to rent a second storage room. So I kept looking for something to add to the business: something that would take up space but not take a whole lot of time. I thought of another golf item.

Just before I retired, I purchased a wall plaque to display some of my prized logo golf balls. It was made from a three-fourth-inch oak plank cut in the shape of a "green," partially covered with green felt, a hole with a flag stick, a "bunker," even a small tree (like the ones found on a Christmas train platform). Short tees were placed in pairs all over the "green." It held sixteen "logo" golf balls. I had made a few of these plaques to be used as prizes for a charitable golf outing sponsored by a club I belonged to. I figured they might be a saleable commodity, especially in a golfing community like The Villages. I gathered the necessary tools and supplies and moved them into no. 2. A table-mounted scroll saw, tees, oak panels, another electric drill and several bits, green felt material, sandpaper, Elmer's glue, fake trees, stain, paint applicators, white sand, a Shop-Vac, and bubble wrap joined the supply of empty boxes on the shelves.

A box of latex gloves (good to prevent getting stain on my hands as well as keeping fingerprints off termination items!), rags, dust masks and paper towels were added. I was good to go. It wasn't long before I had a dozen of the plaques completed (and sold!) and several dozen in process. A local golf shop had placed an order for twenty-four of them. (It made a mess in the shed, but it was a good cover.)

About four months after the manager warned me, I had a surprise visit from two local police detectives. I was listening to the radio while in the process of staining several golf ball plaques in shed no. 2. I had the door closed to keep the wind from blowing dust around. The solitude was broken by a loud knock on the garage door. When I slid the door up, the two knockers identified themselves as police detectives who wanted to ask me a few questions. Fortunately, nothing was being processed for motivational package deliveries. The potions and poisons were all safely hidden.

The two detectives and I stood around (I only had one chair) and chatted for about thirty minutes while enjoying a couple of Cokes. They explained the reason for their visit. Several complaints about possible drug activity at storage facilities throughout the city had been logged. After looking around no. 2 and a short visit to no. 1 shed, the detectives departed (after buying two of the golf ball plaques at a 25 percent discount). It took two cans of beers and a couple hours for my knees to stop shaking. The following month, the manager was able to get me side-by-side storage units, so I moved all my tools and supplies to a new home. I kept my workshops for almost five years while maintaining the cover of eBay purchases and sales, including selling hundreds of the ball plaques and about a thousand of the pull chains. The two detectives returned about six months later and bought three more of the golf ball plaques for gifts. (They received the customary 25 percent discount, of course!)

Apparently there was actually drug activity occurring at one of the storage facilities in town. A couple of months after the first visit by the detectives, I saw a news flash on a local TV station about the capture of four Asian Americans unloading a million dollars' worth of illegal drugs from a U-Haul truck into a storage shed already full of drugs and stolen merchandise.

On the home front, sometime during the middle of the year and unknown to me, Arnie and Barbara, friends of mine in The Villages, conspired to set me up on a blind date. We were introduced at the neighborhood backyard Memorial Day holiday BBQ. It was a nice evening with lots of laughs. We agreed to have dinner at the Cattle Baron Club the following week.

There are eighty thousand people in The Villages. Five thousand are single, and four thousand of them are women. I found I was viewed as a "valuable commodity." I was healthy and single, I had a full head of hair and most of my teeth, I was OK financially, I spoke clearly and appeared to be well educated, my "plumbing" still worked, and I could legally drive after dark! I was "what women want"!

We dated a couple more times: dinner, a movie, and dancing. It was fun, but it also could prove to be dangerous. One evening over dinner, I explained my eBay businesses to my date. She was a very nice gal with not much "baggage." She had two married kids, four grandkids, and she loved to travel. When she heard about the RV and the Honda, she suggested we take a trip ASAP. She also seemed infatuated by the flea market "stuff" and asked if she could help out sometime. That's when the alarms sounded (in my head), and I realized our relationship could create complications I'd rather not get involved in. I couldn't take the chance on distractions or detection. I had a difficult time just scheduling visits to see the kids and grandkids. I couldn't afford to try and hide my activities or gamble someone would accept what I was involved in, let alone assist me. I wouldn't take the responsibility for another person's safety. No! It would be best to remain a bachelor.

O.K., let's move on to what happened domestically in 2014. The top dogs at the SEC seemed to be having a difficult time monitoring or regulating the folks on Wall Street and at the leading financial institutions. I don't know if it was a lack of intellectual capability or simply a lack of motivation, but when it became common knowledge multi-million dollar bonuses had been awarded to eighty executives for Christmas, it left absolutely no doubt what had to be done. The Lists delivered special Christmas packages to nineteen SEC officials, Wall Street CEO's and, of course a few of the bonus recipients. Maybe they would finally get the message.

The Democrats had been defeated in the 2012 elections and the Republicans, assisted by the now influential Tea Party, had gained complete control of Congress as well as control of many states. The economy and unemployment began to show improvement. We still had the same inept, lame duck, executive branch, at least until the 2016 elections. One thing was for sure, the public was fed up with 'same ol' government rhetoric. However, as time went on, Congress was showing signs of what my Grandmother used to call "growing too big for their britches." True, they were addressing issues like health care, social security, financial reform, pollution, immigration, unemployment, renewable energy sources, Iran, Iraq, Afghanistan and North Korea. However, Congress displayed a negative attitude toward any open discussions over methods or new ideas. Compromise was forbidden and this became a divisive issue. The age old problem of 'cliques' was returning. The GOP had translated the election results to mean we had given them 'carte blanche' to do as they pleased. It became 'my way or the highway'.

There was little doubt the American voter had empowered the GOP to make changes, but voters wanted the best possible changes and that wasn't going to happen with a GOP dictatorship. My evaluation of US politics showed The Lists were definitely having an impact, but unless the government adopted a cooperative effort, failure was imminent. The Lists, once again, had to step in to try and correct this situation. The new Chairman of the GOP, along with nineteen prominent government officials, were sent assignment letters from The Lists in October 2013. They were given a year to get their act together.

The Tea Party's influence over domestic politics, while impaired by the negative GOP attitude, continued to grow. This disturbed several right wing groups who attempted to assassinate two of the TP leaders. Unfortunately, one attempt succeeded. Fortunately, it wasn't Sarah Palin but one of her staffers. This action only provided the TP with more influence. Of course, the mainstream media tried (unsuccessfully) to prove these actions were "staged" by the TP as a publicity stunt. (Another conspiracy theory!)

Public indignation demanded media personalities be given a kick in the behind for their so-called fair-and-balanced journalism (more like biased "tall tales"). Wolfe, Katey, Glenn, Peter, Dianne, Piers, Bill

O., and Racheal finally found themselves under long-overdue federal scrutiny, and network sanctions were issued for the first time in years.

"Bobblehead" entertainers like OW, Dr. Phil, Ellen, Charlie, Barbra, Bill C., Bono, Angelina, Ted, Antonio, David, and others were all taking "hits" from a disenchanted public. Turns out most of these self-professed experts really knew little more about the topics they espoused than the general public who they were attempting to influence. Their rationale? Who knows? It could be as simple as being important, again. By creating controversy (as their off-the-wall comments usually did), their names were back up in the lights or on ET. And it was much easier getting noticed than competing on *Dancing With the Stars*! Evidence that The Lists were having an impact came from an unlikely source. It was widely reported that one Hollywood mogul fled to Vancouver, British Columbia (Canada), and claimed refugee status. He stated there had been so many mysterious deaths in the entertainment community lately (actually there were fourteen in about nineteen months), he feared for his life. He needn't have worried; his name wasn't on The Lists.

The government was working overtime to figure out a way to tax us after we made the transition from gasoline to electric to power our cars. When we made this switch, the government would no longer be able to collect huge fees from oil companies for drilling on government lands or for permits to drill offshore. Nor would governments (county, state, and federal) collect gasoline taxes "at the pump." While there was little evidence that the feds were fully behind development of the battery-powered car, it was known they had dropped some of their stonewalling techniques, restricting development by "others," and thankfully, hydrogen fuel power had disappeared from the discussions.

Could it be because oil companies had begun to acquire businesses that would eventually wind up supporting the natural gas or electric-powered vehicles or, in some cases, actually manufacturing them?

The oil lobbyists were evidently reeducating our politicians. I have no idea how we were going to be taxed for not using gasoline, but there's no doubt it would happen. GE was probably going to make a fortune manufacturing, installing, and maintaining all those charging stations! More jobs! They'd probably wind up looking like today's parking meters and would collect a fee for each charge. Hey! What do you want to bet this turns out to be the replacement gas-tax revenue source?

Two large solar-generating stations and two wind farms out west and one hydroelectric generating plant on the Ohio River were getting closer to coming online. Construction management reported they would all be online by the end of 2016. The eighteen thousand employees working on these projects along with another nineteen thousand workers to be added in the next year would continue to build clean power facilities for at least the next six years. At the same time, nuclear and coal generating plants would be mothballed.

The 2010 Gulf oil-spill cleanup was just about completed. The new techniques developed proved to be very beneficial to this and future efforts. About 40 percent of the spilled oil was reclaimed and processed. Even Kevin's method actually worked. If there were a repeat, we'd be much better prepared. The tourist areas (the Gulf Coast beaches) had been restored within a matter of months. Scientists estimated sea life in the Gulf would return to prespill status by 2017, and the damaged wetlands would be cured by 2020. The "greenies" disagreed with this assessment, stating "normal" would not be achieved until midcentury. (I stopped eating Gulf fish and shrimp as a precaution).

The government oversight bureau that looked the other way and allowed the 2010 oil spill to happen, the MMS, was gutted in 2011 and then restored with a new "cast of characters." The bureau now has a split personality. One branch is responsible for permitting and fee collection. A second branch is for enforcement of safety standards. Hopefully, over the next generation, as the demand for petroleum products becomes less and less, offshore drilling and Arctic wilderness drilling will cease entirely.

We'll always need some gasoline, diesel, lubricants, and other petroleum by-products, but 90 percent of the normal demand should vanish when our cars/trucks/buses are converted to battery or natural gas power. With very little effort, I was able to find out three of the head men at the MMS in 2008, 2009, and 2010 had acquired property and other "things" worth about one hundred times more than their government salaries would have allowed. None of them had millionaire wives, and none had won the lottery. Their names were added to The Lists' package-delivery schedule early in the process.

"Notes" from The Lists were sent to the three successors as reminders of what could happen if they "looked the other way." I noted an increase in the number of actual field inspections performed by the enforcement branch of the MMS late in 2013 and ensuing years. One of the enforcers apparently didn't want to take a chance and resigned in September. This caused me more paperwork! I had to send an assignment letter to his replacement.

I should explain that I was becoming more and more adept with computers and use of the Net. They were extremely convenient for a multitude of chores, including information gathering, scheduling, and memory jogging. I rarely used my personal computer for any of The Lists' business. I frequently visited chat rooms or public libraries (in different locations) to conduct Lists business. It was difficult to avoid the thousands of CCTV cameras and not leave fingerprints on keyboards, but it was doable with the help of a few simple disguises and superglue. As a precaution, I never printed documents at these locations or used the same place more than once every five to seven months. I seldom spent more than an hour in one place. The only other electronic device I used was a cell phone. My personal phone was never used for The Lists' business. The NSA was watching. When necessary, I used disposable cell phones to communicate with my network of package distributors.

I continually looked over my shoulder and frequently imagined myself as Jason Bourne, fleeing FBI and CIA field operatives. I kept telling myself I was only doing what a lot of Americans felt like doing. Talk about stress!

While there were quite a few of The Lists' projects underway in 2014 and into 2015, the full effects would not be known for sometime. I wondered if the actions caused by The Lists were being reported in the president's daily briefing? I probably hadn't achieved that level of notoriety yet.

Just about everyone, including me, had given up on develop-ment of high-stack technology for wind turbine generation. A communiqué was sent to the necessary assignees to shift their emphasis (and money) and begin to develop tidal-generating facilities (hydrokinetic power) on both coasts in the next three years. This technology already existed and looked much more promising. Another new technology called space-based solar power was being discussed.

The situation on our southern border had become worse. Immigration, drugs, guns, terrorism, and violence had worsened in spite of the efforts of both the Mexican and US governments. The death toll continued to rise, and the zone was getting deeper into US territory. Even though our military was now involved, this would undoubtedly test the resolve of our government officials. I could only hope they were up to the challenge.

The money set aside for NASA and space exploration were finally being reallocated. "Mars and beyond" would have to wait. The Hubble Telescope was kept in operation. We maintained the space station and actually expanded it (with our financing and the help of our friends in Russia). A substantial portion of US funding would be diverted to locating potentially dangerous (to earth) meteors and asteroids. Development of a means to destroy or divert anything on a collision course with the earth (remember the Mayan 2012 prophecy, now 2032) was being discussed, but very little actual work had occurred. The Lists would only tolerate this delay for another year.

The scientific community was intrigued but at a loss to explain why the ocean waves are becoming bigger and stronger. Then *bang!* Another accidental discovery took place in 2014 when scientists in several countries, studying global warming, pollution, starvation, weather patterns, etc. stumbled across something they had not been looking for. Apparently, the combined effects of three large volcanic eruptions and seven earthquakes above 6.5 in a short period raised concerns and some curiosity. Could these natural disasters be caused by a shifting of the earth's crust? Scientists found no conclusive evidence that the crust had shifted any more than would normally be expected. They were a bit perplexed when they found the magnetic north, the guide post for compasses on planes, boats, the Boy Scouts, etc. had shifted about forty miles in one year versus four or five miles a year previously. Thank goodness for GPS navigation. They could only think that the earth's molten center was sloshing around more than normal. Doesn't that give you a warm (no pun intended), fuzzy feeling? However, these scientists discovered something considered far worse than the magnetic north phenomenon.

They found the earth's axis had shifted about four feet in the last three years! This was truly an aha moment. For this to happen, the earth's balance (its weight distribution) had to be altered. Just imagine a child's top spinning round and round. When it's touched or begins to slow down, what happens? It spins out of control, falls over, and stops. The earth is just like that spinning top. If our planet begins to wobble on its axis, war, global warming, and political or religious differences will quickly become insignificant. This news sure makes one pause to consider why NASA and "the boys" in Washington are pushing for a base on the moon and a mission to Mars. Do they know more than we're being told?

The good news is the earth is spinning at the same rate: one revolution every twenty-four hours (give or take a millisecond). Gravity has not changed. I'm still about ten pounds overweight! Our relationship with the sun and moon seems stable, and the tides are normal. The bad news is that the earth's axis has tilted about four feet. We desperately needed to find out what caused this to happen!

After almost a year of expedited scientific study, it was determined man had helped mother nature make this happen. Over millions of years, "Mother" has changed the course of rivers, caused continental plates to shift and mountain ranges to form. Then there were huge volcanic eruptions and massive earthquakes. Recently, there have been many man-made contributing factors, most dealing with mammoth construction projects starting as long ago as the building of the pyramids, then the Suez Canal, the Aswan Dam, the Hoover Dam, Lake Powell, Lake Mead, the Panama Canal, and most recently, the Three Gorges Dam in China. Each of these projects had caused a major change in the weight distribution on the earth's surface. Over the years, major cities have been built, each requiring the movement of billions of cubic yards of earth and concrete along with millions of tons of steel, wood, and other building materials.

We must consider global warming and the melting of the polar ice caps.

When these manmade changes are added to Mother Nature's activities the combined effect could contribute to the causes for the earth's axis shifting. This situation deserves analysis and answers from folks way above my pay grade. I guess I'll need to wait to see what steps are initiated to keep this phenomenon from escalating. I wouldn't count on witnessing any major projects involving the displacement of billions of cubic yards of earth or millions of tons of steal or concrete in the near future. None of the projects outlined in The Lists would contribute to this problem. Maybe it really is time to rethink a mission to Mars or other missions to try and locate a human friendly place to relocate to.

The founder of Wikileaks has appealed his conviction. Apparently his e-site continues to amass a fortune and he's spending it on the highest priced legal help he can find. The ACLU told him they weren't interested. How about that? The 'black and white' version of his plight is he's nothing more than a cyber terrorist. The 'gray' version is his first amendment rights have been violated, otherwise known as 'he's rich and has a cult following'. His minions continue to publish government secrets (can you believe that his source, a Private in the Pentagon, had access to so much classified material?) and I must confess to reading some on line information as it pertains to the business of The Lists.

Once again the Pacific Ring of Fire acted up. A 7.9 quake occurred in the Gulf of Alaska in August. The epicenter was 25 miles off shore. Sitka and Seward were almost wiped out by the tsunami that followed. More than eight hundred were killed. Fortunately, the 60 foot wave petered out before hitting the Hawaiian Islands. Hurricane season proved to be volatile. There were 22 full fledged storms that devastated most of the Caribbean Islands, the Gulf states and the Atlantic coast. Four hundred and twenty six tornados were reported in April. It could be that the work The Lists is trying to accomplish is too late!

The NSA claimed a major coup after capturing two home grown Muslim extremists trying to blow up the Stratosphere Tower in Vegas just before a large convention of Star Trek enthusiasts hit town. I'm still trying to figure out what they were trying to accomplish. Maybe they were just angry because they'd lost at the slots!

A federal judge in San Francisco surfaced as a pop-up target (#216) for The Lists in late 2013. She adamantly continued her belief that society was responsible for the crimes committed by minority or intellectually challenged criminals and that society should be held accountable, not the actual culprits. I believe the straw that broke the camel's back (in this case the camel's back was my patience) was when she released a murderer, a Hispanic guy who had raped and killed two teenage girls and their dates. The ACLU had taken the case to appeal (as they had with thirteen previous cases). The judge ruled that the DNA used for the conviction had been obtained illegally. A valid search warrant had been issued, but the officers who performed the search did not have the warrant with them. This was the fourteenth time in three years that this judge (the police and DA had christened her the bleeding-heart judge) had released a dangerous criminal on a minor technicality. All fourteen of those released were either black or Hispanic with records so heavy it took two clerks to carry their records into the courtroom.

Nine weeks after this episode, the judge received a box of expensive (See's) chocolate bonbons. An enclosed card stated it had been sent to her by a friend at the ACLU. What are friends for? Eleven hours after feasting on the chocolates, the judge died of "natural causes." We'll keep an eye on her replacement.

As far as I can determine, most federal-enforcement agencies continue to look for terrorist organizations as the "perpetrators" of numerous unexplained deaths of politicians, business leaders, financial executives, entertainment moguls, lobbyists, and several attorneys. Good luck with that!

CHAPTER 22

LOOKING BACK: 2014, FOREIGN

January 2015

Results of 2013/2014 for foreign locations showed little improvement over 2011/2012. It appears that changing the attitudes of corrupt foreign leaders is a more difficult task than in the United States. Between 2012 and the end of 2014, the reliable information I was able to gather showed The Lists to be directly responsible for a multitude of foreign deaths; most of the incorrigibles and another twenty-six nonperformers were immediately eliminated over the course of eighteen months. The Lists were indirectly responsible for about eighteen more deaths chalked up to collateral damage. (This number of deaths caused by The Lists may not be accurate. The more remote the location or the more censored the media, the more difficult it becomes to accurately quantify the number of deaths or the causes.) The loss of these lives was a drop in the bucket compared to the thousands being killed annually by their own leaders, drug traffickers, tribal territorial disputes, terrorist-group attacks, starvation, or for ethnic reasons.

The continued emphasis on eliminating US foreign aid was having a major impact in many locations. A few were a surprise. South Korea, Afghanistan, Yemen, Somalia, and even Israel were all crying foul. The Taliban presence in Pakistan continued. I'd bet that half of our representatives in Congress and probably 90 percent of our population had no idea how much money we were sending overseas (bribes included) to both friends and enemies. They do now! Becoming isolationists is starting to look attractive.

The financial ignorance of our representatives and ourselves doesn't stop here. We are finding out we owe so much money to so many foreign countries, we are on the brink of bankruptcy every day. Between China and the Saudis, we have outstanding trillion dollar IOUs. With rampant inflation in China, international financial stability could be at risk. A common currency for North America is slowly beginning to look attractive to the three countries involved. Then there's Japan and South Korea where we have billion-dollar deficits. About the only place we don't owe money is Antarctica! Of course, many of our friends (current or ex-allies) still owe us tons of money from as far back as World War II, but we don't talk much about that. Japan, France, England, Russia, Israel, the UAE, and a few more owe us billions, and we'll probably never see any of it repaid. Why do you suppose that is? With Japan still recovering from the devastation of the 2011 quake, we'll probably forgive their debt.

The new governments in Egypt and a few other Arab countries continue positive relationships with the United States, but they are tentative at best. If the people do not see the promised reforms within their country, watch out! Other nonfriendly regimes are waiting in the wings to infiltrate the temporary ruling party. Some Arab leaders have seen the light and quietly stepped down. I'm certain none of them left empty-handed, but at least they did leave. Jordan, Libya, and Syria are all undergoing a political makeover.

In spite of antigovernment protests, several regimes continue to hang on to power, and terrorism continues to flourish in Yemen, Afghanistan, Iran, Somalia, and Pakistan. Somali Islamist insurgents began attacking Uganda and are threatening attacks on the United States. This is one reason The Lists reserved the right to initiate terminations for what is called pop-up targets. These terminations were not foreseen, and the targets were not sent assignment letters: the transgressions were so severe, the attempt for immediate termination was more than justified. It's not yet clear which terrorist group was responsible for blowing up a large section of a diversion lock in the Suez Canal, but they managed to interrupt shipping for more than two months. Security was beefed up on both the Suez and Panama Canals after this episode. Oil prices went up again! Need to find out if BP could have been behind the scenes somewhere.

Terrorist activity was evidenced in a few unexpected locations. Hundreds of deaths resulted from bombings at tourist locations in Brazil, Argentina, and Chile: places that had civil unrest but had previously been untouched by terrorist action. Canada saw one of their ferries blown out of the water near Vancouver, British Columbia. A Tokyo airport terminal was heavily damaged by a bomb blast. Another bomb was set off at the Bolshoi Theatre in Moscow. No one was killed, but the theater was shut down for six months. Several bombs exploded in populated market places in Tangiers, Bombay,

Istanbul, and Beijing, killing hundreds. These terrorist activities seem to have no rhyme or reason. There were no demands made, and no one stepped forward to take credit. I think the culprits were only trying to create fear in a society already uncertain of the future. This they undoubtedly accomplished. The "good news" (if anything associated with these events could be considered good news) was nuclear or dirty bombs hadn't been used.

The situation in Mexico has shown some improvement since the US Marines were deployed along the border and were given unlimited access to many areas across the border. The drug cartels aren't dead, but they have taken tremendous losses in Mexico and Central American countries. Venezuela has joined the list of "bad actors." The Canadian border is still full of holes, but the RCMP has shown much improvement recently. This is probably because the Canadians don't want the troublemakers from south of the border entering their territory.

The Russians (and us) were still trying to find the four thou-sand pounds of missing HEU. Apparently, the terrorists didn't have it or hadn't figured out how to use it. Rumor has it the Israelis are now being involved.

The situation in Iraq was about the same. Our troops had been pulled out, but we still had quite a number of advisory personnel and "contractors" on the ground. Afghanistan was another story. The majority of the troops and weapons removed from Iraq were now relocated to Afghanistan. It appears we learned nothing from the Russians' defeat there or our own history from Vietnam. The border with Pakistan did nothing to deter terrorist activity. Terrorists moved freely on both sides of the border, and we seemed unable to do anything about it. (It's the terrain, dummy! Where did we hear this before?) Yemen is in the same class as Pakistan. I still think ol' Harry Truman had the right idea. We're allowing the United States to turn into a nation of benevolent sissies!

Someone (no one was taking credit for it) blew up another nuclear facility being constructed in Iran. Iran claimed it was only a power-generating plant. I'll bet! It really was good news when the so-called president of Iran, the five-foot-five-inch loudmouthed moron who claimed the holocaust was a hoax and who was always trying to grow a beard, was killed in an accidental plane crash. I wonder if the ayatollah had anything to do with it? The Lists didn't.

The Chinese are not bending, even a little bit, on the currency or pollution issues. It appears their sole intent is to dominate the industrial/civilized world, and they're well on the way to accomplishing this task. In the '50s, US citizens started to buy cheap, poor-quality Japanese merchandise. In the '70s, Japanese quality was head-and-shoulders above what was made in the United States. In the '80s, the US quality began to improve, and in the '90s and '00s we were back in the game. Even though we were making quality goods, we began to buy more and more merchandise from China and South Korea because of pricing. In 2014, we're still purchasing more and more from these two countries. Taxes and tariffs do not deter the huge volumes of imports into the United States. Heavy manufacturing in the United States has all but disappeared. Are we dumb or what?

China is continuing to exert some economic pressures on the United States and others by flexing their newfound muscle in the Panama

Canal Zone. Their accumulated acquisitions, shipyard growth, and cross-country railroad facilities in the area (along with their apparent influence on government officials) are creating anxiety in the international shipping community. We may get a temporary reprieve in this area. China's economy is showing signs of stress, and the government is purposefully slowing down unnecessary spending.

NATO is finally showing some signs of life. On three separate occasions during the year, NATO forces responded admirably to calls for help in Europe. Hopefully, this trend will continue and expand to other areas, especially in Africa. The historic 2011 alliance between Russia and the NATO allies to erect a missile-defense shield to help stem the Iranian nuclear threat continues to show signs of a successful coalition. (I still believe it would be much easier and cheaper to just invade Iran and eliminate the threat once and for all.)

The first break in the search for the missing HEU from Russia happened in March. Two Armenians boarded a train in Tbilisi, Georgia (no, not the state), and pulled a box of Marlboro cigarettes out of a railroad worker's toolbox. The cigarette box held nuclear-bomb-grade uranium. Undercover operators had been alerted to the presence of radioactive materials and caught the alleged terrorists red-handed. Several high-profile arrests followed. There was only about an ounce of material involved, but its value could have been as much as $1.5 million depending on who wanted it and why. There's still about 3,999 pounds and 15 ounces still missing! That's a lot of money!

The Russians have been ominously quiet lately. They remain the lifeline to the space station. Of course, the United States still funds most of this effort. The resurgence of the Communist Party in Russia seems to have been halted: at least for the moment. Disney hasn't opted to build a theme park anywhere in Russia, but Chernobyl is now open as a tourist attraction. Oh well. We have the site of the Twin Towers, and they have the site of a nuclear disaster. The Russian Mafia is still operating, but like the '30s, '40s, and '50s here in the United States, they are making a transition to the "quieter" forms of crime like gambling, arms, drugs, and money laundering. Western Europe, Russia, and Turkey continue to employ thousands on an energy pipeline, linking their nations. Some news reports state the reason things are so quiet in this region is the Russian Mafia is one of the investors.

A sale of $60 billion of arms, mostly jet fighters, by the United States to Saudi Arabia has caused quite a stir in the international community. The United States believes it will be a positive step in an unstable region. Iran especially does not like this deal. Of course, Iran could play the same game and provide our unfriendly neighbor, Venezuela, with some Russian arms we wouldn't want them to have. Ah! The game of geopolitics! Or could it be a nuclear chess game?

Venezuela was beginning to be a real pain in the butt! Chavez is a clone of his ex-buddy in Iran and repeatedly threatens the United States with everything from cutting off our oil supply to nationalizing holdings of US companies. He'd already initiated this activity for those who would not agree to pay exorbitant bribes. I wasn't able to find a direct link between Mr. Chavez and Bob Dudley, the CEO of BP, but there were quite a few political/financial rumors floating around the Net. I'm a believer of "where there's smoke it's probably a good thing to find an extinguisher." I set the wheels in motion to find a way for The Lists to exert some influence in this situation.

I neglected to acknowledge the environmental progress made in some European countries. A few of the Scandinavian countries have become almost 100 percent powered electrically by the wind. Even Holland has converted to wind-generated power for the pumping stations that keep the farmers dry. Of course, they kept the diesel-powered units for backup purposes. (The traditional and very picturesque windmills have not been used for this purpose for many years.) France, Spain, and Germany have begun investing heavily in wind turbines. Coal-fired boilers and nuclear plants are no longer being built in these countries. I hope they will begin curtailing the use of the existing polluting facilities in the near future.

The EU, the IMF, and the United States are all participating in continuing efforts to bolster the European economy and stabilize the euro. Bailouts seemed to have become a norm, to make up for incompetence at all levels of business, banking, and government. More and more countries have implemented drastic cutbacks in their social programs. Education, retirements, health care, etc. have all been effected, and public unrest continues to grow. Riots have become commonplace.

Industrial growth in Europe was classified as minimal, yet the published numbers regarding unemployment continued to go down. Perhaps the expansion of efforts in the nonpolluting energy sector was helping this situation, or maybe it was the transition to electric automobiles that was underway. Without a doubt, the need for security personnel had grown substantially just about everywhere.

India had hired thousands of workers to become janitors for cleaning up the entire country. They are generating tons and tons of recyclable material. A large US corporation, Waste Management, has been assisting in this effort. I hope India isn't continuing to dump what's leftover into the sea like many other countries (the United States and China!) are doing. This cleanup project will take years to complete, but it will improve sanitary conditions and the quality of life for everyone in India. Who knows? Indonesia could be next!

The UK, Canada, and Australia appear to be rolling along with only modest internal strife. Australia has uncovered a wealth of natural resources in the center of the island nation where very little population had existed previously. They're advertising for immigrants willing to relocate and go to work in this newly developing area. The packages the Australians are offering are very attractive for young men or women. If I were forty years younger, I'd have seriously considered taking advantage of this offer. Chile and Argentina are in a similar situation. I wouldn't be surprised to see areas in Africa begin this type of growth in the near future. Vast areas of Africa remain untouched, relative to available mineral deposits and other natural resources. The year 2015 will be a turning point for a number of nations. The social / industrial dynamics of the world were changing dramatically because of new energy sources, pollution controls, raw material requirements, job growth, and even immigration regulations. Prosperity was becoming available for most of the world to take advantage of. Observations should be made by the UN (?) in the next few years to see which countries had enough foresight to take advantage of this situation and to assist them whenever possible. Population continued to grow at alarming rates in many countries. This will be the next social crisis.

The law-enforcement agencies of Europe don't seem to have the "mysterious and untimely" deaths of so many of their citizens at the top of their to-do list. Perhaps it's the small number involved when compared to the thousands dying daily.

We all need to recognize a simple fact: our planet is not nearly as large as it once was, or as safe!

2015

CHAPTER 23

LOOKING BACK: 2015, DOMESTIC

January 2016

Year 2015 demonstrated The Lists' message was continuing to have a measurable impact on the lives of folks in the United States. Many good things happened and are continuing to happen. Where should I begin this annual summary? Don't misunderstand; not everything is coming up roses, yet. It was very gratifying to see any improvement, since there was a Democratic Executive Branch still in power paired with a Republican Congress. The intervention provided by The Lists, last year, assigning twenty congressional GOP leaders to cease their dictator strategy, to discuss and, yes, even compromise, was working: they avoided grid lock. Only two terminations were needed to get their attention! The Chairman of the Appropriations Committee and Majority Leader both decided to do the right thing after the loss of two highly valued staff members (in spite of the best efforts of the law-enforcement agencies to prevent it from happening). The question being asked by analysts was "If this mixed marriage government can accomplish so much, what results can we expect when a single party controls the government?" I expected to see politics as usual curtailed somewhat during 2015 as the parties began preparations for next year's election. However, my expectations of seeing an improved governing philosophy didn't happen.

A new (according to Republicans and Tea Partiers) or revised (according to the Democrats) national health care plan was put into effect. The Democrats decided to back off their effort to stall this legislation. Obviously, the DNC was going to use this success as part of their campaign strategy for the 2016 elections. The Supremes finally ruled out mandatory participation. Yet it's estimated 90 percent of our citizens are buying the insurance and are covered for just about everything. (The ACLU was very unhappy that illegal aliens would not be included). It was decided that instead of increasing the rate of federal income tax (ala Canada) to pay for the program, those opting to purchase the coverage would pay a policy premium based on a specific percentage of their annual income averaged for the preceding five years (much like benefit calculation for Social Security). Premiums are recalculated annually for a continually rotating five-year period. The more you make, the more you pay, but the premiums are very reasonable for the coverage provided. Members of Congress must participate in this plan. All military personnel and their families are included in the plan at no cost to them while on active duty and after reaching full retirement (now at twenty-five years of active duty). Insurance or pharmaceutical companies better not be found trying to cheat the system. Those opting to not purchase the insurance were usually treated as second class citizens (doctors and hospitals were not guaranteed payment), but they still received medical care and were billed for it. Collection activity for those who failed to pay for the services was very aggressive. Totally disabled (unable to work) individuals were covered at no cost as was anyone over the age of seventy-five. It became extremely difficult to prove an inability to pay for insurance or claim disability. Was it fool proof? No! But it was much better than what we had before.

This approved health care payment initiative seems to have paved the way for an in-depth discussion regarding the proposal for a flat income tax. While not introduced as a debatable issue in the legislature in 2015, I'm certain we'll hear more about this in the next couple of years.

With unemployment continuing to drop, monthly, the govern-ment's costs for sustaining the health care program will continue to drop. During 2014 and early 2015, The Lists found it necessary to convince a number of AMA members (mostly doctors and administrators), insurance and pharmaceutical company executives and a few lobbyists it would be best for their own health to adopt the new plan. A few didn't subscribe to this philosophy and are no longer involved.

Illegal immigration hasn't been eliminated, but the staggering number of illegal aliens crossing our borders in the '90s and '00s has been significantly reduced, especially those coming from Mexico. The process for legal immigration has been streamlined and contains specific, easily met requirements and timetables. If anyone wishes to legally enter the United States, they can do so in about three months if they meet the criteria. The economic situation south of the border continues to improve with more and more US and Chinese investments taking place. More and better paying jobs have been made available to the Mexicans and their quality of life is improving. The drug problem continues, but with the presence of the US and Mexican military at the border, the cartels are finding it easier to ply their wares elsewhere. A number of foreign countries have seen an increase in drug traffic and the attendant crimes associated with drugs. It wouldn't surprise me to see these countries asking the United States (not the UN!) for assistance in the near future.

As unemployment in the United States continues to drop, new construction projects and expanding or new manufacturing facilities are advertising for employees in every part of the country. Infrastructure refurbishment (bridges, highways, water and sewer systems, parks, reservoirs, etc.) reminiscent of the '30s TVA and WPA programs are in process. Contractors for the new type of energy generating plants (hydroelectric systems on our rivers, grid improvements, fiber optic installations, wind and solar energy farms, etc.) are hiring and training busloads of workers.

The on going conversion from gasoline/diesel vehicles to natural gas or battery power has created thousands of jobs almost overnight. Everything from supplying lightweight composites for automobile bodies to the components for the lithium-ion batteries, manufacturing/installing thousands of charging meters or retrofitting gasoline engines for natural gas is creating manufacturing jobs and most of these jobs are being kept in the United States.

The federal agencies overseeing most of these programs began offering large bonuses for employee inspired innovations; both technical and production improvement ideas will be considered.

While a substantial portion of the wind turbine and solar energy hardware is imported from China, inside the United States the installation, operation and maintenance of this equipment is creating permanent jobs for US workers. With the growing medical problems and deaths caused by pollution in China, the need for nonpolluting vehicles is a very high priority for them. This need is creating a sort of balance of trade between China and the United States; we send them nonpolluting cars and trucks and they send us wind turbines and solar panels. Not a bad deal for both nations. In 2014, GM and Ford began manufacturing electric cars on a limited basis. Then GE, twelve electric utility giants, UPS, FEDX, USPS and nine major cities in the United States placed orders for 250,000 electric vehicles to be delivered in 2015 and 2016. This represents a small percentage of annual domestic vehicle sales. However, it appears that the floodgates for electric vehicles have finally begun to open. Seven large cities and a multitude of utility companies have placed orders for about one hundred thousand natural gas vehicle conversions, which can happen almost immediately. China wants as many vehicles as we can manufacture and willing to pay premium prices for them. The second area for employment growth associated with the electric car is the manufacture of batteries. The third area is the manufacture and installation of battery charging equipment and natural gas filling stations. At current and forecasted growth, by 2020, sustainable employment directly attributable to the electric car will be about seven hundred thousand jobs with another two hundred thousand temporary jobs (for another five to ten years) for natural gas conversions.

This is great news! These vehicles not only create jobs and eliminate polluting emissions, they will also eliminate our continued dependency on foreign oil, often purchased from hostile countries who use profits to fund terrorist activities.

OPEC and the Big Oil companies in the United States aren't very happy with the dramatic drop in revenue because of this transition, but it's not all bad news for them. Most of these companies were smart enough to diversify in the 2013/2014 time frame and invested in this new industry. Their CFOs say it's a matter of covering all bets! So the vultures are not really circling their corporate offices.

Personally, 2015 was a year of highs and lows. The success of The Lists seemed to be assured, at least domestically. The verdict was still out regarding the international scene. Preparation and mailing of a number of justifiable termination packages or assignment letters was almost automatic by now. An individual's success or failure to achieve results was easily evaluated, thanks in large part to information supplied on the Net. I attended college graduations. In Ohio, Buddy and I cheered as Amanda received her diploma. Then, in Florida, Tim, Cheryl and I proudly watched as Christa graduated. Then it was back to Ohio for Christopher's high school commencement. Several family holiday get-togethers allowed me to temporarily return to the normal role of Dad or Grand Dad. I made time to go on a three-day fishing trip with two sons and a three-day camping trip with the youngest grandson's boy scout troop. I polished the Vette and entered a people's choice car show. I won a very nice second-place trophy! Walter and Diana had made the move to The Villages. We traveled together in our Vettes, shared dinners, and hit the little white ball frequently. I kept my clubs clean and the golf cart ready to go. The members of my foursome enjoyed taking my money. I think my best score was a 107! I couldn't stop looking over my shoulder.

I hit a low point three weeks before Christmas. One of my golfing buddies, a great friend for fifteen years, died unexpectedly from a heart attack. When I attended the funeral services, the realization hit me; I was nearing "super senior" status. I wasn't exactly on borrowed time, but it was probably the right time to think about doing some of the things on my bucket list, reducing my workload from The Lists and consider finding a successor.

In between social engagements I was able to take some time to reflect on what I'd accomplished over the past five or six years and what I was planning for the next four or five years. I didn't think of myself as a terrorist, but I realized I was no longer a normal citizen. Nor was I a mercenary, a soldier, a politician, a vigilante, or a policeman. So what am I? I'm certain some would call me an assassin, and I guess I'd have to agree that's justified, but I think I'm in a different category. I'd really prefer a new title: something like geopolitical activist. How's that sound? I have no desire for vengeance. Vengeance is getting even for something. I didn't want to get even: I wanted to win!

The kids invited me to spend Christmas with them, but I decided to avoid the mayhem this year and take a seven-day holiday cruise (no. 3 on the bucket list) in the Caribbean with a bunch of my retired friends and neighbors from The Villages.

Jim and Jan, my neighbors and Buckeye buddies in The Villages, orchestrated the trip. Thirty-one of us decided to board a Holland America ship at Fort Lauderdale, sail (I wonder why we still say *sail?*) around the islands in the Gulf, eat gourmet meals, swim with the dolphins, eat some more, dance a little, gamble a little, eat some more, buy trinkets from island shops, buy booze from the duty free and, in general, have a jolly Christmas and festive New Year. Thanks to the efforts of Joe and Grace we were always on the go. We arrived back at the port of Tampa in early January 2016. I missed the Rose Bowl game but returned in time for about twenty college-bowl games on TV (there seems to be a bowl game for every product and city in the United States), the Super Bowl and the beginning of ads for November's election. I didn't get much rest, but we had a great time, and I was able to forget about The Lists for a while.

My first New Year's resolution was to be certain not to get caught. My second was to find someone to take over my duties as administrator for The Lists.

Resolution #1 was becoming more difficult. The FBI, NSA, Homeland Security and Interpol, Scotland Yard and the CIA were teaming up to locate what they claimed was an international terrorist group operating autonomously and not a conspiracy as originally believed. Their objectives were still unclear, but most of the targets had been prominent citizens, leaders involved in everything from politics to investments. These agencies had interviewed hundreds of persons of interest, but, as yet, were not focused on any group or individual. They continued to follow the traditional investigative protocol: (1) find a link between the victim and the killer; (2) find a motive; (3) verify suspects alibi. I didn't feel nervous about the way they were proceeding.

I know they didn't realize it, but they were actually making my job much more difficult. The publicity given to these 'mysterious and untimely' deaths was making targets skittish about accepting gifts or even eating out. Several of these prominent people who had received an assignment were now 'brown bagging' their lunches to the office or to meetings. This was definitely an indication The Lists was having an impact, at least in the US.

There was some good news to report for a change. No major quakes had hit anywhere and the number of hurricanes had dropped to seventeen. They were still severe, but there were less of them. Also, the number of tornados in April dropped to two hundred and sixty four. Perhaps the efforts to reduce the negative effects of pollution were actually having a positive effect after all.

CHAPTER 24

LOOKING BACK: 2015, FOREIGN

January 2016

As reported for the domestic portion of 2015 happenings, documentation gathered regarding the foreign situation was finally showing signs of improving. The Lists were definitely having an impact, even though not as pronounced as domestically.

Terrorism remained at the forefront of the international scene. Somalia and Syria are the new breeding ground for international terrorist organizations. The $80 billion US intelligence agencies have stated that Afghanistan and Pakistan are no longer their highest priority but neglected to state how they plan to tackle this new situation. There were sixteen certifiable terrorist attacks in Europe originating from these two countries in 2015, proving that much of this part of the world is vulnerable to an attack. I have not found one piece of information showing an increase in antiterrorism efforts in any of these locations.

Maybe they need to enlist the help of Zorro. The Somalis have, as yet, not launched their promised attack on the United States. The Lists delivered four termination packages to Pakistani officials and two to officials in Syria. I could not figure out if anyone was an official in Somalia. There has been no confirmation of the packages being delivered, let alone being successful, but I continue to hope.

The rebellions in Yemen, Saudi Arabia, and Iran were finally beginning to see progress. Terrorist activity declined, and leadership was allegedly undergoing changes. The people wanted a democracy and pledged to making it happen.

The Mexican president and his vaqueros fall into a kind of Shakespearian category, "much ado about nothing," except it should read, "nothing much about ado." Their government continued to state they were doing everything possible to stem the tide of violence, illegal immigration, and drug trafficking on the border. In spite of the increased employment in Mexico (it's the economy, stupid), easier access to legal entry into the United States, and military intervention, violence continues. It's like a losing football team. After three or four losing seasons (and more than thirty-seven thousand dead people), what happens? The coach is fired! It's time to fire the coach in Mexico. In this case, the coach is probably the AG. I think his name was Arturo Chavez. He received an assignment from The Lists in a letter in 2014. Unfortunately, his performance level improved 0 percent. As a matter of fact, as the results show, he went into the negative numbers. Based on the perceived complexity and enormity of the problem, The Lists had allowed some extra time for improvement. Since it didn't happen, it became necessary to initiate a coaching-staff change. Mr. Chavez remains in his position, but two of his lieutenants had to be replaced.

Hopefully, we'll see improvements next year. Terrorists show no interest in Mexico at this time, except as a route into the United States.

Tourism to/from Cuba took off like a bottle rocket. The only commodity Cuba had to sell was tourism (bimbos, beaches, bars, cigars, and casinos), but the Cubans must have been saving their money for years, and when visiting the United States, they began to buy everything in sight. Yes, the junkyards frequently heard shouts in Spanish as another treasured antique automobile part was found. Inevitably, guns and drugs would begin changing hands, but that was a few years away.

An unanticipated development occurred regarding Russia. A highly placed Russian diplomat at the UN suddenly became a very rich playboy (perhaps he'd found some of the missing HEU to sell or brokered a deal for arms to one of the emerging terrorist groups) and blatantly began abusing his immunity status (above-the-law syndrome). This occurred almost immediately after his involvement in finalizing the START nuclear treaty with the United States. In UN sessions, he followed his directive to avoid commenting on Iran and North Korea (siding with China) and to prevent sanctions against either country. He became a pop-up target, and The Lists sent him a very expensive congratulatory package of caviar and vodka. About a week later, he was replaced at the UN. His successor received an assignment letter the following week. I hope he had it translated accurately.

Russia appears to be preoccupied with oil, aluminum, natural gas pipelines, and taking our money to keep the space station alive. Is this the calm before the storm, or are they actually moving toward a more peaceful coexistence? Or is it simply because they have found out that money does talk?

Just a short note: while vigilance was heightened regarding the personal safety of hundreds of dignitaries, it seems that no one thinks it necessary to interfere with the postman. The assignment letters from The Lists always make it through!

It was interesting to read publications from a number of sources, including the secretary general of the UN, that the United States "had lost its position regarding the moral high ground in international affairs." How about that? The translation of this statement simply means we'd stopped paying the bills for the UN! If we'd lost the high ground, I wonder who had won it? After what seems like a hundred years of stupidity, the host country for the UN (us) finally changed some of the rules for visiting diplomats. These rules, established years ago by the Vienna Convention on Diplomatic Relations, were actually a license to steal (or in some cases, kill). I'll bet what really got them PO'd was they were no longer exempted from having to pay parking tickets, and some of the diplomatic privileges at restaurants and sporting events had been taken from them. They could still probably get away with murder, but they couldn't legally double park while doing it!

It was well beyond time (and patience) to deal with Iran's nuclear aspirations. Several of their so-called power plants had been blown up in the last two years, but they plodded on. So in 2015, three more of their nuclear chiefs were eliminated (three had already been killed or had fatal accidents in the preceding two years). The Lists accepts responsibility for only one of the 2015 terminations. The chief of nuclear ops, Ali Salehi, was our target, but we welcomed the other two, regardless of who was responsible. Time will tell if this has deterred Iran's ambitions. Americans are persona non grata in Iran. My goodness! Iranians are actually allowed to "profile"! United States, AG, and ACLU, take note!

The Saudis continue to be a work in progress and are being affected by the situation in Egypt, Libya, and Algeria. We're not sure at any given time if they are for us or against us. It's like the CIA knowingly putting up with a double agent in the hope he/she will provide them with something of benefit. (Almost what my captors are doing with me!) Of course, it's difficult to reprimand an entity that holds a mortgage on your country and still ships oil to our refineries, although not so much as a few years ago. I had no idea how successful it would be, but two highly placed sheiks were sent assignments in 2015. I couldn't imagine them leaving their fancy palaces, but who knows? So I used a very expensive courier service to deliver the letters to their palaces or locate them in a tent the size of the one used for the Barrett-Jackson automobile auctions at some desert oasis. In either event, if they continued to support the "bad guys," terminations would be issued next year.

China continues to be an enigma. What are they doing? Who are they supporting? What aren't they doing? Who aren't they supporting? They keep on truckin' with their industrial revolution, aggressively controlling population, and doing very little about pollution. They continue a $150-billion project (lots of jobs) that will transfer water from the dammed-up Yangtze River (the Three Gorges Dam is a recently completed $25 billion project) to arid locations in the north. They don't seem to feel any regret that their polluting the earth has had something to do with global warming. Apparently, their nuclear program, whatever it is, remains on track. At least our satellites are giving us some details as to what's going on behind the Great Wall. One thing is very well known: they keep on buying US treasury securities. We now owe them more than $900 billion. They are starting to buy our electric cars, at least until they learn how to clone them. The Politburo Standing Committee, the real power in Communist China, spent much of their energy and resources hacking into Google because of detrimental comments about government officials. Wow! Because of the First Amendment, all we have to worry about is Wikileaks! Rumors are flying about China's growing interest in the Panama Canal. They've already announced financial backing for a $3.4 billion Caribbean hotel/casino complex on Nassau called Baha Mar. We'd better keep a close watch on Cuba!

In North Korea, "Junior" might have some say on what's going on, but I think Daddy is still pulling the strings. The United States continues to use sanctions but to little effect. We're still not giving up. The newest sanctions include such drastic measures as a refusal to ship luxury items or gourmet foods to the ruling elite in Pyongyang. There's no way to get to either of the Kims or any of the Politburo members. But like with Russia, there's always hope of reaching a diplomat or two at the UN. Eliminating a diplomat at the UN is about at par with swatting a mosquito, but it's the thought that counts. I'll consider this as an objective for The Lists next year and try to select targets whose loss would be the most detrimental. It's beyond my realm of understanding, but now there are strong rumors that South and North Korea are looking at the benefits of reunification.

The Lists had steered clear of attempting to influence decisions made by our friends in South Korea, but it looks like it could be time for a change of philosophy if they start holding hands with their northern neighbor.

It's widely reported our Central American friend in Venezuela continues on his path to nationalizing all foreign interests within the country. This was an oversight on my part: I thought he'd already succeeded in accomplishing this.

It might be in everyone's best interest to allow this to happen as long as he stays out of Cuba. If Cuba and Venezuela team up, we could see a different kind of cold war beginning. Anyone from the CIA listening? Does the Bay of Pigs ring a bell?

Overall, the international economic situation is still in a state of flux. The dollar, the yen, the euro, all currencies appear to be stabilizing, but none are really secure. The EU, the IMF, the Federal Reserve, and other banking institutions remain vigilant but are still pessimistic at this time. However, the continued growth of industry in the United States and steady reduction of unemployment seems to be having a positive effect on the economy in other countries. The bailouts provided by the EU and IMF seem to have been the proper move. Most European countries are showing signs of economic recovery. The effects of the US reduction or elimination of financial subsidies continue to have a lingering negative effect but are less and less as time goes by.

Global warming continues to be of prime interest in much of the international community. Several small islands and a few coastal villages have all but disappeared due to the rising level of the oceans. Food and water are not a concern today, but European countries are growing nervous about what may happen in the next ten years.

While signs of improvement are noted, it looks like the problem areas for the next three or four years are going to be the following:

1. China-pollution and currency value

2. North Korea—aggressive pursuit of nuclear missiles and reunification with South Korea
3. Pakistan, Syria, Somalia, and Afghanistan—terrorist support
4. Iran—Nuclear arms and terrorist support
5. Venezuela—arms, drugs, and nationalization
6. Mexico—violence associated with arms, drugs, and immigration
7. Egypt—establishing a true democracy
8. Libya—still a work in process

The diplomatic relationship between the United States, the UK, Canada, Australia, Spain, Germany, Italy, Israel, Japan, Brazil, Argentina, Chile, South Africa, and the Scandinavian countries remains strong.

US ties with Egypt, Libya, India, Saudi Arabia, Mexico, Russia, and France were still considered tentative.

2016

CHAPTER 25

(LOOKING BACK-2016-DOMESTIC)

January, 2017

This was a difficult year for me personally, but it was rewarding on a professional level. It began with the normal requirements for managing The Lists and ended with me recuperating from a broken ankle while in the process of training my replacement. Here is a brief summary of the significant happenings for 2016.

Beginning in 2013 the legislative branches of the federal government were controlled by the Republicans (with the assistance of the Tea Party) and they were continuing to implement needed changes. The only thing that could have prevented them from succeeding was infighting or an internal power struggle. (This could easily occur as the GOP began to deliberate who would be selected to run for president.) If this happened, their ability to override a presidential veto would be impaired. The Republicans would undoubtedly be supported by the American public unless they did something really stupid.

At the beginning of the electoral process, the list of candi-dates had to be trimmed from twenty to twelve. The GOP had given up on Mitt after his poor showing in 2012. Newt and Marco had moved to the front of the pack. Everyone waited anxiously to see if the Democrats nominated Hillary or another female. August through October were interesting, to say the least. The November results were announced and, because the Democrats had lost all credibility with the voters, the election was a lo-sided victory for the GOP and TP candidates. In spite of an all female Democratic ticket, Marco (a descendent of Mexican immigrants) was elected president and Rick Santorum was now the VP. Quite an interesting combination. Most of the GOP and TP jumped on the band wagon. Good old Rush was at a loss for words. Glenn started knitting another Christmas sweater. Sarah went moose hunting and Newt returned to his part time gig as a consultant/commentator on FOX. If the GOP honored their commitment, the next four years should be something great.

The banking and business communities continued to meet their moral and legal obligations. I firmly believe the actions of The Lists over the past few years had something to do with this improved behavior.

A media hyped negative was the change for SS eligibility to seventy. The change applied to those under age fifty five as of June 30, 2017. Without any doubt, this change was necessary. There were fifty five million 'boomers' and more on the way!

Global warming was still a major problem. It continued to get warmer and dryer in the summer and wetter and colder in the spring and winter. There were some positive signs as we eliminated major sources of air pollution. Water pollution was another problem not adequately being dealt with. We were making the efforts, but were we going to run out of time?

The necessity for population control worldwide was being well communicated. Even the Pope halfway endorsed the use of condoms albeit for the prevention of AIDS. Many third world countries continued as the primary concern for overpopulation with Africa leading the way. I was waiting to see if Obama joined Bono or Carter for missions to Africa.

Security forces in the US finally said "The hell with the ACLU. Let them fight it out with the Supremes!" They began using racial profiling as a strategic means to identify potential terrorists. Unfortunately, this change in philosophy came a little late in the game. Terrorist recruiters were becoming more successful in recruiting 'home grown' US citizens joining their cause. (I still haven't quite figured out what their cause is).

Congress passed flat tax legislation to replace the antiquated federal income tax. This new tax structure eliminated the majority of age old loopholes for individuals and businesses. No longer was it going to be possible for 47% of working individuals to avoid paying one dollar in income tax and for 17% of the working population to carry the burden of providing our government with 95% of the necessary tax revenue.

The flat tax was pretty simple: every individual would pay a flat 20 percent of their income to the federal government. There would be no tax exemptions to list. Active-duty military personnel were to pay a 10 percent flat tax. This flat tax would be locked in for a minimum of twenty-five years. Every business or corporation would pay a flat tax of 30 percent of their profits to the federal government. This included foreign owners/investors. Expansion, training, charitable contributions, etc. would not affect the amount paid in taxes. This percentage tax rate was locked in for ten years. Without all the loopholes and quagmire of exemptions, the IRS would have a lot less work to do in the future, and it was forecasted there would be a 60 percent reduction in employment for this monstrous bureaucracy within two years. Fortunately, many jobs were being created in the United States (thanks to The Lists?), so if you worked for the IRS, it was a good time to start looking for another job. The SS tax (FICA) remained "as is."

The new government continued tackling the old problems. At the top of their list was employment. For a change, unemploy-ment wasn't the problem: finding qualified people to fill the multitude of open jobs was the issue. Education and job training moved to the front of their agenda. If this problem wasn't solved, the long-term economic impact could go the wrong way. No one wanted that to happen. Job openings existed in almost every industry, both manufacturing and service. Everything from janitors to electronic technicians to rocket scientists was needed. The health—and human-services job market was booming, thanks to the upgraded national health care legislation.

Since the laws for immigrants to legally enter the United States were changed, making the process much easier, quite a few vacant jobs were being filled by the growing immigrant population. However, since industrial growth had mushroomed in Mexico, the migration of Mexicans into the United States had slowed considerably, and violence at the border was disappearing. The Mexicans were finally finding decent-paying jobs and staying at home, and the absence of migrant workers, especially in California, opened a whole new problem area. We began to see an influx of immigrants from Venezuela as a result of the continued dictatorship and escalating violence in that country. World economies were showing sustained growth, and this was creating an international labor shortage not witnessed in the past. For the first time in history, prosperity was causing problems!

The transition from an economy led by oil, coal, and nuclear to solar, wind, water, and batteries was definitely having an impact on the national and international economy. Employment, pollution, population growth, and even politics were improving. The flat tax coupled with unprecedented employment began filling up the government coffers.

The positive economic trend for all of North America offset the immediate need for the three countries to look at merging the three currencies. However, I think the US Secretary of the Treasury was still entertaining the idea since the international clout gained by the merger could be a huge benefit for everyone involved and possibly begin reducing the imbalance of trade with China.

Global warming showed no signs of slowing down. Perhaps we had gone past the point of no return. Only time would tell. There could be no doubt that the planet was getting warmer and dryer. The number of hurricanes, volcanic eruptions, earthquakes, floods, and rogue ocean waves continued to increase in frequency and severity. More of the smaller islands were evacuated due to rising ocean levels. Coastal communities were spending more and more to shore up reefs, barriers, and dikes. The great glaciers were melting, and the level of the Great Lakes and river systems were dropping. The existing desalination facilities located on both coasts were adequate for now. Additional units would be required in the near future. Asia, Africa, and parts of Europe were now engaged in building strategically located conversion plants. The Lists did not become involved.

Terrorist activities had not disappeared. We were witnessing smaller and smaller homegrown attacks in the United States. Fringe groups still existed and were populated by disgruntled (delusional?) citizens, protesting ideals like abortion (Yep! Still there), ethnicity, class structure, gay rights, or the ever-present "haves" versus "have nots." The leaders of these local factions were usually US citizens who had been courted by Muslim or Islamic terrorist organizations and converted to extremist ideals with the promise of God (or Allah) only knows what. Fortunately, not many of the homegrown converts believed in blowing themselves up for the cause (whatever the "cause" was).

Our youth are finally getting the message about physical and mental fitness although, as yet, only about half of the population under twenty actually embraces physical fitness as a way of life. No one seems willing to give up twittering, facebooking, tweeting, texting, IMing, or as a last resort, cell phoning. However, about 90 percent of the population over fifty-five seems to be gung ho for the fitness programs. In our retirement community, The Villages in Florida, there are about 100,000 people, and 99,999 of them are trying to stay physically fit. Academically, high school and college test scores are showing improvements. The pay for performance endorsement by various teacher unions (after some prodding from The Lists) has raised the bar. Generous merit raises are available for the best-performing teachers (and professors). This program has restored some pride in the profession. Retired professionals are also being utilized instead of sidelined as in the past.

CHAPTER 26

LOOKING BACK: 2016, FOREIGN

January 2017

Those who received foreign assignments did not fare as well as their domestic counterparts. The major deterrent to success continues to be terrorism. In spite of the stepped-up security measures after the attack on the Suez Canal, a group of terrorists from Asia (that's as close as officials could get to identifying what was left of them) hijacked a vessel traveling through the Panama Canal and blew the doors off one of the leveling locks. It took almost four months to clear the wreckage and repair the lock. Fortunately, traffic through the canal was only interrupted for about a week. The Corp of Army Engineers finally decided to increase security on the locks on the river system inside the United States.

To prove that no nation is immune to terrorist activity, I'll point out what happened in China. The eighth man-made wonder of the world, the recently constructed Three Gorges Dam, was targeted for destruction by a group of Islamic militants. They almost succeeded in setting off a bomb being carried in a thirty-five-foot cabin cruiser while going through the locks. The bomb was made from various fertilizers, diesel fuel, and other ingredients. (More info is readily available on the Net if you're really interested in the recipe.)

Apparently, the reason their attempt didn't succeed was due to a faulty cell phone they were using as a detonator. The cell phone being used as the trigger had been made in China, but the receiver, another cell phone being used as the detonator, came from South Korea. There was an electronic compatibility problem! A multilingual security guard heard a group of Muslims on a boat in one of the locks, yelling at each other about a cell phone. While this heated discussion was going on, the guard heard the word *bomb*. He alerted his captain, who took immediate action to apprehend the suspected culprits. Only two of the six on the boat survived, and I'd bet they wished they hadn't.

Another group of Muslim extremists or jihadists weren't anymore successful in their attempt to blow up the Eiffel Tower even though their bomb did go off. None of the hundreds of brainiacs in government service, intelligence agencies, or even TV anchors have figured out what strategic value blowing up this structure could have been, but the attempt was made.

Apparently, the terrorists didn't have a civil / structural engi-neer in their group. They managed to blow a large crater in the area adjacent to the tower but did no damage to the structure itself. No one is claiming responsibility for the attempt: probably too embarrassed. Perhaps this will convince the French to assist the United States and NATO in dealing with terrorists and those who support terrorism.

In Russia, ethnic clashes are becoming commonplace. Xenophobia is in process. The Slavic nationalists desperately want to eradicate infiltrators from the Caucasus region. This internal conflict has had no effect on the START nuclear treaty with the United States or Russia's ability to support the space station (as long as the United States continues to pay for the taxi service). Everyone is still looking for about four thousand pounds of missing HEU.

Then there's the game of "chicken" between North and South Korea. A couple of years ago they were discussing unification. In 2016 they were engaged in a nonnuclear war, although everyone, including the UN, shies away from calling it anything more than a border dispute. Russia and China are not involved (Yah! Right!) I wonder who the combatants are obtaining arms from. A prudent individual might ask, "What happens to me if this conflict escalates into a nuclear confrontation?" Hey! Maybe we can find some workers and resurrect another industry: building bomb shelters. It's more than a bit worrisome when refugees from North Korea tell us they are starving. North Korea, a country of twenty-four million people, is ruled by a dictator and an isolationist government, hence the nickname the "hermit kingdom." They have very little to trade or barter. They are hungry, and they see their neighbor to the south "fat and happy." Not a very stable situation, especially when the neighbor used to be a part of their kingdom. Once again, I took the time to update the survival supplies and hurricane gear in my walk-in closet, now also known as a bomb shelter.

Of course, Iran, Syria, and Pakistan continue the internal strife that began one thousand years ago and their external conflict with the rest of the world. The Lists are having a very difficult time trying to convince these martyrs to shape up. It's difficult to threaten someone who has a suicide bomber mentality with termination? Threats against the family are always a viable option. Iran continues to "march to a different drummer" even though their moronic "little leader" was eliminated. Each day they become more and more of a nuclear threat.

Somalia hasn't given up piracy, but they've added the use of terror tactics against their neighbors. They continue to train and support terrorist organizations, especially any individual or group who commits to blowing up the United States. Apparently, one or two "leaders" are emerging. I need to find out about their vices, so when they become pop-up targets, I'll be prepared. There's no sense trying to send them assignment letters. Termination packages may not do any good, but I'll feel better for having tried.

Most world economies are showing distinct signs of improvement. A few are slowly improving while others are already overflowing. China, Venezuela, the UAE, Saudi Arabia, and others are in the overflowing category. The EU, the World Bank, the IMF, and the euro remain stable, at least for the moment. It seems as though anyone who wants to work can now find a job.

The effects of global warming on international communities are identical to those being experienced in the United States, Canada, and Mexico. In spite of the tremendous efforts to reduce pollutants, the warming trend continues, and catastrophic storms pound coastal regions everywhere.

An extremely large piece of the Antarctic ice shelf broke off early in the year and drifted north into the Atlantic Ocean shipping lanes. Its presence created some delays in cargo-vessel transport and even cruise line crossings for months. The scientific community was dead set against using explosives to get rid of the nuisance. They actually put an expedition onto the "floating island" for about two months to gather information about our ancient planet and about the ocean currents of today.

CHAPTER 27

2016 (LATE)

The tale of my successor

It was sometime during 2015, I realized sooner or later I would need to cease my involvement with The Lists. When I decided it was time to "retire," I would need to have a well-trained replacement lined up to take over: kind of like "succession planning" in any organization. My health was still very good, but I was getting older, and while I wasn't becoming disillusioned, I was getting tired. Living a double life came with a price. With everything I'd invested in The Lists, obviously I wanted the work to continue until the needed results were achieved, and that would most likely take a few more years. The allowable time frame to locate someone to take over for me would have to be within the next couple of years, before burnout (or capture). It was a bit of a dilemma trying to figure out how to locate qualified candidates, let alone how to safely interview them. This wasn't the kind of "job" advertised in the classified section of the newspaper or any of the online services. The job was nerve-racking, it was against the law, and my successor could wind up in prison or even wind up dead. There was no salary. Actually, there were quite a few out-of-pocket expenses, so whoever was selected would not only need to be dedicated to the cause, he/she would need to be able to finance their involvement. Candidates needed to be footloose and free to travel, not have an IQ of 160, but they would need to be intelligent, possess a highly developed sense of right and wrong with no religious hang-ups. Only self-starters with common sense, the ability to communicate, recognize pending problems and solve them would be considered.

During my career and travels throughout the United States and other countries I'd met hundreds of people from many walks of life. I spent hours searching my memory banks thinking who, if any of these acquaintances, could be a candidate. My old friend, Roy, was a great DC insider, but I didn't think he could handle the demands of The Lists. I could think of no one who fit the overall requirements.

It's like I'd heard someone on a CSI episode say, "The answer was in plain sight all along." On a Tuesday night in March, at a weekly poker club gathering, I had an epiphany. Sitting directly across from me at the poker table was an obvious candidate for a successor: my friend Mike. He was in his mid '50s and was a retired FBI agent. He and his wife, Claudette, moved from Ohio to The Villages four years ago. Claudette was the athlete in their family. I didn't have the opportunity to get to know her very well: she died of an aneurysm a couple of years ago while they were playing pickleball at one of the recreation centers. Pickleball is an extremely physical game and is usually played by four to six people armed with a wooden paddle a little larger than a ping-pong paddle. Teams hit a wiffle ball back and forth across a net on a miniaturized tennis court. The game is similar to doubles tennis matches—only faster. Safety-minded players wear knee pads, elbow pads, and eye protection. They always have a towel handy and drink gallons of water or Gatorade. That's why I stuck to playing golf and drinking cold beer.

Mike and I had been acquaintances prior to his wife's passing. We golfed together, and he joined me once in a while when I took my Corvette to car shows. After he became a widower, we became friends. We spent time together when I was in town. We'd go to dinners, movies, a local sports bar to watch football games, or try to beat each other on the golf course. Mike had two grown children, no grandchildren (yet) and, as he stated, "no other baggage."

During our time together, I found Mike and I shared many of the same beliefs regarding the problems in the United States and in the world in general. We thought we knew what to do to solve the problems. More than once I recall him saying, "We'd be much better off without that a—hole!" I'm sure there were occasions when his FBI instincts kicked into gear, and he wondered why I disappeared for a couple of days or even a week or more without notice, but he never pried.

After I realized Mike could be a candidate for the next administrator of The Lists, I conducted a lengthy (almost four months) and very clandestine evaluation process. At first I was more than a little bit worried about his previous law-enforcement background. Hell! He could just arrest me while I was talking to him! I accomplished a silent interview without Mike realizing what was going on. A couple of times, after sharing a six-pack of Coors Light while watching an NFL game or the NBA playoffs, we'd chat about our beliefs, our background, and some of the humorous or bizarre things we'd managed to do. Mike had been in the army prior to joining the FBI. I kidded him about my being a Marine and him being a boy scout. We'd both gone through training at Quantico, Virginia, so we had lots of stories to share. We'd traveled all over the world but for different reasons.

Most of my travel was for business or for vacations. His travel was for investigations, law enforcement, or security. Neither of us saw combat in the service, but Mike had seen more than his share of violence. As an agent, he'd been shot at and had to shoot two people, killing one of them while on a DEA assignment. I owned several pistols, two rifles, and a shotgun.

Compared to my inventory, Mike owned an arsenal. He also had access to the local law-enforcement shooting range. We practiced there a few times a year. Mike was a better shot with a 9 mm pistol, but I took honors with a .30-06. He helped me obtain a concealed weapons permit.

It wasn't until September that I felt comfortable enough with Mike's attitude and capabilities to broach the subject of The Lists. I'd rehearsed my "speech" at least three or four times before the discussion began. One afternoon, following nine holes, we were sitting on his lanai, drinking a couple bottles of Samuel Adams. It was a relaxed setting, and hopefully, we wouldn't be interrupted. As soon as I began my tale, whatever I'd rehearsed was immediately forgotten, but I had no trouble keeping his attention.

Going into the discussion, I believed there were three possible outcomes from what I was about to reveal. Mike could hear me out, and then any of the following could happen:

1. He would decline the offer and forget the conversation took place.
2. He would accept the position and begin training.
3. He would arrest me or arrange to have me arrested.

After my presentation, he surprised me by not doing any of these things. He was very quiet for about a minute and then told me he'd begun to suspect me of some kind of CIA involvement. My mysterious comings and goings and the amount of knowledge I had regarding national and international affairs weren't normal. He hadn't anticipated what I just shared with him, but it did explain my behavior. We had a lengthy discussion over a few more beers and a pizza we'd ordered sometime during the afternoon. Finally, he introduced a fourth option:

He would take the job offer under advisement and reserve the right to ask more questions and check out some things. He would give me his answer within a week. He committed to secrecy and further, whatever his decision, he would not divulge anything I'd told him to anyone. I breathed a sigh of relief, knowing at least I wouldn't be arrested.

It was going to be a long week. I thought Mike might call me with questions, but he didn't. We had no contact for three days. I remember when he finally phoned me. It was about 10:00 a.m. on a Saturday. He asked me if I wanted to have lunch and then "go hit a few balls at the driving range." Naturally, I said yes.

We agreed to meet at our local sports bar, Beef O'Brady's, for a beer and a burger at eleven thirty. We each drove our golf carts. During lunch, we steered clear of any mention of The Lists or the job offer. We talked about his new driver and my problem getting out of sand traps. After lunch, we headed to the driving range located behind our local Walmart.

It was a beautiful afternoon, and fortunately for us, there weren't many folks on the range. We picked out two spots off to the left side of the range where we could talk without interruption or being overheard. Mike opened the discussion with a number of pointed questions. Why, what, and how did I get involved were at the top of his list. Then, "Why did you pick me?" "What's expected?" "Who else is involved?" "What's the timetable?" He told me, "I think I have a pretty good idea of what the risks are, and I don't expect to see any rewards." Needless to say, we didn't hit many balls, but we did have a lengthy and frank discussion. We adjourned to my lanai and continued our talks until dinnertime. We had another pizza delivered. There was enough beer in my fridge. The longer the discussion went, the more frank the Q&A session grew.

It became more and more obvious Mike and I had the same concerns and shared the same moral and patriotic values. Mike had seen it all during his FBI days, and he was fed up with the whole federal bureaucracy and all the BS good law-enforcement people had to put up with. He confided that he had seen really bad guys just walk away after being caught red-handed because they had DI (diplomatic immunity), were CIs (confidential informants) for someone high up in the organization, or were well connected to somebody in the Senate. It didn't take much convincing on my part, but it took some time to answer his growing list of questions.

It took a couple of hours to explain how The Lists came to be and what I felt the short and long-term objectives should be. He seemed genuinely interested in the objectives of The Lists and was amazed that no one had found out about my involvement. I held back telling him how many deaths had been initiated by The Lists. I'd confess later.

Mike's years of training in law enforcement had provided him with a wealth of knowledge and understanding in many fields, including national and international politics and security and terrorism: in general, the "good guys" versus the "bad guys." His exposure to the details on issues like the environment, energy, population controls, etc. was minimal. I knew he was showing interest in the job when he informed me he was a "quick study." Mike confided to me that he wasn't wealthy, but he was "OK, financially," and he was in excellent health (physically and mentally) and wanted to stay that way.

We took a look at the financial requirements for maintaining The Lists. Since I'd completed most of the groundwork, continued operational expenses would be minimal. Excluding the storage sheds (I believed it was about time to get rid of them), expenditures should be about $5,000 a year unless it became necessary to issue a massive number of termination packages. There was an adequate supply of the motivating powder on hand, but the high-end gift inventory was always kept at a modest level. So the dollar value for expenses could jump quite a bit if the number of "bad guys" grew or if assignment letters were ignored. Near midnight we called a time-out.

The following morning, Mike and I resumed our conversation over breakfast at the local IHOP. By midafternoon, Mike seemed to withdraw from the talks. He informed me that this was a lot to digest and a lot to commit to, if he decided to join me. I told him honestly, my involvement would cease within a year or so, but only after I was certain my successor was thoroughly trained to take over. I'd even help out with the finances if needed. Later, after selling the RV, the proceeds went into the operating budget for The Lists.

Mike thanked me for my honesty and for confiding in him. He told me he understood why I was doing it and wanted us to remain friends whatever he chose to do. When he left, I wasn't sure what he would decide or when. He called me at 9:00 p.m. and simply said, "I'm in!" His training began the next day. The timing for bringing Mike onboard couldn't have worked out any better. It was late October 2016 when we began his indoctrination, a couple months before I ended the year with a bang: literally.

Mike's training went quickly. We decided it was time to shut down the eBay flea market business and the golf ball stuff. We moved out of the sheds before the end of the year. Mike volunteered the use of his second garage for storage of the inventory and preparation of the packages. We agreed to take time off from The Lists, enjoy the holidays, and regroup in early January for the 2016 evaluations, 2017 assignments, and any needed package preparations.

About this time, my youngest daughter, Kimberly, in Uniontown, Ohio, contacted me regarding Thanksgiving. She wanted to act as hostess for the entire family and also intended to include a seventieth birthday celebration for me. After a couple of IM discussions, I finally agreed to fly up for the festivities. There weren't any major chores left for The Lists, and Mike agreed to handle any last-minute carryover Christmas orders coming in for the golf ball plaques or light pulls (still had a couple of dozen on the shelves). I packed a bag, took The Villages shuttle to the Orlando International Airport, and off I went. It was a beautiful

75-degree day in Florida. The five-day forecast for the Akron area called for highs in the '50s and lows in the '30s. The good news was that no snow was predicted. Sure enough, when I landed in Ohio, the sun was shining, and it was a balmy fifty-four when the kids and grandkids met me at baggage claim. After a minireunion, we hit the road for grandson Christopher's basketball game before dinner. He made two great shots, missed four others, and his team managed to win their third game in six tries. Joshua, Brittany, and Johnny thought it was a great idea when I bought ice cream cones to celebrate the victory.

Most of the gang (twenty-eight people) showed up for a grand Thanksgiving dinner and my birthday celebration. Knowing I'd be flying home, everyone bought me something small: golf balls, golf gloves, and golf tees. It seemed like only ten minutes after dinner and dessert, everyone was sound asleep in various parts of the house.

The next day, it was 26 degrees and snow was falling. We were all bundled up (I borrowed a parka and gloves from my son-in-law, Chris) and, over my objections (I wanted to watch football on TV), crowded into their SUV and headed to the mall for the traditional Black Friday Christmas shopping and an animated movie the grandkids had been waiting to see. It turned out to be a pleasant afternoon. It was about five o'clock when the show was over, and I joined Chris for a trek across the snow-covered parking lot to fetch the SUV. I didn't make it!

We were twenty feet from the SUV when I hit a patch of ice, went "a—over tin cups," and *wham*: I hit the pavement. Most of me landed flat on the asphalt, but my right ankle managed to land on the curb, and as I found out an hour later at the hospital, it broke in two places. Everyone helped get me into the SUV (I wanted nothing to do with an ambulance) and away we went to the Akron General Hospital. After surgery (two pins were needed) and two days' R & R, a walking cast was installed over my ankle after the swelling subsided. I received two minutes' training on the use of crutches before being discharged. My daughter wanted me to stay and convalesce at her home, but all I wanted to do was get home and warm. So it was back to the airport, a quick flight south (they even gave me an exit row seat) to Orlando where it was warm and sunny. Mike was waiting for me with a wheelchair at the airport. I spent the next five weeks, hobbling around and recuperating over the Christmas and New Year holidays. The cast was removed, and I was pronounced healthy just before the Super Bowl.

Sometime later, Kimberly asked me to explain something I'd said about breaking a promise. I told her about the pact that Barbara and I made right after we moved to The Villages. The Christmas holiday plan that first year was for us to load up the Grand Cherokee with suitcases and presents, leave Florida on December 20, and take two or three days to drive to Akron. That's what we did. It was 70 degrees and sunny when we left. Three days later, after battling snow, wind, cold, and ice across the Virginia and West Virginia mountains, we arrived. It was 17 degrees. We celebrated Christmas and left Akron on December 28 and set the GPS for home. We arrived just in time for New Year's Eve at Katie Belle's with friends and neighbors. It was 68 degrees.

After that trip, we made a promise to never travel north between November 1 and April 30. The kids would have to come visit us for Thanksgiving or Christmas. I had broken my promise and wound up with a broken ankle. I never want to see snow again!

2017

CHAPTER 28

LOOKING BACK: 2017, DOMESTIC

January 2018

We began 2017 in our new quarters, Mike's golf cart garage, and me recuperating from a broken ankle. The first order of business was the annual chore of evaluating the nonperformers for 2016. Mike was truly a quick study and not a bit shy when it came to enforcing the rules. He prepared fourteen termination packages for poor performance during 2017. Then he sent eighteen domestic and six foreign assignments for 2018. As the year began, we found ourselves spending more time for leisure activities than time devoted to the business of The Lists. I think it was a wise decision to get out of eBay craft business (the golf items) and move out of the storage sheds last year.

Thankfully, the number of packages needing prepared for The Lists' nonperformers began to decline dramatically. I believe there were two reasons for this reduction. One reason was an exposé that appeared on

60 Minutes in February 2017. It informed the public that "Homeland Security, the FBI, NSA, and other international law-enforcement agencies were searching for members of a vigilante organization [they stopped referring to us as terrorists] who were targeting hundreds of people, both political and nonpolitical, and exterminating them because of their alleged detrimental behavior toward society." The report went into a detailed explanation of those believed to have been on this mysterious death list and the reason(s) they were eliminated. Almost overnight this news spread across the globe. The report appeared in newspapers, online, and on TVs everywhere. Many of the previously identified potential targets on The Lists, those who had already received assignments and seemed reluctant to perform the task, began to comply. This was true domestically and in quite a few foreign locations. It was one thing to be on a list for an Oscar, an Emmy, best dressed, or the most eligible, but who wanted to be on a hit list? I considered this the good-news part of the story. The bad-news part was the number of copycats who crawled out of their hiding places after the broadcast and began to settle personal vendettas. Over a six-month period, the media listed sixty-two mysterious deaths. The Lists had nothing to do with twenty-three of them but appeared to be getting all the credit.

The second reason for a reduction in the need for terminations seems to be because the Republicans now ran the entire federal bureaucracy. They were actually implementing projects/ changes that were spelled out as assignments by The Lists. I had no idea if this would go on for more than the four-year election cycle, but their current efforts were very much appreciated.

When we moved the supplies associated with The Lists from the sheds, the plan was to use Mike's garage and continue the business.

His Village home had a full two-car garage and an attached golf cart garage. Mike only owned one car and a golf cart. We moved into the cart garage since we really didn't need a whole lot of space, and the cart garage was large enough for our purposes. Mike seldom had any visitors, but we thought it would be prudent to buy a large metal cabinet so we could lock up The Lists' "sensitive" items and keep them out of sight. We stacked the flea market items on the shelves and work tables in plain sight.

Mike and I bought and sold flea market items more as a hobby than a business. But even as a hobby, it gave us a reason to frequently go traveling and a legitimate need for the boxes and shipping supplies in the garage. When it was just me managing The Lists, I worried about getting caught but had made no provisions for it. What was the sense of worrying about being arrested or worse? Now that there were two of us, it made sense to think about a different plan. So Mike and I developed a what-if scenario. The what-if dealt with detection. The plan simply stated if one of us was arrested or mysteriously vanished for more than a twenty-four-hour period, the other one would immediately grab two small boxes of incriminating materials locked in the metal cabinet in the garage (mainly the poisons and the laptop: the flash drive records were already stored at an off-site location) and get them to another previously identified and nontraceable location. I will not provide any details for the location since I have no way of knowing if Mike implemented the what-if plan and if it was in use. None of the items specific to The Lists had ever been handled without any of us wearing latex gloves and dust masks, so we were pretty sure if the items were found, the CSI folks would have a devil of a time tracking back to us using fingerprints or DNA.

If this did occur, it didn't necessarily mean The Lists were permanently out of business. Whoever was left standing would determine *if* and *when* to retrieve the materials and reopen the business of The Lists.

The number of terrorist organizations seemed to be getting smaller. The problem was the remaining groups seemed to be getting smarter. They were being well trained, were well supplied, and were not easily detected. Homegrown terrorists, usually disgruntled US citizens, seemed to be growing in numbers. True, some of these would undoubtedly be diagnosed as sociopaths, but what about the rest? Were they brainwashed or perhaps just looking for an adventure? Whatever their rationale, at least most of them weren't totally nuts: the reasonably intelligent ones refused to blow themselves up and settled for planting remotely activated bombs or dumping poisonous chemicals or assassinating people from a distance. As evidenced by their lack of success, I'd guess many of these folks had a negative IQ. However, there were exceptions to this belief.

And we need to remember there are just some plain bad people in our world. Here's an example. Fifteen men and five women, dressed in casual attire and armed with automatic assault rifles (terrorists or mercenaries?), quietly and ruthlessly robbed a casino in Southern California about three thirty one afternoon. They had no difficulty eliminating the nine members of the casino's security detail or disconnecting the alarm systems and the surveillance equipment. Everyone in the casino kept right on losing money and had no idea what was happening. Next they entered the counting room (where all the money is kept, counted, and stacked). The four people in the room were easily incapacitated. Apparently, two of the female intruders knew their way around casinos and computers because in the next fifteen minutes they took 50 percent of every account held by the casino at various banks and transferred it to untraceable offshore banks. Transfer of more than 50 percent would have raised a flag at the banks. Next they put every bit of the cash on hand in three wheeled suitcases, tied and gagged everyone in the room, then sat and waited about three minutes until the armored car they had been waiting for showed up. Yep! After shooting the guards and driver, they drove the armored car to a rear-loading dock and took more than seven million dollars in cash out of the truck. They must have known this was the truck's last stop. They stripped the dead guards and put on the uniforms. Ten of them remained behind to keep things quiet at the casino while the others took the truck to the central armored car company's main distribution center.

Arriving right on time, according to the company's pick up schedule, they were waved through the guard gate and into the loading-dock area of the building. (Think this might have been an inside job?)

Thirty minutes later, they drove out of the building in three armored trucks, taking different routes. They left with about $70 million and fourteen people dead. At the same time, those who stayed behind at the casino left the office, walked to the parking lot, and drove off in ten full-size stolen cars. Everyone in the counting room had been shot twice.

The three armored trucks and the ten cars were found torched late that night. The twenty thieves/murderers and about $77 million disappeared. The authorities are still looking for them. This will undoubtedly be the next action flick we'll see in 3-D at the Old Mill Theater in The Villages.

Why did I include this story? I guess I did it to put things into the proper perspective. These weren't terrorists. They didn't have a cause. They were crooks who killed twenty-seven innocent people for one reason: money. The Lists have been responsible for the deaths of over four hundred extremely corrupt individuals for one reason: so the bad things affecting society get changed and we all survive. Which reason do you think is more acceptable?

OK, let's get back to the story of The Lists and 2017 in the United States.

Federal, state, county, and local governments still require funding for operations. True, the federal government has dramatically reduced its size and spending habits. The new flat tax has had immediate benefits for both the taxpayer and the government. Everyone is now paying a fair share to keep the federal machine running. There is still a large deficit, but it is dropping much quicker than anticipated. Enforcement is a necessary evil: at least for a while. The main problem is rich folks and businesses are still trying to find ways to beat the system. As The Lists identify these people, assignment letters will be issued and then followed for adherence.

Quite a few states have shown the desire and ability to cut their spending. A few began to evaluate a flat tax à la the new federal income tax method. Some have implemented a 5 percent flat tax based on income, doing away with a state income tax, sales tax, and luxury tax. I was fairly certain the rest of the states would soon follow this fair and simple tax trend. Without the traditional loopholes, the amount of tax money collected will double or triple in a short time but only if enforced. Given time, we may be surprised with lower real estate taxes.

Scientists have been predicting a megaquake would hit the coast of California before 2030. By definition, a megaquake is an earthquake of 10.0 on the Richter scale. The anticipated quake would cause about one-third of California's land mass to slide into the Pacific Ocean. This event would have a devastating effect on the rest of the country. Silicon Valley, Napa Valley, and the breadbasket of the United States would be obliterated. Obviously, this hasn't happened, yet! What did happen was the megastorm. This was a tropical storm—similar to the one that devastated the northern coast of Australia in 2011—that hit Northern and Central California in February 2017. This storm was much worse than the one in Australia. Scientists called the storm "an atmospheric river," moisture that originated in tropical Pacific regions and gathered in ferocity as it approached landfall a little bit north of center of the California coast. This storm covered about 60 percent of the state with hurricane-force winds in excess of 130 mph and dropped almost ten feet of rain in less than seventy-two hours. The flooding, mudslides, coastal erosion, business loss, home damage, and crop damage amounted to more than $400 billion. Around 1.5 million people were evacuated, six hundred thousand were homeless, and two hundred thousand were killed. Power would not be totally restored for months.

What caused this catastrophic megastorm? Scientists could not reach an accord, but a general consensus was that global warming brought on by atmospheric changes caused by pollution was the culprit. I wondered if we were too late in our efforts to reduce pollution?

What about evolution? We have pythons in the Everglades and predatory snakehead fish in our lakes, rivers, and streams. Zebra mussels are clogging intakes at municipal water plants and power plants. Manatees are dying in record numbers due to colder weather patterns in Florida. Dead dolphins and whales are showing up on our coastal beaches. How about the threat of killer bees?

There are examples of massive agricultural changes as well. If you've ever driven the north-south interstate highways near the East Coast during the summer months, you must have noted the growth of the Asian kudzu vines everywhere. These growths are so prolific they can take over mile after mile of other growth, including large trees, and cause them to die off. To me, pollution is just like the kudzu vine. Pollution has become a "growth," covering the earth like a blanket, slowly killing our planet and us. There is little doubt this is a contributing factor to climate change and the cause of these killer storms!

Let's not forget the opposite of the summer megastorms: the monstrous winter weather that dropped four and five feet of snow and ice on Canada, most of the northern United States, the UK, Russia, China and other regions. These storms didn't just come and go: they came and stayed. They were accompanied by 50-mph winds and temperatures near zero. The civilian populations in these areas were immobilized for weeks. People couldn't get to work. People couldn't get medical care. People died from the cold. Mountains of garbage appeared and so did the rats and then disease came.

Resources were strained beyond the breaking point. In spite of the best efforts of the National Guard, looting was commonplace. The economic impact was immeasurable and the death toll astronomical. Remember the 2011 warning from The Lists: "It's getting dryer and warmer!" The Lists forgot something: while it had been getting dryer and warmer in the summer months it's now getting windy and wet. Then along comes winter, and it's getting a whole lot colder!

There is the possibility of a major new survival problem. This problem hasn't made it to the front page, yet. Is our supply of oxygen being depleted? So far, the apparent loss of breathable oxygen on our planet is only having a negative effect on the birds (they're dying). That's right: the birds! Scientists haven't figured out what is causing hundreds of thousands of birds to just drop out of the sky, dead. Apparently, this is occurring in many locations—not just in the United States. The Audubon Society is alarmed because of this situation. Are you?

Humans and animals breathe oxygen and exhale carbon dioxide. Plants breathe carbon dioxide and exhale oxygen. We also need plants if we want to eat. In the past, there were no problems meeting these needs. Now, there's a delicate balance. Each year there are many more us and fewer plants on our planet. If overpopulation or pollution continues to kill off the vegetation, where is the oxygen going to come from? Where will we get our food? Are we sure we're doing everything possible to reduce air pollution, reduce deforestation, and control population? I think not!

There's another problem caused by pollution. Humans, animals, and plants require water to live. While we are addressing the issues causing air pollution, we'd better not forget about water. The largest polluter of air and water is Mother Nature. Man is next. Since we have no control over Mother, we'd better be doing everything we can to control what we are causing!

Every living thing on our little planet has to breathe, has to eat, and has to drink. We are entirely dependent on each other, yet we humans seem to be ambivalent to the needs of the others. We'd better change our attitude and do it now!

We now have a federal government totally controlled by the Republican Party (with the assistance of the Tea Party), and expectations are high. We expect to see a reduction in taxes, continuing increases in employment, smart spending on education, a continuation of social benefits like Medicare and social security, as well as a strong military and controls over financial institutions who previously caused so much grief. Terrorism is always a consideration. National security is an issue as is instituting some method for population control, including immigration. I expect to see an adherence to the plan outlined by The Lists during 2016 and 2017. Improvements have been noted, but much more work is needed. Perhaps a short recap (a list) of these successes is justified.

Pollution (no. 1 problem) in the United States is being addressed by several continuing programs. Here's the status on a few of them.

Sources of electrical power continue to improve. Free, nonpolluting, and renewable generating facilities continue to be installed. The sun (solar panels), the wind (turbines), and the water (river dams or tidal units) are becoming the primary providers. Coal, diesel, or nuclear units continue to be phased out. Scientists continue to work on solar fusion and Tesla's idea to find even better methods, but for now, I'm satisfied we're on the right track.

The process of eliminating the old gas—or diesel-guzzling cars, trucks, and buses continues. New battery-powered vehicles in all sizes and shapes are becoming available at affordable prices. The safety, speed, and distance issues are well on the way to being solved. New battery packs are lasting about five years, and replacement cost continues to drop. Charging stations / meters have sprung up everywhere. They are installed and serviced by the counties where they are located. Set up like parking meters used to be, nominal charges are paid at the meter by using your newly designed driver's license as an energy debit card (EDC). The proceeds are divided up just like they used to be when the gasoline-pump tax still existed. Unleaded gasoline is still available, but its use is restricted to things like golf carts or antique automobiles. The oil companies reported a drop of about 45 percent in US gasoline sales, so there are still some polluters out there while the transition continues. I sold my Vette and bought a used 2014 Tesla! I loved my Vette, but it did cause pollution.

To maintain the new batteries, all you need to do is charge them every day (just plug it in) and check the tires monthly. Every three or four years, new tires and brake pads will be needed (about fifty thousand miles). The battery packs will require replacement about every five years (about seventy-five thousand miles). Remember what you needed to do to maintain your gasoline-driven car? Remember how much it cost to keep it serviced and fueled? When doing a comparison of costs for a battery-powered car (nonpolluting) to a gasoline-powered car (polluting) of the same size, driven similar distances each day over a five-year period, we find that the total cost for the battery-powered vehicle (including the cost of a new battery pack, charging costs versus the cost of unleaded regular gasoline, and normal maintenance for each) is approximately $6,500 less. Wow! That's a savings of $1,300 a year with zero pollution.

Trucks, trains, and even cruise ships are being converted to natural gas. The factories making the changeover equipment are working 24/7, but this is a huge undertaking and will take about ten years to complete.

The airline industry is a true dilemma. Short of going back to dirigibles, there really isn't a good way to convert the jet engines from the fuel (high grade kerosene) being used. However, we can look at alternative means of travel such as high-speed rail. A grid of high-speed rail systems crisscrossing the United States and Canada, looking something like a tic-tac-toe game, would provide basic travel routes, at least to/ through the larger cities. This could substantially reduce the need for long-distance air travel in North America and create a lot of jobs. For now, we'll just have to accept status quo.

Population continues to grow but at a reduced rate. Apparently, the national sex-education program is paying off. Obviously, the government's blessing for civil unions or same-sex marriages has put a dent in the number of births. Speaking of "blessings," when the Vatican stated the use of condoms was approved by the church ("to help stop AIDS"), the Catholic birthrate dropped about 15 percent the first full year and continues to drop. We still have to watch the immigration situation, but legal applications for citizenship have started dropping about 10 percent last year as Mexico, Central America, and several African countries improve employment opportunities and living conditions for their citizens. This is a very favorable trend for the United States. Unfortunately, I don't feel we're seeing the same results in many foreign locations, especially in Muslim countries where population growth seems to be about the same as it was in 2012. Allah (or Muhammad or the ayatollahs) need to intervene for those who practice the Islamic religion.

There are still episodes of terrorist activity in the United States. Two large ships were blown up in Long Beach Harbor. One was a container ship bringing goods from China. The other was a tanker carrying about two million gallons of crude oil. The reaction to the "spill" was instant: harbor crews had been practicing a response to this kind of episode for years. Containment was estimated at 99 percent. In the first instance, the bombers escaped. In the second, it was thought the terrorists "went down with the ship." Vigilance at all harbors has been intensified. Pleasure boats endure hours of delays, trying to enter a marina anywhere near a major port or at locks on our rivers.

A bomb was planted at the Saints' football stadium in New Orleans in November just prior to an NFL game. Then a bomb threat was phoned in to the local police, the FBI, Homeland Security, and two TV stations just before halftime. The bomb turned out to be a fake, but thirty-four people died in the stampede caused by an announcement to evacuate the stadium. The bomber turned out to be a fifteen-year-old boy who was considered a nerd by his classmates. He actually posted his success on Facebook. He's now waiting to be tried as an adult for terrorism and multiple murders but no longer thinks of himself as a nerd!

Things were going so well by midyear. I thought seriously about taking the RV out of storage and taking another vacation. Maybe I'd repeat the trip that started the whole thing. The more I thought about the work it would take for a trip like that, the more I convinced myself it was time to relax. I sold the RV. The proceeds went into a lockbox inside the locked cabinet in Mike's garage. This money was to be used to continue funding the work of The Lists. It should last for as long as Mike kept The Lists going.

I had my Honda motorcycle cleaned up and serviced. Then I drove it to Cincinnati and presented it to my grandson for his high school graduation. (Jim and Trina had given me the OK to do this). Taylor was a good kid. He played baseball and football and had good grades. His Dad was OK with it, but his Mom took some convincing and a lot of "Please, Mom" with promises to be careful, always wear a helmet, study, and get good grades (he was off to Ohio State in the fall). His older sister, granddaughter Amber, thought it was "cool." She was OK with me giving Taylor the Honda, but she appreciated the new tires and the brake job I paid for on her used Nissan Leaf. (She was proud to be a "greenie"). I stayed for four days and then flew back to Orlando.

My involvement with The Lists would continue throughout 2017, but beginning in 2018, I planned to become more of an adviser than a doer. By the end of the year, Mike was doing a great job and required very little input from me.

CHAPTER 29

(LOOKING BACK-2017-FOREIGN)

January, 2018

With so many of the bad actors removed from the international picture, conflicts seemed to diminish. Terrorist activities still happened, but political turmoil was substantially less than in previous years. Iraq, Yemen, Libya, Egypt, Bahrain, Jordan, Tunisia, and Saudi Arabia had undergone dramatic reforms or were still in the process of changing as demanded by their citizens. Many of the missing despots had been in power for years. Some had been backed by the good old USA because we needed their oil and their land for military bases. Now, after many years, our foreign policy was coming back to haunt us. Most of these fledgling democracies needed our assistance and were willing to forgive and forget. US foreign policy was being rewritten on a daily basis. Pockets of resistance (predominantly old Muslim regimes) still existed, but they were becoming less and less influential in the mid-east.

Iraq continues to be a problem for the US. We keep trying to let them do their own thing and they keep screwing it up. Osama is dead, but Afghanistan remains an irritant to us. NATO continues to increase its presence in both locations. Since Osama's death in Pakistan, relations between the US and Pakistan have been strained, but, as of this moment, Pakistan still needs us on their side. I wonder how long that's going to last?

Iran is a thorn in everybody's side. Even with their fanatical leader gone and the people revolting and demanding reforms, government officials continue to seek ways to develop nuclear capabilities. Russia, China and North Korea seem to be getting involved. What do they know that we don't?

Somoli pirates surface from time to time but their modus operandi has changed. They no longer attack large container ships belonging to the major shipping companies since the companies joined together and hired their own naval strike force who hunt down and eliminate the pirates. They have been very successful. The pirates decided it was much healthier to board private vessels, mostly yachts, put the crew and passengers adrift, and take everything else. They seem to be very successful in collecting modest ransoms for the yachts from insurance companies. If I owned a yacht, I believe I'd be smart enough to avoid waters frequented by the pirates no matter what kind of insurance I carried.

BMW, Jaguar, Fiat, Volkswagen, Volvo, and several other automotive companies have entered the electric-car industry with a vengeance. Russian, German, Swiss, and French aluminum companies are working diligently with the manufacturers to assist with this transition. I'm certain in a few years they will be attempting to sell into the US markets. I must confess, some of their offerings are much more attractive than what's currently produced in the United States. The exception to this statement is the Tesla being made in California.

The major obstacle they are faced with is obtaining the raw materials needed to manufacture the lithium-ion batteries. The United States and China have most of these mining areas committed to long-term contracts. The European manufacturers are desperately looking for another source of supply (explorations are taking place in Australia and Africa) while developing new battery configurations to power their vehicles.

Europe is way ahead of us in utilizing wind and water for electrical-powered generation. In some areas, solar power is readily available, but wind and water-driven turbines now supply approximately 70 percent of the electricity to the UK, France, Spain, Portugal, the Netherlands, Italy, Germany, Austria, Switzerland, and parts of Russia. India and Japan seem to be the only holdouts for nuclear-powered generation. Africa remains in the dark ages. I fear that diesel generators and coal-fired boilers will remain in use here for years and years.

South American countries are gradually moving into the twenty-second century. Brazil, Chile, and Argentina are investing heavily in hydroelectric generating plants on their rivers and along the seashore.

Iceland thrives on its geothermal generating plants. The steam coming off the underground semivolcanic rifts is another source of free, nonpolluting power. Australia, Greenland, and other isolated geographic locations will undoubtedly remain as is for years to come.

If my memory is correct, there was a major terrorist threat in 2017 to an area of the planet not previously targeted. The authorities involved believed the target was the seaport at Perth on the western side of Australia. They were mistaken. This time the bomb used didn't arrive on a ship: it was in the cargo bay of a commercial airplane. There were two people in the cockpit who failed to respond to calls on the radio, a normal practice for aircraft entering Australian airspace twenty miles offshore. Two Aussie Air Force fighter jets scrambled immediately and intercepted the lumbering cargo plane just as it crossed the coastline near Perth. The pilot still didn't acknowledge radio inquiries. The flight path showed the plane would soon pass directly over a new nuclear-powered plant located seven miles to the north of Perth.

When the cargo plane refused to respond to a last try by the fighters, they shot it down with conventional firepower instead of blowing it up with air-to-air missiles. This proved to be a very wise decision. The plane crashed seventeen miles outside the city and twelve miles from the power plant. Then it exploded! It was loaded with a dirty nuclear bomb that would have wiped out five or six blocks of Perth or wreaked havoc on the power plant. It was estimated that two hundred thousand people would have died. There were fourteen people killed on the sheep ranch where the crash occurred. One thousand five hundred square miles is now off limits to humans, sheep, and "roos" for the next fifty years.

The investigation of this event proved the plane had been purchased by a Saudi oil company several years ago. Last year they leased it to a firm allegedly based in Tripoli, Libya, who stated they were going to "perform aerial explorations in various parts of the globe." No one has any information about what they were exploring for. The flight originated in Malaysia, showing a load of repair parts for a shipping company on the manifest. The shipping company knew nothing about the shipment, the plane, or anything else.

The outcome of this attack was nothing short of a miracle. I wonder if anyone in authority has stepped up security measures at other nuclear facilities, especially in the United States? I also wonder if the US Air Force would have been permitted to react the same way under similar circumstances? I've found out that a bomb capable of leveling three or four city blocks could be carried in a two-passenger Piper Cub. How do we prevent something like this from happening? The only possible way is to keep terrorists from obtaining the materials to make a dirty bomb. Let's not forget the missing 3,999 pounds of HEU still missing from Russia! It's hard to get a good night's sleep, thinking about this potential.

When comparing population control with a nuclear threat, it doesn't seem nearly as important. Don't be fooled. Uncontrolled population growth has as much potential to kill us off as a nuclear blast: it's just more subtle. The Chinese still have the best idea for controlling population. Unfortunately, their enforcement lacks consistency. City dwellers are permitted to have only one child unless the first child is a female. The penalty for disobeying this law is very stringent: loss of all social benefits, loss of a job, no education for the child, etc. This is why so many female babies are killed at birth. Farmers are permitted to have many children to help with the work on the farm. So a rich Chinaman simply buys a farm or two and is allowed to have more children.

The Muslim countries show no signs of restraint regarding population growth. As a matter of fact, some of their leaders are proponents of paying their people large sums for each child born. Apparently, the objective is to eventually outnumber everyone else on the planet.

Foreign financial institutions continue to prosper. With everyone who wants to work working and most economies stabilizing, companies and individuals are putting their money in the bank or investing. The euro is once again stronger than the dollar, and the UK is again considering switching the British pound over. I don't think this will happen in my lifetime, but who knows?

It's surprising, but there are finally some signs of life for the UN and NATO. Excluding Iran and North Korea, the UN position regarding many of the sensitive issues spelled out by The Lists are now being supported. NATO is becoming a force to be recognized. They have become a lean, mean, fighting machine. They are well-trained and well-equipped soldiers with the capability of rapid (and deadly) response. There's still some infighting regarding who's in charge at times, but this happens less and less frequently now. With the United States supplying the fighter jets, troop ships (air and sea), and 25 percent of the troops, we manage to exercise a controlling interest most of the time.

Mike will probably need to spend more of his time on foreign development than on domestic issues. We've already made arrangements for him to do some traveling next year (2018) in Europe and perhaps to Asia if things work out. He plans to leave in late February for Switzerland and try some "real" skiing. Then he's off to Germany, Russia, and the UK. I've already schooled him on how to recruit folks to remail termination packages. This way he'll have his own contacts and organization for operating the foreign portion of The Lists over the next three or four years.

I'm sure I've missed mentioning some important happenings for foreign locals during 2017, but as of this moment, I can't think what they could be.

2018 AND 2019

CHAPTER 30

LOOKING BACK: DOMESTIC AND FOREIGN 2018/2019

(sometime in 2020)

I know the month, day, and date when I was captured, but as for today, I have no idea what time it is, let alone what month or day of the week I'm in. I disappeared from The Villages on February 1, 2018.

Mike and I had completed the review of 2017 performance for the List. He was in the process of preparing a few termination packages for 2017 transgressions. We had already mailed assignments for 2018. Things appeared to be reasonably quiet. There was no hint of detection.

The end-of-the-year holidays were over with, and the Super Bowl was only a few weeks away. The snowbirds had returned to The Villages right after Christmas, so the roads, golf courses, and restaurants were crowded. If 2018 was the same as previous years, the snowbirds would all drive back north by mid-April, and those of us left (we were called frogs because we were here until we croaked!) would get back to normal until after Christmas.

Ninety percent of managing The Lists had been turned over to Mike. I felt comfortable being relegated to a consultant role. I was involved in establishing the assignments for 2018. There weren't as many as in previous years. A lot of what previously would have become assignments from The Lists were already being taken care of by people who were responsible in the first place. Quite a few of these responsible entities were what I referred to as the new people. The old regimes were gone. Some had been voted out. Some had resigned. Some had died of natural causes. A few had been overthrown. Some had been terminated. We made certain their successors knew about The Lists and the rules!

We collected information from 2017, regarding terrorist activities. We needed to decide if there might be something The Lists could do to deter future efforts by an individual or group. Our list had eleven terrorist episodes, ranging from pouring chemicals into a public water supply in France to a bomb made of two pounds of C-4 that failed to explode in Union Station in DC. We came up with an estimated 1,100 deaths caused by these roving terrorists. We didn't feel competent enough with the information we possessed to have The Lists try to intervene. The decision was made to rely on the various security agencies to perform their jobs. We were prepared to act if additional information provided a means for us to do so.

With the work completed for The Lists (i.e., 2017 evaluations and 2018 assignments), we were ready to take it easy. Mike was closing up his house and packing his bags for a seven-week tour of Europe. His first stop was scheduled in Switzerland where he was looking forward to trying out the ski slopes. I planned to wax the Tesla and drive down to the Keys for a couple of weeks. I now owned a slightly used 2014 sports model, a beautiful silver/black convertible. It was battery-powered and 100 percent environmentally friendly. It would go 110 mph with no problem (except for the highway patrol) and almost four hundred miles on a full charge. At times I felt like a traitor to my Corvette and The Village Vettes Corvette Club, but other "E" cars or hybrids didn't appeal to my taste. If a battery-powered Corvette ever does come to the market, I might reconsider. In the meantime, I considered starting an electric car club.

That's why I was having dinner by myself at Red Sauce the afternoon of February 1. Thankfully, Mike was somewhere in Europe at the time. I hope he remembers the protocol we established in case one of us disappeared.

You'll have to go to chapter 31 to finish the story of The Lists.

CHAPTER 31

(THE FINAL CHAPTER-OR IS IT?)

(sometime during 2020)

Things were going along pretty well except for my being in prison. The authorities thought I was writing my memoirs, but I'm sure they were growing impatient: I hadn't provided them with any incriminating evidence. I'm at the point where I'm on my fact-finding mission in 2009 and 2010. I'm certain there isn't anything they don't already know about my personal life, but they continue to hope I'll make a mistake and reveal something. I wonder what would happen if I told them about The Lists, the nine hundred assignments or the four hundred terminations?

Then one afternoon, when Pete delivered my lunch tray and I noted something different: my milk shake had two of the red and white stripped straws. I wondered why? I unfolded the napkin and found this message: "pub 7 wks-I go n 2". WOW!

At my current pace, I figured I would need another three or four months to finish my book. Now, I only had two weeks to finish. Was this possible?

I was working on 2018 and 2019, but in my situation, accurate reporting wasn't possible: I had no access to any news sources. My narrative would consist what I was able to recall prior to my capture and then I would have to hypothesize regarding any successes of The Lists for 2018 and 2019. It would be up to the editor or publisher to correct errors or fill in the blanks. Mike was unaware the book was to be published and the publisher had no idea who Mike really was.

So, for expediency, I decided to lump together 2018 and 2019 for the final chapter. I wanted to include a summary of comments for both the domestic and foreign portion of The Lists for both years, but concluded that this effort would be a waste of time (and straws).

Deep down, I guess I didn't want the book to end. It was my job. It was something to look forward to each day. I realized I had no choice. I was certain if I didn't supply the end in two weeks, the book would be finished by the publisher. I didn't want my book finished by someone else. Like Frank, 'I wanted it my way!' The good news was the story of The Lists was going to be published. My family and friends would at least know I was alive in about eight or nine weeks.

I had two weeks before Pete received a substantial check and disappeared. I finally figured out why Pete was giving me two straws. He was telling me to get busy and increase my production. Writing one or two sheets every couple of days and then forcing them into a straw was one thing. Writing two or three pages every day and then squeezing them into two straws was another thing all together. Could I do it? What happens if I get 'writer's block'? Did I have a choice? It was time to get busy!

From the beginning of my captivity, I've had no contact with the outside world except through Pete. That was about to stop. As a matter of fact, I was sure my situation would only get worse once The Lists was published. I'd find out in about eight weeks.

I only hope it was all worth it. That I've accomplished what I set out to do and the public will understand why I did it; maybe even endorse it. I read a quote somewhere that's stuck with me. "When the mission of one is for the good of all, no one can lose."

I feel sure Mike was following our plans for The Lists. My interrogators continually demanded information about my accomplices. I recently found out I wasn't the only suspect Homeland Security (or whoever they are) had picked up. They began apprehending people in mid-2017. A dozen or so had been released quickly and a few others had been freed over the last year. They're obviously planning on keeping me and the others if the terminations were still happening.

I've been offered a "deal." I'm sure the remaining prisoners have received the same offer. If I tell them who's helping me, they will see to it that my living conditions are improved. What a deal! I keep telling them, "No, thanks." For the moment, they are permitting me to write my memoirs. Here's the last chapter of The Lists.

The many positive changes that have taken place over the last decade have had an enormous impact on civilization. Could these accomplishments be attributed to the actions caused by my grand plan, The Lists? Naturally, many changes would have happened without outside assistance, but I don't believe they would have occurred in the same time frame. We aren't living in Utopia, but there's no doubt The Lists contributed to changing our lives for the better. My rationale?

Quite simply, The Lists altered the philosophy of quite a few leaders in many arenas, including geopolitics, industry, religion, finance, and human rights. Even the entertainment industry was influenced by The Lists. Leaders in all capacities were reminded their positions existed to serve the best interests of the society they worked for, not vice versa! Some of the leaders took their assignments as nonsense or a prank. Others turned over the information to the authorities. Still others took the message under advisement and actually began to conform to the changes demanded. I'm sure some were influenced by the first 161 terminations that occurred early in the program. I came to realize the more corrupt an individual, the more vain he/she was. The more vain they were, the more invincible they felt. This feeling made them very easy targets for termination. All I needed to do was prey on their entitlement mentality.

This is probably the correct place to review some of the biggies: things having the most profound impact on society.

The categories for domestic and foreign consideration included renewable energy sources, energy independence, the economy, pollution, unemployment, human rights, overpopulation, immigration, terrorism, government-funded construction projects, state and federal government administrative changes, quality-of-life items, and lastly, sustainable-life issues. Most of the items I refer to received lip service from corrupted officials for years, but that's changed over this last decade.

Today, in the United States, in spite of years of oil—and coal-company negative advertising, manipulative lobbying campaigns, and government foot dragging, alternative / renewable nonpolluting energy is being supplied to various parts of the United States from four enormous wind turbine farms located in three western states and two offshore facilities along the New England coast. Yes, the Indians (not the MLB or NFL team) and the advocates for the Eagles (not the NFL team) dropped their objections to these installations. They are supplying cheap, nonpolluting electricity to more than one million homes and businesses. This new industry has created direct employment for thirty thousand people and another fifteen thousand indirect jobs in the United States. It's unfortunate we are still purchasing most of the hardware from the Chinese because they managed to corner the market more than ten years ago.

Huge solar-generating complexes have been installed on Indian reservations in six southwestern states. The Native American Indians living on these reservations no longer feel that the only way to make a buck is to open a casino. These solar systems have created tremendous employment opportunities and substantial revenue for Native Americans. Direct employment is close to forty thousand with another twenty thousand indirectly supporting this industry. These installations are providing low-cost, nonpolluting electricity to millions of homes and businesses in Albuquerque, Phoenix, and Vegas.

Nineteen hydroelectric generating stations were constructed adjacent to existing flood-control dams on three of the nation's rivers. These units supply cheap, nonpolluting power to fourteen municipalities and 1,180,000 homes and businesses.

Eighty-five thousand direct employees and twenty-five thousand indirect employees service this expanding industry.

The electrical power being generated by these new facilities has resulted in mothballing 25 percent of the nuclear-powered plants that existed in 2012 and has reduced the need for dangerous long-term storage or the potential illegal and extremely dangerous use of spent nuclear waste. No new facilities are planned.

Additionally, seven coal-fired generating plants have been shut down, ending the tons and tons of pollutants discharged daily from their stacks. The displaced workers from the old plants were given the opportunity for training, job transfers, and relocation. There are four more hydroelectric generating stations under construction along the Mississippi River at this time.

These new clean energy sources are still considered a stopgap in the overall scheme of things. The ultimate solution for a never-ending clean energy source is called laser fusion, and unless the folks in Walnut Creek, California (at the LLL), know something the government doesn't, that's probably twenty years away.

Following the disastrous oil spill caused by the collapse of the BP drilling rig in the Gulf of Mexico in 2010, existing deepwater drilling rigs were inspected, to be certain adequate safety equipment was in place (and operating) so there would be no repeats. It took three years and billions of dollars from BP (they had more money in their coffers than most industrialized nations) to clean up the mess from the spill. The federal government stopped issuing new offshore deep-drilling permits for about a year but finally "caved in" to pressure from the oil companies and lobbyists in 2011 and began permitting new drilling sites.

There were seven major companies when The Lists originated. Early on, six were required to contribute 15 percent of their annual profits to an escrow account set up specially to fund construction of wind—and solar-powered generating facilities along with expedited development of the electric automobile. This fund was managed by a blue ribbon five-person team consisting of extremely knowledgeable and dedicated citizens and chaired by none other than Bill Gates. Mr. Gates, a staunch supporter of both human rights and environmental improvements, volunteered for the position after finding out about the intent. There were no politicians, lobbyists, financiers, or industrialists on this committee. Initially, BP was granted a two-year exemption from contributing to this account so they could fund the Gulf cleanup 100 percent. At first, the other six companies balked at paying their share. The Lists terminated the services of eighteen of their top executives, and the successors happily approved the escrow payments. In the middle years of the last decade, the smart people working for the oil companies decided to do one of two things: diversify the company portfolio (get in on the ground floor of wind/ solar power companies, join those companies manufacturing the electric car or developing profitable mass-transit systems for major metropolitan areas) or seek employment elsewhere. Some of the "Disneyesque" monorail systems we see in LA, San Francisco, Chicago, DC, New York, Seattle, Toronto, Florida, and Phoenix are owned by smart oil companies.

The federal subsidies and tax breaks the oil companies had received for years were stopped very early in this process. Salary caps were instituted, strict bonus guidelines were introduced, and gold/platinum parachutes were eliminated. Any of the top executives caught trying to cheat the new system were eventually eliminated.

The switch from our gluttonous appetite for oil benefited the United States but created economic havoc in many foreign countries. We managed to avoid the necessity to open the Arctic to drilling and issuing permits for offshore drilling. Today, we continue to reduce our dependency for foreign oil imports, eliminate our debt to foreign corporations or governments, and reduce our exposure to man-made environmental disasters.

Improved manufacturing techniques for lithium-ion batteries over the last six years has led to a major expansion of the electric automobile industry. Today we see safe and attractive two, four, and five passenger electric cars running around in cities and 75 mph on interstate highways for up to three hundred miles without needing a charge. Many delivery trucks, taxis, and buses have been converted to electrical-drive systems. The new batteries have eliminated range anxiety and the need to have an onboard gasoline motor should the batteries run low. Natural gas continues to be another source of clean burning fuel. We have avoided the disaster of trying to adapt to hydrogen fuel cells for powering our vehicles.

Batteries are 97 percent recyclable and have a life expectancy of about eight years. Replacement cost is $1,500 or $15 a month. WOW! I used to spend over $200 a month for gasoline. It takes two hours for a full charge if plugged into a 220-volt charger or four hours on a 110-

volt charger. The cost is about $2 at any of the millions of charging "meters" that seem to have appeared overnight. We see parking lots everywhere with three types of marked-off parking areas. The local McDonald's and Walmart, highway rest stops, hotels, stadiums, theme parks, hospitals, factories, etc. display "handicapped," "charging," and just plain "parking" areas. The $2 charger fee has replaced the pump tax used to pay local, state, and federal governments. When you charge your batteries at home, you avoid the $2 fee, but it does cost $1.25 for the electricity used. Think about that! $1.25 or $2 for three hundred miles. Not bad! And there's zero pollution.

The electric car has had quite a few benefits beyond almost eliminating foreign oil imports and dramatically reducing pollution. Thanks to a $7,500 federal-tax credit for purchasing an all-electric car, we've seen strong sales in the United States, and Detroit is back in full swing, producing the new vehicles at rejuvenated manufacturing facilities. Foreign sales continue to grow. Five hundred thousand jobs have been created in the United States and Canada in manufacturing, sales, and service for the "E-cars." Clean burning gasoline, diesel, and natural gas-powered vehicles are still in use, and there are about one million jobs still tied to them. It will take another ten years to improve the design and convert the remainder of these vehicles to battery or natural gas power.

The AIV (aluminum-intensive vehicle) was refined even further and introduced new "composite" materials to reduce the weight of the cars and improve the mileage range of the batteries. The designs used had no negative effect on comfort or safety (the age-old argument of steel versus aluminum construction) and actually improved crash ratings. The cars last much longer (don't rust) and are 93 percent recyclable.

The raw materials needed for US production of aluminum car frames and lightweight composite bodies along with the requirements for battery manufacturing has expanded in Mexico and created new industries in Argentina, Chile, and several African countries, places where jobs were greatly needed. The quality of life in these areas is improving daily. We need to keep an eye out for corrupt leadership appearing in these infant economies. The UN and NATO need to stay awake!

Global warming is still with us. It took 150 years for the industrial age to make the mess we're in; it's going to take awhile to clean it up. This is especially true since one of the most powerful and polluting nations in the world isn't cooperating. China has stated, "you've got yours, now we want ours" more than once. As China continues its manufacturing growth, this philosophy will only add to pollution of the earth's atmosphere (global warming) and the rivers and oceans their waste runs into. While most of the industrialized nations of the world continue to eliminate pollutants, their successes are offset by what's happening in China. North Korea isn't far behind China although they currently generate only about 15 percent of the amount of pollutants China does.

In 2010 and 2011, China experienced intense rainfall. The Yangtze River flooded, and the pollution on the three-thousand-mile-long river was so bad that when it hit the new Three Gorges Dam, it clogged the intakes to the generators and gates to the locks, stopping electrical generation and blocking shipping on the river. Authorities stated they removed about six million pounds of trash every day in an effort to reopen river traffic. The garbage was about two feet deep and covered an area the size of one hundred football fields. Now that's pollution!

Glacial melting continues, and the earth's surface temperature has risen 2 degrees in the last decade, and alarm bells continue to sound! The effects of El Niño and La Niña appear to be about the same, and the various climate-controlling ocean currents seem stable, for now. Our planet is still getting warmer and dryer.

International regulation of the fishing industry continues, and the development of "fish farms" is being expedited to help meet the growing global demand for food. Exploration of our oceans continues. We need to understand the 60 percent of our planet that's underwater and figure out how to use the resources we find. This is much more important today than space exploration.

It's gratifying to see reforestation efforts have trebled over the last eight years. Unfortunately, the South American rain forests are still being cut down, but the negative effect is being offset by massive replanting there and elsewhere.

Nationally, the railroad companies have begun to clean up their act. Pollutants have been substantially reduced while the pick up / delivery schedules have improved to 91 percent on-time performance for passengers and for commercial hauls (almost as good as the world's best performers, Japan and Germany). The shift of long-distance hauling from trucks to rail continues. It used to take three weeks to ship goods from Chicago to LA by rail. Now it takes about three days. Trucks continue to be used to transport the goods to/from the rail depots and seaports, but they have been converted to clean burning fuels. Railroad workers now total about two million. Their benefit costs were finally reduced to an affordable (and realistic) level to keep costs competitive. Yes, it was necessary to use a few "motivational packages" for certain arbitrary union leaders and corporate moguls in order to get agreement on the reduced benefits, but ultimately, agreement was reached.

Ocean transport has become much more environmentally friendly. Cargo vessels no longer sit in port or just offshore with engines holding them in place, spewing tons of pollutants into the atmosphere for hours or even days. They are now required to anchor the vessel and to use clean burning diesel generators for their electrical power until underway. The fine for dumping sewage or debris into the water is now a flat $100,000 for the first offense and $250,000 for a second. A third offense results in the arrest of the captain and the vessel and its cargo impounded until a $500,000 fine is paid. No one has reached a stage 4.

A study is now in process to see if the costs for another widening/expansion of the Panama Canal for even larger vessels and increased traffic flow can be justified. This study has turned up some interesting and disturbing facts. It seems that the Chinese government has been quietly buying up large parcels of land adjacent to the canal and gaining a substantial foothold in this commercial lifeline area. I believe we need to be wary of this and to see what other strategic areas China is acquiring worldwide.

Several saltwater-to-freshwater conversion plants (desa-linization) are now online on both coasts of the United States. The water level in the Great Lakes continued to drop. This was undoubtedly caused by the warmer weather patterns (much less snow accumulation) and the melting of the polar ice cap (global warming?). We were running out of drinking water! Direct employment at these facilities is now at eighty thousand with anticipated growth to well over one hundred thousand in the United States. The output of the units on our West

Coast resulted in a 20 percent reduction in the amount of water California drained from the Colorado River. This avoided what could have been "water wars" between the western states. On the East Coast, the new installations have improved the availability of freshwater to the point that the ancient underground piping systems supplying water to major cities from inland lakes can be shut down for long overdue repairs. Florida is currently evaluating similar installations. The Sunshine State has exceeded the build-out capacity for potable water and can no longer issue building permits for new retirement communities or amusement parks.

Development and implementation of water-conservation techniques still receive low priority from the various government agencies, but they are at least looking at the problem with more vigor than in past years. It would be a very good idea if the public began to take a more active interest in the preservation of this life-sustaining resource. How many of you look at anything on your monthly water bill except the amount due? Have you any idea how many gallons of water you use, or for what? Did you realize that every time you flush a commode, the amount of water that goes down the sewer would have kept you alive for two days?

Water-saving commodes have existed for years. Do you have them in your bathrooms? What about a nonflushing urinal for the guys? How long are you in the shower? How full do you fill the tub? Do you leave the water running in the sink while brushing your teeth? It's estimated that in the United States, we could reduce our freshwater use by as much as 50 percent overnight just by putting a stop to these things and not wasting our precious water. One nonblushing conservationist suggested we begin a club called the PTFO for "pee twice, flush once"! I see "PTFO" coffee mugs and T-shirts in our future.

Earlier, the potential use of thermal high-stack technology looked very promising for generating electricity, but it now appears that power generation will be supplied by wind turbines, solar systems, and perhaps a developing technology for tidal generators or hydrokinetic power. There is no need to spend any more time or money on high-stack generation. In the next twenty years, laser-fusion technology will begin replacing most of these power sources. Buy stock, now!

The development of a uniform packaging code was very successful. With the exception of India, North Korea, and China, the world currently generates less than 50 percent of the landfill trash we did ten years ago. Biodegradable packaging; 100 percent recyclable materials; container-deposit programs with a twenty-five-cent deposit on each aluminum can, glass, or plastic bottle; and elimination of plastic grocery (polluter) bags and paper ("save the forests") bags at the grocery stores have all helped this endeavor. (If you don't bring a canvas/cotton reusable shopping bag for your groceries, you'll need big pockets. Plus, you receive a 0.5 percent discount for bringing your own bag). I remember when I was a kid looking for pop bottles to cash in for two cents at the local grocery store. I'll bet kids and grandkids are really cleaning up today, in more ways than one! Have you seen any empty cans or bottles lying around lately?

The funds Congress allocated for NASA and space travel were suspended almost eight years ago. NASA was permitted to maintain the space station and the Hubble, but 75 percent of the remaining funds were diverted to restoration of infrastructure system such as railroads, major highways, and bridges. This put a lot of people to work. Twenty-five percent of the money was set aside for development of a rocket-response shield. It was not directed at Russia, China, Iran, or

North Korea! (Perhaps it should have been!) It was directed at outer space. There are literally thousands of large meteors and asteroids speeding through the universe and no one (not even Steven Hawking) knew what the odds were of one of them colliding with our planet. We still need to find out if there are any of them on the way here and develop the means to destroy them or redirect them before they can impact the earth. I don't feel like joining the dinosaurs. It's fair to say, today, we know a lot more about what threats are out there than we did ten years ago. I read recently that NASA and the military think they have a way to detect and eliminate a rogue meteor or asteroid. We may find out since NASA believes they have detected an asteroid threatening to hit the earth sometime this century. This is a job for the space station inhabitants and astronomers everywhere. Space exploration is scheduled to be reinstated in the late 2020s. I believe we should continue to "hold" exploring the universe and look at something much closer to home: the oceans. Sixty percent of the earth is covered by water, and we know next to nothing about our oceans. Don't you wonder what's down there?

Immigration has been a very volatile issue for many years, and it remains an issue today. During the first ten or twelve years of this century, protests, boycotts, riots, media-inspired events, and celebrity sound bites were the norm. Another cause was the absence of federal government enforcement at our borders. So a couple of the US states bordering Mexico passed laws to stop illegal immigrants from entering our country. They arrested and deported them. The media exploited both peaceful and violent demonstrations, which were usually attended by bleeding heart liberals, illegal immigrants, over-the-hill entertainers and politicians looking for a way to get at the growing Latino vote.

The situation on the US/Mexican border was finally declared a war zone after more than thirty thousand deaths occurred at the hands of drug lords. Drug cartels / gangs began to terrorize communities on both sides of the border. It looked like Iraq and Afghanistan. For some unknown reason, our federal government's reaction was minimal. The Mexican government was either overwhelmed or just incompetent. The Lists attempted to intervene very early in the game by eliminating leaders of the noisiest immigration protest groups, biased media personnel, several drug pushers, and inept Mexican officials. This action had almost no effect on the border problems. It wasn't until 2013 when the US and Mexican governments began to fully cooperate and use combined military forces that the problem began to subside. It took more than six years, but we've managed to drastically reduce the drug traffic, murders, prostitution, terrorism, and the human suffering they cause.

Immigration problems still exist, but they have substantially diminished. Mexico has become more industrialized, creating many good-paying jobs and improving the quality of life for the Mexican citizen. The US immigration policy for legal entry into or becoming a citizen of the United States have been modified and the time requirement shortened. It's now more difficult for a US citizen to enter Mexico or to become a citizen of Mexico than the other way around. There had been two attempts to change the Fourteenth Amendment of the US Constitution. This amendment states that whoever is born in the United States is automatically a US citizen. The process necessary to change the constitution makes it virtually impossible to do so. Both attempts failed. It literally took an act of Congress to pass legislation to record the fingerprints of legal and illegal aliens. This is hilarious! Every US citizen has been fully documented for years. We're all numbers in the system and can be tracked anywhere! From footprints at birth to fingerprints to dental records to driver's license, AAA no., AARP no., Social Security no., Medicare no., passport no.—everyone of us is a number, and it took Congress years just to approve taking fingerprints of aliens entering our country! Boy, were we stupid or what? The ACLU continues to have lots of fun with this situation.

The US census predicts that the Latino (Spanish-speaking or Hispanic) population will become the majority by 2030 (if not sooner). Immigration problems will then become nothing more than a footnote in US history. Mexico, most Central American countries, and the United States will probably merge sometime during this century. Watch out, Canada!

The health care system in the United States has shown drastic improvement since 2010. The federal government finally faced the reality of health issues created by obesity and by the boomers' explosive aging population growth. They implemented changes, using the positive aspects of Canadian and European socialized health care plans as benchmarks. Medical equipment manufacturers, pharmaceutical companies, hospitals, physician associations, and their lobbyists vigorously fought the changes but thankfully lost the battle to common sense and public pressure on politicians. Even the fast-food industry (or was it the fat-food industry) has modified their marketing techniques and menus to promote healthier (but still profitable) selections. Most public school systems have reinstituted their Phys-Ed (physical education or gym) programs and modified their cafeteria offerings to improve the long-term health of our youth. The military has noted an improvement in the physical condition of enlistees in recent years.

New construction for or expansion of existing mass-transit systems for major metropolitan areas in the United States has progressed but at a snail's pace. Resources, money, and personnel have been in short supply due to the magnitude of other higher-priority projects. I did not anticipate the short supply of free world-qualified engineering and construction manpower to support this effort. It should come as no surprise there is an abundance of this talent in China and India.

The free world countries need to take notice of this and get their educational priorities in order.

Most of the old problem areas are under control, and some have been relegated to a priority 3 or 4 status. Are there new concerns popping up? Absolutely! While we've witnessed several conflicts over the past twenty-five years, we really haven't had any major wars. That's good, right? Not altogether.

If we go back in time to the war between the States, then travel forward through history, we'll take note of World War I, World War II and the Holocaust, Korea, Vietnam, ethnic cleansing in Africa, Iraq, the Cold War, etc., and plot statistics for a few things like population, economics, technological advances (weapons, medicine, transportation, communications), we'll find a very distinct correlation to "before/during/after" the war. (For ease of analysis, I've discounted the additive effects of a couple of plagues that happened in this time frame, but it is interesting to note that the Spanish Flu epidemic of 1918 killed more than four million people.)

The first major impact created by war (and cleansing) regards population. If these had not happened, we would have four hundred million (plus or minus a couple hundred) more people on our planet today. Think about that. They're not here because the people who died during these conflicts did not "go forth and multiply." This was "birth control by default." Now think of all the things we enjoy today because government, military, science, and industry worked harder and smarter during the war years in order to beat the enemy. The list of the items developed directly related to war is phenomenal. Would they have been invented/discovered without wars? Probably. But without the urgency inspired by war, it would undoubtedly have taken many more years.

So if we agree population was controlled and technology advanced because of war, what else happened? Many governments became entrenched and stable. When the threat of war loomed on the horizon, populations became easy to manipulate, and citizens allowed their governments greater latitude; governments became very powerful, very controlling. During and for years after wars, economies exploded. Military spending was unrestricted. Everyone made money, except the soldiers. Those in the know in government and on Wall Street made millions (they continue to do so today) by manipulating the public, using the media to communicate the victories and the losses at the appropriate times.

Without war, without an enemy, the public becomes less docile and focuses on regaining control of their elected government officials, cutting waste and taxes, reducing unemployment, improving health care, controlling immigration, questioning the wisdom of the media (beginning to sound familiar?), etc.

Governments, military strategists, historians, psychologists, and economists know that society needs a common enemy to prosper.

If we don't have a national goal like freedom or "defending our way of life," what's going to draw us together? If we aren't engaged in a war and no pandemics are threatening us, what happens? Does the economy revert to depression? How do we justify spending billions on the military? Do we begin to control population growth the way China does? Where do new jobs come from?

The good news is, even with the massive quality of life improvements we've seen in the last decade, we still have a few common enemies to deal with.

Terrorism is a real enemy; it's not a figment of our government's imagination in spite of the multitude of conspiracy theories that abound. Is it big enough to replace the positive effects of war? No one can be sure, but our military and national security agencies are spending like drunken sailors. Keep up the good work, fellas!

While many global economies are still on the mend, we have other 'old' enemies to contend with. Pollution, global warming and over population are today's enemies: we just can't fire missiles at them.

We have to learn how to live smarter, eliminate waste, provide clean electricity and manufacture tons of birth control devices. Without a major effort by everyone we're going to run out of food and water. In the summer it's going to get hot—really hot! And it's going to get dry—really dry! In the winter and spring it's going to get cold—really cold! And it's going to get wet—really wet! It may take twenty years or it may take fifty years, but if we don't eliminate our bad habits we will not survive as a species. Remember the dinosaurs? Tomorrow's people may not approve of the methods used by The Lists, but they should appreciate the intent and the results.

I don't have anything more to add except this: I've done my job or what I believed was a job that needed to be done. With the time and energy I've devoted to The Lists I feel like I've earned a master's degree in political science and international studies. I only hope you, the reader, don't view the story of The Lists as a civics lesson.

I doubt I'll be able to communicate with my family except through the publication of The Lists. I want them to know I've missed them very much and love them all. Hopefully, the royalties from book sales and the sale of my 'worldly possessions' will provide money for college tuitions, weddings or other expenses.

I'm tired. I'm in prison and I've resolved in my own mind that I'll probably be here until I die. I'm proud of what I know has been accomplished by The Lists. I believe the world has become a much better place in the last ten years. I hope the story of The Lists makes a positive and lasting impression on today's and tomorrow's society and history won't repeat itself.

EPILOGUE

I returned from my afternoon workout and shower. My job had ended when the final pages for the story of The Lists were slid into the straws two weeks ago. I wondered what was going to happen to me in about five or six weeks when the book was published. It was due out in early November, just in time for Christmas shopping. I doubted I'd ever be able to read the book.

My daydreaming ended abruptly when my door banged open and the new guard told me to follow him. I'd learned months ago not to ask questions and to follow instructions quickly. I had no idea what was happening. It wasn't the normal time of day for an interrogation (maybe Mike had done something major?). The guard led me down a different hallway. What if they had found out about the book being published?

The guard stopped in front of a glass door mounted in the center of an all glass wall. Inside the wall was a conference table with eight leather chairs, a credenza with a coffee pot and cups. One large window was at the side of the room and there were no bars on it. The guard instructed me to enter and sit. I did as told while my stomach started to churn.

I sat alone for what seemed like an hour. I saw two men approaching. They were dressed in black suits. One carried a cardboard box. The other had a briefcase. There were no introductions. I was told to listen. If I had questions, I'd have an opportunity at the end. After their presentation (I can't think of what else to call it) I sat there, shocked and surprised. In less than thirty minutes my personal situation had drastically changed.

After being 'detained' for almost two years, I was to be released. No apology was offered.

Of course, there were strings attached to my being released. The 'strings' were carried in the briefcase. Suit #1 opened the case and pulled out three documents I would need to read and sign. Document #1, once signed, would get me $250,000 in cash and tax free (no paper trail). Document #2 stated that I agreed never to divulge what had happened to me over the last twenty three months. Document #3 stated that I acknowledged that if I violated Document #2 provisions, I would be immediately arrested and tried for treason. The briefcase also held twenty two social security checks and twenty two retirement checks. All financial accounts would be returned to normal status within twenty four hours. If I agreed to the terms I would be taken immediately to a military air base nearby and flown to my choice of a US destination.

Wow! This was a 'no brainer'. I signed the three sheets as fast as humanly possible. Not only did I want to get out, I had to get out quickly. If I didn't disappear before the book was published I'd be toast. I wonder where Pete had gone? Suit #1 handed me the briefcase with watch, wallet, passport, keys, etc. Suit #2 gave me the box and said "Get dressed". The clothes I'd been captured in were in the box.

In less than a minute I was ready to go. When I looked up from tying my shoes, the suits were gone. My clothes were a little big, but I didn't care. A minute later a guard asked me to follow him to the garage. Forty minutes later I was the only passenger on an Air Force transport on my way to Orlando. I decided to stay overnight in a motel near The Villages and take a look around before actually returning home.

I bought a sub-sandwich, a beer, a tablet and three Bic pens. I ate my gourmet dinner in my motel room while watching T.V., reading the newspaper and contemplating my next move.

The Lists would become public in less than five weeks. I needed to wrap up my personal affairs and quickly disappear. I didn't want to involve friends, family or Mike so going directly home was out of the question. I also needed to get this latest information to the editor and publisher to insert it at the end of the book. So, I finished writing these last few pages and faxed them the following day to the editor. I'll bet he was as surprised as I was.

I developed my escape plan. First I'd quietly get rid of as much of my old life as was possible in three weeks (I allocated a maximum of three weeks before I needed to vanish) and turn everything possible into cash. This would go into the infamous off-shore secret bank account. I'd make sure I kept an adequate supply of cash with me at all times. Over time I'd learn how to develop a new identity, get credit cards, etc., but that would happen later. I filled out the legal documents for transfer of various properties into trusts.

If I managed to avoid capture, perhaps in a few years, I'd write a sequel to The Lists and tell the story of my new adventure. Goodbye, for now.

POSTSCRIPT

This is just a short note for anyone who's read The Lists and is inquisitive enough to try to validate certain facts. This bit of information could save you a lot of time.

You'll find that a place called The Villages does exist in Central Florida as do many of the landmarks I've mentioned in the book. You'll find I do (did?) exist and that I really did mysteriously disappear when I said I did. If you dig hard enough, you'll be able to locate friends, neighbors, my children, and grandchildren, although they will not be able to provide you with any more information than furnished in the book, so please, don't pester them. Unless my circumstances drastically change, no matter how hard you look, I'll make sure you don't find me. Nor will you find Mike. Don't misunderstand, there's definitely a successor managing The Lists: it's just not Mike. But you must admit, it was a good story. Good luck!

You'll better understand the world you live in if you study the message below and realize there are millions of people who unquestionably accept this message as gospel. I feel sorry for them! This depicts a black-and-white analysis of life, and life actually exists in many shades of gray.

"That, that is, is. That, that is not, is not. Is not that it? It is!"

Think about it. Perhaps it should read like this:

"That, that is, is. That, that is not, is not. Is not that it? I don't think so!"

ABOUT THE AUTHOR

Tom was raised in the South Hills area of Pittsburgh during the World War II era. He attended the University of Pittsburgh and served in the United States Marine Corps. His career began in the steel mills while going to school. The last thirty-five years, he managed aluminum-producing plants in Ohio, West Virginia, and California.

Tom and his wife, Barbara, have six children and eleven grandchildren between them. They reside in The Villages, a retirement community of eighty thousand golfers and thirty thousand golf carts in Central Florida. They continue to travel all over the world, enjoy golfing, driving their Corvette to car shows, and visiting with family and friends.

Tom contemplated writing *The Lists* for several years. The hardest part was taking the time to sit down and write the first paragraph. It's a subject near and dear to him, and he hopes it will become so for you after you read *The Lists*.

He's begun writing his second novel, another thriller titled *What If?* Watch for it sometime in 2012.

Milton Keynes UK
Ingram Content Group UK Ltd.
UKHW042005281024
450365UK00003B/196